A L

To ~~XXXXXXXXX~~

Wish you
were here.

by

Mark J. Okrant

Wayfarer Press

Mark

WAYFARER PRESS
PLYMOUTH, NEW HAMPSHIRE
USA   03264

A Last Resort

Okrant, Mark J.
Murder Mystery
1. The BALSAMS Grand Resort Hotel
2. Historic resort

ISBN 0-9646061-4-3

Produced by Preseps, Ltd.
Printed in Warner, New Hampshire USA

**"All saints can do miracles,
but few can keep a hotel."**

*attributed to St. Francis of Assisi
by Mark Twain, 1898*

This volume is dedicated to the memories of:

Warren Pearson, at the helm as this voyage
commenced, but sorely missed at its mooring.

Dennis Joos, a great writer and a better man.

and

Shirley Chatzek, a fundamental ingredient in our lives.

Foreword

Writing A Last Resort has been a labor of love. First, it provided an excuse to make multiple visits to the setting of the novel, the wonderful BALSAMS Grand Resort Hotel in northern New Hampshire. Second, it allowed me to work with some people I treasure.

As a novelist, I have been influenced by three outstanding writers. James Michener inspired my habit of researching every nuance of a subject...now, if I only had his investigative staff. Like Susan Isaacs, my lead characters are professional people whose vocation is not police or detective work; and, like Isaacs' lead character, Judith Singer, Kary Turnell continually wrestles with self-doubt. Also, similar to Dana Stabenow's mysteries, the geographic setting of my crime scenes is as important as the characters in the two books I've written to date.

There are so many people to thank. I begin with three people-all no longer physically with us-to whom this book is dedicated. Warren Pearson, longtime general manager of The BALSAMS, was a dear man who provided numerous insights about the resort business. Dennis Joos was a writer for the News and Sentinel, a northern New Hampshire newspaper. He also was a real life hero: months after Dennis interviewed (and encouraged) me about the book, he was killed attempting to stop a crazed killer from further terrorizing the community of Colebrook, New Hampshire. Shirley Chatzek, my wonderful mother-in-law, was the first member of our family to stay at The BALSAMS. Our relationship was such that I entrusted her with reading the manuscript, a responsibility I never assign lightly. Shirley played a larger role in both of my novels, by finding me quiet refuges where I could write in peace.

Thankfully, most of the people who contributed significantly to this effort will have an opportunity to see it in print. First, there are three dear friends who served as my editors. Darla Anderson, a mystery buff, and the barrister who I trust more than any other; Sally Stitt, another mystery buff, and a woman who is incredibly conversant in the worlds of words and numbers; and Steve Barba, president of The BALSAMS, who is as much a philosopher and sage as a world-renown resort manager. Steve demonstrated his belief in both The BALSAMS and yours truly by permitting my murder mystery to be set at his resort. I have paid tribute to both Steve and Warren by creating the character of general manager Warn Barson, who is actually a composite of their names and personal attributes. Alma and Chuck Grand thoughtfully allowed me to use their cottage in Vermont as a refuge; it was owing to their kindness that my initial draft was completed faster than I ever dreamed possible. And, a special thanks goes to the grand dame of Alaskan mystery writers, Dana Stabenow, who encouraged me from the get-go.

Then there are the three members of my immediate family who served as editors, and who contributed significantly to my quality of life in the process. First, there is my wife, Marla, who I cherish like no other. I can assure you readers that Kary's marital difficulties are by no means autobiographical; I am indeed the most fortunate of men in that respect. My favorite older daughter, Robyn, is a creative genius, who inspires me through her example. And, my favorite younger daughter, Elisabeth, claims she learned syntax from me; however, Elisabeth's wonderful intellect could only have come from her mother.

Mark Okrant (2005)
Plymouth, New Hampshire

Cast of Principal Characters

Kary Turnell . . . . professor, former crime writer, and one time wonder award-winning novelist

Nya Turnell . . . . Kary's long overlooked wife

Warn Barson . . . . general manager of The Balsams, and Kary's old friend

Tom Barson . . . . Warn's easily agitated son, grew up at the resort

Edna Connor . . . . a bored, naïve housewife sent to the resort by her husband

Al Connor . . . . too busy with his business to care for his wife

Richard Tomquist . . . . a former employee at The Balsams, had troubles with management

Billy Fenton . . . . local ne'er do well, now employed at the resort

Reg Gill . . . . superintendent of services, a good man in a crisis

The Others (in alphabetical order)

Bob Clay, director of tennis services

Fran Golloway, orchestra leader and music director

John Gray, maitre d'hotel

Lucy Laflamme, executive housekeeper

Paul Leonard, executive chef

Jeff Milk, laundry manager

Sue Nesson, director of personnel

Bill Norman, night security man

Jim O'Neil, assistant director of golf

Jay Olds, registration manager

Shannon Parton, director of recreation services

Rolf Vernon, head of maintenance

Dave Watson, business manager

Chapter 1

Dixville Notch, Friday, July 14. It was a great day for some and a good day for others, but, by all appearances, a terrible day for one guest at The Balsams Grand Resort Hotel. The story I'm about to tell you may seem too strange to believe. But, I swear, every last word of it is true. This entire episode began as a badly needed diversion for my wife Nya and me, but it turned out to be one of those life-changing experiences.

My name is Kary Turnell. Twenty years ago, having earned an MFA in creative writing from Princeton, I took a job as a crime writer for a major Philadelphia newspaper. I left the paper under less than favorable circumstances. For the last fifteen years, I've been teaching sociology and criminology at the brick and mortar campus in Plymouth, just south of the White Mountains in New Hampshire. While I love teaching, the fact of the matter is I'd rather be writing novels, award-winning, money making novels.

Ten years ago, I wrote a really good murder mystery. It was so good that it stayed near the top of the New York Times Best Seller List for six months. It had been so popular that it paid for a house Nya and I coveted for years. The royalties also made it possible to send our two daughters to the private, overpriced colleges of their choice. More to the point of this story, it was so good that my picture adorned The Balsams' Wall of Fame, the corridor where the resort's management has placed the signed photographs of their famous past guests. Very few things-the first time I made love with a woman, any time I spend with my daughters, eating a cheese pizza at Sally's in the Elm City, the perfect Fireball-have given me greater pleasure than walking along the corridor that connects the Dixville House and Hampshire House, and seeing my smiling face hanging near pictures of Babe Ruth, John Philip Souza, Art Linkletter, and Ken Burns. Too much time had passed since I last made that walk. Why, you ask? Because I'd been too caught up in trying to write the sequel to my prize winner.

Way deep down, I've known that it was my twenty-something year friendship with the resort's general manager, Warn Barson, that had earned me my exalted spot on the Wall of Fame, not being a one-shot novelist. Warner S. Barson, "Warn" to his friends, and I met in the early eighties at some now obscure meeting. We had hit it off instantly.

One day, Nya, out of the clear blue, suggested that we head north to Dixville Notch. Nya was born and raised in Venezuela, the daughter of an American diplomat. She attended an ivy-covered campus in Boston, and with hard work, had become a successful publicist. Nya was-still is-bright, pretty, completely faithful and more energetic than anyone I've ever known. We chose to live in New Hampshire because I love the lifestyle here. We don't live in western Connecticut or on Long Island, closer to the action in Nya's world, because I just couldn't stand living anywhere near the Big Apple. Too many people might recognize me. Then they'd ask, "When's your new book coming out, Kary;" or worse, my closer acquaintances would make comments like, "Don't worry Kary, at least Nya's earning a buck." People in the Big Apple can be so damned obnoxious. So that's the real reason we live in New Hampshire. Throughout our marriage, if something has made me feel comfortable, Nya has been all for it. Bless her heart.

For ten years, Nya endured my writer's cramp and everything that went with it. I hadn't been able to write a solid paragraph since the early nineties. Yeah, that's the nineties...nine-zero. You don't need to say it; my one whiff of success was during the last century! But, do you know the amazing thing? Throughout this prolonged period of my personal agony, Nya was an angel. Her career had taken off like an Apollo rocket; being here in New Hampshire certainly hadn't slowed her down. She put up with my late night hours, the reams of wasted paper, the boozing and the swearing. But, what had been the worst for her was my total failure in the bedroom. Simply put, I had lost interest. Whether it had been because of her professional success, my lack of it, or a combination of the two, I had taken leave from my wife's bed-figuratively speaking, that is. And, while she seldom confronted me about it, Nya had become increasingly anxious and frustrated by my functional disappearance from the bedroom.

Finally, one day last June, Nya recommended a change in scenery. So my love-starved spouse secretly made arrangements for the two of us to spend an entire month at the one place on this planet that gives us peace of mind-The Balsams. All she told me was to plan absolutely nothing between the fourteenth of July and the ides of August. We were going on what she termed "a retreat". She insisted that I bring nothing remotely related to my teaching duties or my feeble efforts to write again. Nya agreed to leave the trappings of her successful business behind as well. So, when it was time to pack for our retreat, I reluctantly left my notebook computer on the table in my daughter's old bedroom, which now doubles as my home office. Our trip to The Balsams was strictly about R&R. No work . . . particularly on novels . . . was going to be permitted. And, there was to be no booze. I promised both of us that any drowning of angst would be limited to one, or more, of the resort's award-winning desserts.

Chapter 2

Early morning, Friday, July 7th. Edna Connor finally faced the realization that her sixteen year marriage to her husband Al was in dire straits. Edna had met Al Connor at a church dinner, almost a year after she had finished high school in the small western Massachusetts community where she was born. Edna hadn't exactly been swept off her feet; Al Connor wasn't the sort of man who could sweep any girl off her feet. No, it had been a matter of Al arriving at a time when Edna realized her prospects were limited. So, when Al, a large fastidious man who was fifteen years her senior, showed an interest in Edna, she'd realized this might be her one chance for marriage and a family. Al and Edna were married by the local justice of the peace, ten months to the day after they'd met.

From the beginning, Edna had doubts. It wasn't that Al treated her badly; it was that he barely paid any attention to Edna at all. During their first year together, he had seemed somewhat interested in her physically. They had made love once every week or two. However, within a year, it had been once a month, then every two months, then barely at all. And, it wasn't long before Al had responded to Edna's pleadings about children by stating flatly that he was too busy trying to grow his business to be a good father to children. At first, Edna held out hope that Al would change his mind once the business was doing better. However, it had been more than eight years since he had turned the small, solid waste management business he'd inherited from his father into one of western Massachusetts' most successful enterprises. But there still were no children.

Now thirty-five, Edna was beginning to feel and act much older. With no need to impress her spouse, Edna became careless about her appearance. She rarely had her hair done and stopped covering the gray that was very gradually replacing her natural auburn hair color. While Edna had given up all hope of having children, she still harbored the hope that Al would begin to take greater interest in using the bed for something other than a place to sleep. One night, when Al came home from work in a particularly good mood, having closed a big deal to handle much of Springfield's solid waste, she decided to make her move. Placing her hand on Al's large, hairless chest, she began to kiss him, first on the cheek and then moved toward his lips. His reaction had stunned her. Instead of sweeping her into his arms, he stood up and headed to the bathroom, announcing that he was tired and had to pee.

Al Connor was not a totally insensitive man; and, he really did love Edna very much, but in his own way. He simply was one of those people who lived to work and worked to live. He had not been cheap or selfish when it came to Edna, save with his affections. To the contrary, Al had forever been telling her, "Honey, I earn plenty of money; why don't you go and buy yourself something nice?" Once, when he could no longer stand the sight of the wreck of a car Edna had been driving for years, he bought her the yellow

Volkswagen Jetta that soon became her most prized possession. No, Al Connor was not a man without feelings for his wife. Al was simply a single-minded individual; and his mind was solely on his business, not on satisfying his wife's needs.

So, when Al came out of the bathroom and saw Edna sitting on the sofa, fighting back tears, he said, "Edna, you need to take yourself a vacation. Why don't you let me send you to someplace nice?"

Bringing a copy of the Worcester newspaper over to the sofa, he said softly, "This looks like a great place for you to go for a couple of weeks. It's called The Balsams Grand Resort Hotel."

Edna's sadness slowly turned to surprise. "Why, Al; The Balsams is one of the finest hotels in all of New England! We can't afford to go there."

"Oh, yes you can; I'm making good money now. You'll have a wonderful time. And I'll even buy you some nice clothes for your trip."

"But," sniffed Edna, "won't you be coming, too?"

"Oh, I couldn't possibly go away this time of year. No, you just go; it'll do you a world of good."

Edna had protested to her friend Jessie that she couldn't possibly go to such a big, fancy resort, not by herself. But, the more she thought about getting a new wardrobe and a complete makeover, in addition to the chance to visit such a fine resort, she had decided to take Al up on his offer. After all, there were no children holding her back; and it was apparent that not even The Balsams could arouse amorous feelings in her husband. Besides, she might make some new friends at the resort.

Thus, Edna agreed to her husband's offer, making plans to stay at The Balsams between July 10th and the 25th. The timing was perfect; it would allow her to return in time for her mother's birthday on the 27th of the month. Edna still loved celebrating birthdays with her mom.

Chapter 3

1 P.M., Friday, July 14th. Our drive to Dixville was as uneventful as any trip through New Hampshire's north country could be. It was one of those beautiful, clear summer days when you can see for miles. Before long, we passed through that beautiful glacial relic known as Franconia Notch, which had been produced by the incredible powers of the most recent continental glacier, more than ten thousand years earlier.

Several towns, Whitefield, Lancaster, Groveton and North Stewartstown, flew past the window of Nya's Lexus. We stopped in North Stewartstown so Nya could visit a convenience store. She'd had a sudden craving for something salty and promised to be "back in a jiffy." I had insisted that we stop in Columbia, so I could satisfy my curiosity about their legendary motorcycle shrine . . . talk about unique! Before long, we were distracted by the sound of sirens. A New Hampshire state police car flew past heading south. A few minutes later, the first car was followed by a second. I remember thinking that they must have been doing seventy.

Dixville, New Hampshire's northernmost notch, has the appearance of a gigantic jawbone replete with great rock teeth. The sheer rock cliffs are forested in conifers and hardwood trees. For more than a century, The Balsams resort, which was named for the balsam trees that populate the area, has been serving the needs of travelers and vacationers.

The management was very smart. In order to compensate travelers for locating in the middle of nowhere, guests were provided with the best food offered by any resort in New England. If hard pressed, many guests would tell you the meals at The Balsams were better than sex. Both Nya and Edna would have agreed.

★   ★   ★

Chapter 4

Having traveled for a little more than two hours from Plymouth, we reached the access road to The Balsams. Just as Route 26 was about to enter the rugged notch, a white, wooden sign with green letters and the hotel's crest, three balsam firs-hand carved and accented with gold leaf-informed us that we had arrived. Turning left, we were able to see the resort across the clear, blue waters of Lake Gloriette. The combination of the lake, the green lawns, the red shingled turrets of the Dixville House, the tall, stucco towers of the Hampshire House, set against the notch's high, gray granite cliffs provided an imposing, yet welcoming site for weary travelers. Nya's Lexus couldn't cover the tree-lined, undulating half-mile road fast enough. The trees soon gave way to flowers and the sight of a thirty-foot waterfall cascading down a series of rocks. We entered a semi-circular drive, stopping at the portico, with its four white wooden columns, which functions as the point of welcome for arriving guests. There, we were greeted by a tall, dark-haired doorman, garbed in gray slacks and a green blazer, bearing the resort crest. We left the Lexus in his capable hands, then walked hand-in-hand up the long, enclosed corridor, and entered the hotel.

Once in the hotel foyer, Nya remarked at how familiar everything appeared. Since the management and staff were fastidious about keeping the resort in mint condition, The Balsams looked as perfect as it had during our previous visits years before.

Taking a right turn, we passed the familiar sign listing the day's arrivals. Sure enough, under the date Friday, July 14, 2003, were our names, D/M K. Turnell, among a list of approximately forty other arriving parties. Like every guest who has ever stayed at The Balsams, our arrival had been expected.

The lobby was like another world. Brass chandeliers topped off the elegant American furniture that strategically adorned the lobby. We moved past the little gift shop and the bellmen's station, and went right to the long registration counter. Here, a woman who looked like a teacher from an old country school greeted us warmly. The badge on her burgundy vest told us the woman's name was Marriam. Marriam welcomed us to The Balsams. But, before calling the bellman over, she handed me a small white envelope. The envelope appeared innocent enough; but, the look I read on her face suggested there was some importance attached to it.

I excused myself for a minute and crossed the lobby to sit in one of the plush chairs opposite the registration desk. I suddenly had an uneasy feeling. Tearing open the envelope, I recognized the messy scrawl of Warn Barson. The note did little to allay my anxiety. It read simply, "Welcome back. Must see you immediately after dinner this evening. Warn." Shaking my head, I refolded it, then walked slowly back across the lobby. Nya turned to face me, getting a good look at my body language. My stomach was churning . . . the last thing I needed was the slightest indication that anything other than one hundred percent R&R was in the offing for the Turnells.

"What's going on, Kary?"

"It's nothing to be concerned about," I lied.

Nya didn't seem convinced . . . or pleased. This would have been a good time to remind myself why we were at the resort: to, hopefully, rejuvenate our static marriage. Unfortunately, I didn't.

★   ★   ★

In retrospect, it's quite likely that Nya had been preparing herself to terminate our marriage should this retreat fail to produce the desired results. Who could blame her? The last ten years had been tough. I'm sure, if you asked our family and friends, they would have described ours as a secure marriage. However, only Nya knew how depressed I had been growing about my inability to produce a second novel. At first, Nya had taken shelter in the children's affairs and her own prospering business. But, with the children grown up and living on their own, her awareness that there was very little *us* in our day-to-day relationship had increasingly frustrated her. Nya had become increasingly discouraged by the absence of physical intimacy on my part. If indeed this vacation was her last-ditch attempt to save us, Warn's note was not going to help matters. Before we'd even had the opportunity to unpack, Nya was seeing the same distant, depressed look plastered on my face. Of course, if I hadn't been so preoccupied with Warn's note, I might have seen how unhappy she looked and tried to make things right.

To be honest, I still barely remember the elevator ride to the fourth floor of the Hampshire House. And, I know I didn't even notice when our bellman inserted a modern plastic coded card, rather than the traditional Balsams brass key, into the computerized room lock. I do vaguely recollect having seen a small green light flash when the bellman removed the card. I was in such a fog that Nya didn't even try to ask me for tip money; she simply removed a ten-spot from her handbag and gave it to the grateful bellman. As the door closed behind him, I realized for the first time that Nya was glaring at me.

Chapter 5

Nya wanted an explanation; and, she didn't want it later. "Okay Kary, what on earth is going on? Why did you zone out like that? You embarrassed me." Nya was pouting. Our retreat was off to a terrible start.

"Here." I offered her the envelope containing the note. "Something must be the matter for Warn to send me this note before we even checked into the room."

Nya read the note, pondered for a few moments, then replied crossly, "I'm certain it's nothing. My guess is that your old friend just wants to give you a warm welcome; after all, we haven't been here for years."

"Sure, I suppose that's it," I lied. Thinking I meant it, she kissed me on the cheek.

We spent the next hour unpacking and familiarizing ourselves with the room that was to be our home away from home for the next four weeks. The room was spacious. There were three cedar-lined closets, two of which were filled with Nya's garments before I could blink. Each closet door had a full-length mirror built into the front. A few days later, I was to make the mistake of staring at my reflection while standing there totally in the raw. It was a brutal reminder that some things had become too large while others had remained too small.

Our bedroom contained two double beds; and, at my present rate, I was going to be spending a lot of time alone in one of them. To the left of the beds sat a mint green wooden dresser with three drawers and a matching mirror. Nya commandeered the majority of this space, too.

I had always liked the little extras The Balsams offered its guests. The desk top contained historic pictures of the resort and postcards from turn-of-the-century guests extolling the hotel staff and services. There was a small bud vase containing a few fresh flowers, and a bottle of pure maple syrup. Attached to the bottle was a short note from Warn, "Welcome back to The Balsams; looking forward to our discussion." That little reminder plunged me back into my gloomy state, and Nya into her annoyed one.

As I brought my dopp kit into the bathroom, Nya commented that the wallpaper had been changed recently. Leave it to Nya to notice these things. I simply shrugged. However, in an effort to score a few points with my spouse, I commented about the way the chrysanthemum wall paper complemented the medium blue carpet, the pale green furniture, and the white bell shaped lamps. This attention to detail on my part made Nya smile.

I made a visit to the bathroom, a place where I had been spending more and more time the last several years. So, it was only natural that I should get acquainted with this one right away. The étagère contained bathroom amenities-the usual hand-and-body lotion, shampoo, bars of soap, a sewing kit, and so forth. Knowing that I'd have to arm wrestle with Nya to get my hands on most of this stuff, I ignored it.

The bedroom had one very interesting attribute. Each unit was linked to its neighbor through a small vestibule by two adjoining doors, each with its own bolt lock. During visits to the resort when our daughters were younger, we would lock the main door, then open both locks and leave the doors ajar a crack. With this arrangement, Nya and I were afforded a modicum of privacy, as well as the assurance that our treasures were sleeping safely in an easily accessible, adjacent room.

Chapter 6

3 P.M., Monday, July 10th. Edna Connor could hardly believe what she saw as she drove up the entry road to The Balsams. The scene across Lake Gloriette reminded her of the pictures of Switzerland her friend Denise had brought back from a summer vacation, several years earlier. She couldn't believe that the resort was actually more magnificent than the advertisements showed. What made her arrival all the more exciting was that Edna had long since given up hope of experiencing anything like it. While taking in the view, she couldn't help but feel a twinge of sadness because she was experiencing all of this alone. As had become her habit throughout married life with Al, she scolded herself for any thoughts of self-pity.

"Al's a good man, and a generous one . . . even if it's only with his money." In spite of Edna's efforts to combat her mushrooming melancholy, a stream of warm tears briefly flowed down her cheeks. Then, perhaps owing to the distance from her husband, Edna became determined to meet new people, make new friends . . . and enjoy herself at The Balsams.

"I will not allow anything to ruin this experience for me." Blotting her tears and blowing her nose with one of five lace handkerchiefs she'd recently purchased at Marshall's, Edna Connor sighed and accepted the fact that she would experience everything this wonderful resort had to offer, even if it meant doing it alone.

★   ★   ★

Although it certainly hadn't been her intention, it didn't take Edna long to call attention to herself. While not a beautiful woman, with her new makeover and wardrobe, Edna presented something of a striking figure. Her newly styled, shoulder length auburn hair and freshly glossed lips would, by themselves, have been enough to draw attention. But, the size-too-small wardrobe that the teenage saleswoman at Marshall's had convinced her to buy had accentuated the fullness of her breasts and the generous, but not excessive protrusion of her rear end. While Al Connor no longer took notice of his wife's physical attributes, they were not lost upon other guests at the resort, nor some of the staff.

In truth, Edna was something of a fish out of water at The Balsams. Not having any experience with resort hotels, she spoke to the registration desk clerk in a voice that was louder than normal. And, as she stood in the lobby awaiting a bellman, the combination of her tight-fitting white cotton dress, broad-brim, blue straw hat with an orange head band, and her matching set of faux leopard luggage, had been looked upon with amusement by the staff and a few female guests. Each had to suppress a smile when Edna informed her bellman that she didn't need help carrying the leopard skin monstrosities to her room. However, when the clerk told her about the resort's check-in policy, Edna had exclaimed with a big smile on her well-glossed lips, "Oh, I'm sorry; as you can see, I don't get out much." Indeed, she had spoken the truth.

Despite any initial misgivings people may have had about her, it would not take Edna long to make a number of acquaintances among the resort's population-staff as well as guests.

Chapter 7

4 P.M., Friday, July 14th. I had had quite enough of unpacking and exploring our room. Three things were on my mind: eating one of Chef Leonard's extraordinary dinners, talking with Warn, and taking a stroll along the Wall of Fame, but not necessarily in that order. I wasn't fooling myself. When Nya initially mentioned the idea of taking a long vacation, I hadn't been all that excited. However, when she said we should visit The Balsams, I jumped at the opportunity to see my picture hanging in the shrine of past greats who have visited the historic resort. Don't get me wrong; this wasn't about some gigantic ego trip. Well, okay, maybe it was. I had been so low for so long that I was counting on the Wall to inspire me to reach creative heights I hadn't visited in a decade. It may sound crazy, but I felt that seeing my picture hanging there next to Jerry Lewis and Admiral Elmo Zumwalt would inspire me to write again.

I didn't have to convince Nya to come with me to the Wall. The Wall was located one floor below us, along a corridor connecting the third floor of the Hampshire House and the Dixville House. This heavily trafficked hallway led to the main stairway to the dining room. I totally failed to conceal my anticipation from Nya by taking her hand and literally running down the single flight of stairs to the Wall's entryway. As I approached the Wall, Nya stood facing me with the strangest expression on her face.

"Kary . . . it's gone!"

"Wow, that's a good act, Nya; they should have your picture up here, too."

"You don't understand; there is no picture of you here anymore, Kary."

Sure enough, in the place where my picture had hung was a blank space. Looking carefully, I could see that the white background of the wallpaper's floral print was a bit fresher than the area that surrounded it; and, the aberration was exactly the same size as the frame of the adjacent photograph.

"Damn! Look at this, Nya; the nail is still in the wall!"

Poor Nya looked panicked. After all, the real purpose of this visit had been to bring me back to earth, not send me into orbit. Nya tried to calm me. "I know you're upset, Kary. But, please keep your voice down. There has to be an explanation; and we'll find out what it is."

It was immediately clear to both of us that this terrible act had not been perpetrated long before. By all appearances, the picture had been removed within the past several days or weeks. My heart sank; how could this be? Hadn't I been a great writer? After all, I'd won several prizes for my first book. Was I being penalized by my friend because I hadn't written a second one?

All at once, everything made sense. Warn's note hadn't been intended to welcome me back to Dixville Notch. It was his way of softening the blow. One thing I could say for Warn, at least he had the guts to tell me face to face. However, it appeared obvious that he hadn't expected me to take this route to the dining room; certainly not before he had a chance to break it to me in person. It had been a random act that had placed Nya and me in the Hampshire House. And fate had taken us along the Wall prematurely. Well, if that's how he wanted to play it, I really was looking forward to my conversation with Warn Barson. In fact, I wanted no part of waiting until after dinner. But, as I started for the stairs leading to Warn's office, Nya's hand grasped my arm.

"Kary, please let me deal with the photo. You need to calm down. Losing your cool will accomplish absolutely nothing. Aren't you the father who always told Rachel and Lisa that a person who loses her cool is someone who has lost the battle before it begins?"

The last thing I wanted at that moment was to be reasonable. After all, had Warn been reasonable when he removed my photograph from the Wall? I was ready to argue everything from the Ten Commandments to the Bill of Rights when, unexpectedly, Nya gave me a gentle kiss, this time on the lips. How strange; at that very moment I realized that we hadn't done that in God knows how long. Of course, as usual, Nya had been right about waiting to see Warn. Unfortunately, the thought of eating dinner . . . even a Balsams dinner . . . suddenly did not appeal to me. But, for once, I was determined not to ruin Nya's evening just because I was feeling sorry for myself. With great reluctance, I joined Nya and slowly descended the Dixville House's long main staircase, with its sweeping balustrade; and we made our way toward the resort's elegant dining room.

★　　　★　　　★

Nya was still concerned that her careful plans were about to become unraveled. So, as we stood in line waiting to greet the maître de hôtel, John Gray, Nya whispered, "The critics all said you've lost your passion, Kary. You need this time at The Balsams to rediscover yourself. Besides, you know very well that arguing with Warn is not going to help you get back into the right frame of mind to write." Then, taking my hand, she added, "So, why don't you eat a nice meal and then go visit Warn. I still say there's a simple explanation for all of this."

We ate dinner in silence. Other than the fact that it was excellent, I couldn't tell you what I ordered. I didn't even notice the look of concern on Nya's face when I excused myself without taking so much as a bite of the delicious desserts. My mind was on two things: Warn Barson and my missing photograph.

8 P.M. As I walked out of the dining room, deserting Nya in the process, I took a right turn and headed down the long, staircase that connects the dining room to the hotel lobby. Striding deliberately through the lobby, I nodded to the bellman who had carried our luggage to our room. He barely seemed to notice. Passing by the bellmen's desk, I could clearly see Warn Barson's profile through the large picture window forming the west wall of his office. The resort has had a longstanding tradition of making the general manager enormously visible, and easily accessible, to guests. By seating its senior manager in a veritable fish bowl, there is no way for him to avoid his clientele-whether they are complaining or complimentary. This policy has been tantamount to an open invitation to bend the general manager's ear about everything from the quality of the golf course to the flavor of the evening's soup. As I walked toward our meeting, I remembered reading about how our seventh president, Andrew Jackson, once had an open door policy for his public. According to some historians, you could simply drop in and say hello to 'Ol Hickory, regardless of whether you were the sire of a Boston Brahman or an Ohio River pirate. In contemporary times, Israel also has maintained this tradition of exposing its prime ministers to the public. After what happened to poor Yitzak Rabin, the latter policy must have been changed by now. Apparently, The Balsams management was confident that resort managers were not at similar peril from the vacationing public. Given my state of mind at that moment, they probably should have given this a second thought.

As it turned out, this was the one time I was grateful for Warn's open door policy. As I strode toward his office, what I had it in my mind to say doubtlessly would have threatened a wonderful, twenty-year friendship. However, just as I was about to enter, an octogenarian nearly knocked me on my derrière in her haste to see Warn. Knocking while she opened the screen door, she screeched, "Mr. Barson, I have something to say to you!"

Warn stood up immediately, but did not appear the slightest bit ruffled by this sudden change of agenda. Maintaining a professional, but hospitable presence, Warn invited the woman, Mrs. Gertrude Plessence, to take a seat. As she sat down, Warn remained standing and looked out at me through the screened door, then stated, "I'll be with you in just a few moments, Professor Turnell." This message was really being directed at Mrs. Plessence; it was his way of saying, "I'll talk to you briefly, but others are waiting." His tone nearly made me laugh in spite of myself. Warn Barson had called me a lot of things during the last twenty years, but Professor Turnell was not among them.

Taking a chair outside Warn's door, I listened as Mrs. Plessence, whose surname could not have been any less appropriate, railed on and on about not receiving her popovers during breakfast that morning. "Mr. Barson," she fumed, "I've been a loyal customer of this resort for a lot longer than you have been its manager. I simply won't tolerate being treated like this."

Although my back was to the office, I imagined that Warn's face must have been the color of the cabbage roses adorning the carpet in the John Dix Social Room. To be honest, the thought of his annoyance gave me some solace, given my own attitude toward him at that moment. But, my minor victory was to be short lived. To my dismay, Warn's voice betrayed none of the irritation he must have been masking. As he responded to her charges, Warn's tone was more like a minister privately counseling a member of his flock than that of an admonished general manager. His reply was gentle; there was even a hint of humor in his voice.

"Now, Mrs. Plessence, as one of our senior . . . not to mention favorite . . . guests, you know very well that popovers are only served on Tuesday and Sunday mornings. If the pastry chef made them for you more often than that, there wouldn't be enough time to make those small éclairs that you love so much. Those are your favorites, aren't they Mrs. Plessence?"

When she responded, you could hear a noticeable change in the old lady's tone. I was disappointed, for I wanted Warn to have a taste of the stress I was feeling at that moment.

"Why Mr. Barson," she cooed, "You remembered my favorite. That's so sweet of you."

However, Mrs. Plessence wasn't quite through. "I still think you could have my popovers more frequently than twice a week," she said with a pout in her voice. However, finally satisfied that her point had been made, Warn pushed open the screen door for her to leave. As I rose to enter Warn's office, my timing was off by two seconds and Mrs. Plessence knocked me sprawling back into the chair as she burst past. She was still talking to herself about the elusive popovers as she moved toward the Hampshire House elevator at a pace that would have made Carl Lewis envious. Given what I'd just witnessed, my attitude toward Warn had mellowed dramatically by the time I stepped into his office.

Chapter 9

Warn Barson was the prefect man to run a complex business like the Balsams. He was the grandson of a Scottish immigrant. Like millions of other immigrants, Warn's grandfather had arrived in New York harbor and had been processed through Ellis Island. His brogue had been so thick that the immigration officer completely misunderstood when he pronounced his surname, MacPherson. Thinking that the young man had called himself Mack Barson, the official had listed him in this manner. As he walked away from the entry point, still shaking his head about what the immigration official had just done to his family name, he heard a familiar woman's voice say, "Well, if that's as well as you hang onto things Mack Barson, y'll sheerly have trouble amountin' to much heer in this new lan'." He turned to face a young woman whose long red hair and beautiful freckled face had attracted his attention during the crossing from Britain. In fact, he had spent a large share of the considerable leisure that a transatlantic voyage provides attempting to impress her.

Six months later, they became man and wife; and, it wasn't long before the couple had their only child, a boy named David. David would grow up earning his own money, something that his parents had insisted upon. As a young adult, he became a talented printer. It wasn't very long before David realized he had something in common with his father, an affinity for red-headed Scottish women. A year after David met Julie MacTavish, they were married. The couple was to parent two boys, Harold and Warner.

While Harold followed his father into the printing business, Warner was enthralled when his father had introduced him to Mr. Tillson, the owner of The Balsams. A successful industrialist who had purchased the rubber glove factory on the Dixville, New Hampshire property, Mr. Tillson's investment had made him the owner of a failing grand resort hotel along with the very successful glove plant. Mr. Tillson had been impressed by Warn's excellent manners, keen mind, and sense of humor. Soon after their initial meeting, he invited Warn to spend the following summer working in the fresh air at the resort. Warn couldn't resist; and, as they say, the experience was to shape the rest of his life.

Mr. Tillson gave Warn the job of assisting the greenskeeper to remove dead and unwanted vegetation from the Panorama Golf Course. The weather was unusually hot when Warn reported for his first day of work. As the groundskeeper handed him a set of considerably oversized overalls, he advised Warn to remove the shirt and pants he had donned that morning, and just wear his shoes and socks with the overalls. Warn had followed his new boss's instructions to the letter. Then, while moving a large tree stump from the edge of the sixth green on the golf course, Warn had become so focused on coaxing the stump out of the ground that he hadn't heard the greenskeeper yell for him to move out of the way. When the tractor started forward, Warn stood up and looked over his shoulder, just in time to see the tractor, the stump, his overalls, and one work shoe disappear into the woods. It took Warn about five seconds to comprehend that he was standing along the sixth green wearing nothing but a shoe and a sock. Realizing that he needed to take refuge immediately, he ran, as yet unnoticed, up the path leading to a storage shed hidden in the woods behind the seventh tee. He had nearly reached safe haven when he ran headlong into two golf carts that were occupied by Mr. Tillson, his wife, and another couple. Quickly removing the shoe and sock and holding them strategically, he stood embarrassed, but outwardly calm, before his employer.

Mr. Tillson fought back the urge to laugh, and instead assumed a stern demeanor. "Where are your clothes, Warn?" he asked.

The youngster wanted nothing more than to take advantage of the shack, but could not be rude. Thinking quickly, he replied, "I traded my old overalls for this shoe and sock. One of the caddies offered me a better fitting pair in trade."

Now Mrs. Tillson was curious. "But, Warn, you have only one shoe and sock."

Thinking quickly, Warn replied, "Um, yes, ma'am, but the caddy has only one leg."

Now Warn had everyone's attention. He wasn't going to get out of this mess easily. "How can the young man caddy if he has only one leg, Warn?"

"Because no one's told him that his other leg's missing, yet. You folks won't tell him will you?"

Warn was smiling now, clearly pleased with his little joke. Now he disappeared into the shack, traveling at full speed, while covering as much of his buttocks as he could with the shoe and sock. Warn wouldn't learn until several years later that his grace under fire had made a lasting impression upon the Tillsons and their friends. It was a direct result of this encounter that Warn was later propelled up the hierarchy of the resort.

After Warn had graduated from college, Mr. Tillson told him that the tasks he had filled during previous social seasons-groundskeeper, bellman, and waiter-were to be assigned to others. If he had been concerned that his tenure at the resort was about to be terminated, he needn't have been. Mr. Tillson instructed Warn to learn all there was to know about running the resort's Wilderness Ski Area, which was operated for its guests. He was a fast learner; and, before long, had assumed complete control over the operation of the ski area. This, too, proved to be a fortuitous turn of events.

Like so many others in his age group during the mid-sixties through the early seventies, Warn was faced with the military draft; for, this was the era of the Vietnam War. Despite the fact that he had married and was helping his wife Nancy raise three very young children, he now had a difficult decision to make. Nancy and Warn had spent several sleepless nights trying to decide what to do. One thing was for certain, there would be no running off to Canada or Europe for Warner S. Barson. Finally, rather than risk being drafted into very uncertain circumstances, Warn and Nancy decided that it would be best if he volunteered to join the army. His first several months were not much different from the experiences of any young recruit. He marched, learned to fire an M-16, peeled his share of potatoes, and cleaned more than his share of latrines. Following basic training, however, Warn's company commander learned that there was an experienced ski area manager in Platoon C. With a couple of well place telephone calls, Warn's army career took on a whole new thrust. Instead of being assigned a military MOS that would have meant a ticket to a tropical jungle, he soon found himself operating ski areas on military outposts in Germany and Alaska. Therefore, unlike so many others whose lives were permanently disrupted or terminated by military service during that period of armed conflict, Warn Barson returned from his army duties with an even better set of ski operator's credentials than he had possessed before volunteering for active duty.

As he signed the papers releasing him from further military service, Warn was prepared to live his dream of operating one of the large, new ski resorts that had sprung up in Colorado and Utah. But, Mr. Tillson had other plans for his young protégé. Soon, he made Warn an offer that he simply could not refuse. Warn was offered the opportunity to operate the Balsams Wilderness Ski area while he learned the duties of the resort's general manager. You see, it was Mr. Tillson's brilliant plan that Warn, Chef Leonard, and the resort's groundskeeper would become managing partners of The Balsams. Each of these three men had already invested a number of years restoring the old resort to its past glory. Therefore, Mr. Tillson reasoned, a partnership of these three men, each with his own professional and personal strengths, each with a financial stake in the enterprise's success, would greatly enhance the resort's long term prospects for success, while eliminating the necessity that Mr. Tillson supervise the day-to-day operations of his acquisition.

*   *   *

And so, before the 1970s were half over, Warn Barson, not yet 30 years old, found himself occupying the general manager's chair at The Balsams Grand Resort Hotel. As the years passed, Warn's reputation among the region's community of hoteliers grew tremendously. By 2003, Warn had held numerous community, state and national positions, and was highly respected internationally as a resort property manager.

*   *   *

Clearly, the success that Warn and his partners were experiencing was built upon a spirit of mutual respect and trust that emanates from the front office all the way to the kitchen, laundry room, and every other corner of the resort. The same attitudes and values shared by The Balsams general manager and his staff are requisite of successful marriages, or so I would learn. In each case, the failure to communicate effectively is a path to an unfortunate outcome.

Chapter 10

"Kary!" Warn Barson greeted me with a heartfelt smile, handshake and an embrace. How was I supposed to stay angry at this guy? After all, Warn and I had traveled that delightful road known as middle age together. We had met when each of us was in his early thirties. I had had a great bush of salt-and-pepper hair and a beard to match, while Warn exhibited a hint of gray hair and a body that had become muscular from years of skiing and participating in all sorts of outdoor recreation. Since that time, however, my beard and most of my hair had disappeared. And, what remained affixed to my scalp had turned snow white. Warn, that lucky SOB, had retained most of his hair, which had turned a classic shade of gray. On the other hand, if I must say so myself, I've retained the advantage from the scalp down. I have remained slim, while Warn hasn't.

Warn began the conversation with the usual small talk.

"So, how was the trip up; did you see any moose?" I informed him that we hadn't seen any moose, or anything else out of the ordinary, except for a couple of patrol cars with their lights flashing. Warn seemed to focus on that bit of information momentarily; but we didn't discuss it any further.

"How are Nya and the girls?" he continued.

"Fine," I replied. "Nya's here; I'm sure she'll drop by to say hello. How are Nancy and the kids?"

"Nancy's great; she's been running the new adventure center we've just added. In fact she's in Denver, teaching new applications for a rock wall technique she recently developed. The kids have been scattered all over the place. But Tom works here now; he's our hotel projects manager. If you have a few minutes later on, I'm sure he'd love to see you."

"Yeah, I'd love to see Tom; I think he was a junior in college the last time I was up here."

"Well, I have a bone to pick with you about that. Why do I have to head south every time I want to see Nya and you, Kary? I thought you liked it up here in God's country."

"I do, Warn, I do. But, the truth is, I've been struggling. It seems like every waking hour brings an aborted start to my second novel. I sit down, write a page, then delete it. Then I start again, and again, and again. But, it's never right. So I take a day or two off, then start the whole process over again. If we were still using electric typewriters, I'd have needed a second mortgage just to cover the cost of paper and ribbons. Maybe I should just give up and concentrate all of my efforts on teaching?"

"How is the teaching going?"

"It's great. You know me, I love having a captive audience."

Warn laughed. "Well, Kary, teaching takes a lot of creativity. So, if you're doing well in the classroom, it means that great mind of yours can't have deserted you, yet." Then, looking at the melting snow on my roof, he added,

"Even though you may look like a candidate for an old folks' home." I just smiled. But, of course, Warn was correct that my most productive years should be ahead of me.

"So, why now, Kary?" Warn asked.

"Why what?" I asked.

"Why, after nearly a decade, have you decided to honor us with your presence?"

"I came all the way up here just to see my picture next to the Babe's on the Wall of Fame," I lied. But Warn had given me an opening and I wasn't about to let it pass. He broke into a sheepish kind of grin, and just when it appeared that he was about to come clean, the telephone rang.

Picking up the receiver, he said, "Mister Barson." For the next two minutes Warn listened while I watched his facial expression change from one of mild interest to genuine concern.

"What! Are you sure? Okay, let's keep a lid on this for now. It's probably nothing, but keep me informed about any developments. Thanks. Bye."

The telephone conversation had been none of my business; but Warn seemed strangely anxious to share his conversation with me, despite what he had said to the caller about keeping a lid on things. He looked grave and remained quiet for about a minute or so. Then looking me in the eyes, he said, "If I tell you something, Kary, will you promise it won't leave this room? You won't even be able to share this with Nya."

I sat staring into Warn's steel blue eyes, expecting him to continue explaining. But he just sat there waiting for my assertion. So I nodded.

Thus assured, Warn continued, "That was the maître de hôtel, John Gray."

"I know John, the tall distinguished looking guy with a cookie duster mustache," I replied.

But Warn didn't hear me. One of the traits that had made him so successful as a general manager was his ability to concentrate when the pressure is on; and, in the resort business, that can be a daily occurrence. I had little doubt that Warn Barson could read the Wall Street Journal in the middle of Times Square at rush hour, and answer questions afterward.

"John called to tell me that one of our guests has missed the last two meals."

"I suppose that's unusual," I offered blandly. However, the thought of any sane person missing a meal at The Balsams, let alone two, was completely beyond my comprehension.

"Very unusual," he replied matter-of-factly.

All of the instincts I had developed as a crime writer, rusty though they were, began to kick into gear. After a minute passed, I asked, "How could John know that someone has missed both meals? How does he know this person didn't eat in the café above the Wilderness Lounge or take meals in the guestroom? Are you certain that none of the other guests has seen this person in the last forty-eight hours?"

Warn didn't answer me. The way he looked at me, I could tell that there was more to this disappearance than he was telling me.

"Look, Kary, I need your help." I had never seen my friend so deadly serious.

"Me? But isn't this a matter for the police?"

"Normally, yes. But there are two problems. First of all, the police are involved in some big case down in the Twin Mountain area."

"And second?"

"Something like this could damage our reputation." Then, after a brief pause, he added, "The captain at the Twin Mountain state police barracks isn't expected back until mid-afternoon on Sunday."

"Is that supposed to mean something? They do have other officers."

"The guy who's left in charge of investigations when the captain's away is Lieutenant Morgan."

"Yeah, so . . .?"

"Morgan's a jerk. He worked here for a year while he was studying to be a trooper. He was honest enough; but, he bullied the staff to the point I had to fire him. And from what I hear, time hasn't softened Jim Morgan a bit. Besides, the guy's something of a bungler; he loves to stride into a place, flash his badge and make a commotion. I'm sure he'd love nothing more than to come in here and raise a fuss."

"So, you think it's better to do nothing until the captain gets back?"

"That's not what I'm saying at all, Kary."

"Then, what . . ."

"Look, the staff and I take personal responsibility for every one of the guests. Besides, our guests don't simply disappear like this. They haven't since I've been working here nor, I'd wager, at any time before that. "

"You mean, no one's ever strolled out of the hotel without telling someone?"

"Not in more than one hundred and thirty years. Jesus, Kary, we're a full service resort in a remote destination; there's nothing around here but fifteen thousand acres of woods, ponds, streams and black flies."

"Okay, so does your missing person have a name?"

"Her name is Edna Connor."

"Then I'll ask the obvious question. Has anyone actually checked to see if this Ms. Connor is simply playing golf, or maybe is holed up in her room with a stomach ache or morning sickness, or . . .?"

"The housekeeping staff goes into every guest's room twice a day; once to clean the room and then to do turn downs."

"And they didn't see any trace of her?"

Warn shook his head. "Her bed was made."

"How about the shower . . . no soap residue or hair in the tub?"

"Lucy . . . she's the head housekeeper . . . said her girls told her the room looked like they'd just finished cleaning it. There wasn't a wash cloth, an article of clothing, or even a soap wrapper out of place." He paused to allow me to absorb all of this.

"So, will you help me, Kary?"

Nya was not going to be thrilled with any of this.

Chapter 11

Let me tell you a few facts about myself. My folks, Henry and Lois Turnell raised five children, two girls and three boys, of whom I was the youngest. My dad was a cop in Philadelphia. Within five years, he took and passed his examination to be a detective. Dad was a highly decorated member of the force who openly expressed his desire that all of us boys, but definitely not our sisters, would follow in his footsteps. As it turned out, I was the only one who came close to making my father happy. My older brothers didn't want any part of it. After I completed my degree in sociology at Temple University, the pressure was really put on me to become a crime fighter; however, I decided to get a master's degree in creative writing instead. But, I did end up with a career in crime, just not quite the one my father had planned.

I'd always been a voracious reader, with interests ranging from Charles Reich to Dashiell Hammett. Hammett's novels and my father's police experiences inspired me to take a job as a crime reporter for the Philadelphia Inquirer. I wrote stories that praised local police work despite the tough neighborhoods many of them patrolled. Of course I was perceived to be too "pro-cop" by some of my colleagues at the rival papers. At first I was very happy with the direction my career was taking. The writing was a piece of cake; and I've always had a keen sense for details, which made me a perfect candidate for the paper's crime desk. I probably would have continued as a reporter until my arteries hardened; but this was not in the cards, for a couple of reasons.

First, and foremost, there was Nya. Call it fate; call it luck, or whatever else you'd like. After I'd been sitting in my room night after night and week after week, my former college roommate, Dave, called me. Dave asked if I would be willing to double date with his fiancé and him. Diane, his intended, had a friend visiting her and they had agreed that it would be fun to go out as a foursome. I was all set to decline; but, for some reason that I still don't understand, decided to accept at the last minute.

It didn't take me long to realize that Nya was someone special . . . bright, beautiful, with a terrific sense of humor. More to the point, she actually liked me. We dated steadily for a year before we were married; and before we had really gotten to know one another as husband and wife, she was expecting our first daughter. Shortly thereafter, Nya began to pressure me to leave the Inquirer. Her argument was simple; my long, late hours were making her feel like she was raising our daughter alone. I probably would have resisted Nya's entreaties were it not for one particular case, a case that still haunts me.

There had been a bizarre killing in south Philly that involved an eastern European immigrant and his family. Without warning, the patriarch of this family had attacked his wife and mother-in-law, killing them both. He had hidden the bodies in the debris of a construction project that was being done on the family's garage. Several weeks passed before my father and his partner,

24

using an anonymous tip, narrowed the alleged perpetrator's location to a boathouse along the Schuylkill River. Catching the man sitting in a parked car near one of the boathouses, they used the element of surprise and arrested him after a brief struggle. Unfortunately, in the heat of the moment, my father had neglected to read the man his rights before he opened the trunk of the car, where the perpetrator had foolishly stored the murder weapon. Within twenty-four hours after making the arrest, the two partners were being hailed as heroes. Unfortunately, this fame was to be short-lived. It's a fact of life that headline cases attract the attention of headline-seeking defense attorneys. And the perpetrator in this instance had hired one of the best. It didn't take his lawyer long to learn about my father's error at the crime scene. Within days, the lawyer was working the press . . . successfully. Naturally I was reluctant to join in the feeding frenzy and my boss pulled me off the story, citing conflict of interest. In the end, the judge was given little choice and had to side with the defense attorney's arguments about abusing the accused guy's rights. Without the weapon as a key piece of evidence, the case had been dismissed. In the aftermath, my father had been suspended for three weeks without pay, and I had received a stern reprimand from my editor. The final straw for me came when I was accused by the crime reporter from a rival paper of being gutless and incompetent, "Just like yer old man."

I was told by witnesses that he had "gone out like a light" after I cold-cocked him. The worst of it occurred a year later to the day, when the perpetrator who had been set free on that technicality committed another set of murders. Hearing this, my father had resigned in disgrace and, a short time later, had a heart attack and died while reading an account of the story in the Inquirer.

With Nya's encouragement, I gave the Inquirer my notice. It didn't take long to realize what I wanted to do with my life. I had loved my college major in sociology; and, researching the impact of crime on society was in my blood. So, I returned to school and, shortly after the birth of my younger daughter, had earned my doctorate in Sociology with a specialization in Criminology. After a couple of years teaching at South Dakota State, I had been offered and accepted the position here in New Hampshire. I loved teaching, but could never shake the impact that case had on my father. A recurring dream–where the murderer walks by my father and me in the courtroom, with a cold, vicious smile on his face–had frequently awakened me in a cold sweat. This went on for months; then one evening, Nya had come up with a brilliant idea.

"Kary, you have to find a way to let the past go," she had said. "Your nightmares will never cease until you get the entire affair out of your system."

"We've been having this conversation for the past two years, Nya. Nothing I've tried has helped. I've spent countless hours in counseling. I've tried large quantities of Johnny Walker Red. Nothing's worked."

"I think I have a solution, " Nya offered patiently.

"I'm willing to try anything," I said, while staring intently into her eyes.

"You should write a book about your dad's career and the way it ended. Writing about it will get it out of your system."

"No good," I said, as I stood to refill our coffee cups.

"But, why not?" Nya asked.

"Where would I find the time? I'm up to my eyeballs with students' projects now. Besides, if I tell the whole story, we could be facing a lifetime of lawsuits from my dad's partner."

Nya was quiet for about a minute. Then, all at once, I could see her eyes light up and a broad smile flash across her face. "Write a novel."

"What?" I exclaimed.

"Write the story as crime fiction. Be accurate with the facts, but change the names and the settings. This way, you can get the story out of your system and no one will be able to sue you."

"That's an interesting idea. But what if no one reads it?"

"It doesn't matter, Kary. You're doing this for its therapeutic value, not for monetary reward."

And so, I took my wife's advice and wrote a murder mystery, A Hot Night in South Philly. And, to my total surprise, Random House had published it. Before long, Hot Night was being hailed for its realism; soon I was being mentioned in the same breath as John MacDonald. For more than six months I was on press trips, did every major talk show; there were book signings. To satisfy all of the requests for personal appearances necessitated taking a semester's leave of absence from my teaching duties. Random House knew a good thing when they saw one and signed me to a contract. I was to develop a series based upon the lead character in my book. Everything was going great. I had supplemented our income handsomely and, more importantly, rid myself of the nightmares. It's hard to describe just how great that entire experience felt, and even tougher to explain how circumstances changed so quickly. There is a scene in the movie, Titanic, when the lead character, played by Leonardo di Caprio declares, "I'm the king of the world!" You remember what happened to him, right? My situation is sort of similar.

It wasn't long before my world also began to sink to the depths. Within another six months, it had become evident to me and to everyone else that something was dramatically wrong. Random House was the first to comment publicly when I continued to miss deadline after deadline. For reasons neither Nya nor I have ever understood, I had developed a prolonged, incurable case of writer's cramp. Perhaps it was deep-seeded guilt of riding to fame and fortune on the blood of all those victims, not to mention my father's bad luck. Or, maybe I really was just a one-book wonder, as the New York Times Review of Books had speculated. Whatever the cause, I had failed to produce . . . not a single chapter, not a sentence, not a word . . . not even a prospectus. Strangely, the affliction had not affected my ability to produce publishable academic articles; but these did not satisfy me. I was obsessed with writing another bestseller. As the years passed, my relationship with Nya began to suffer. My guilt at letting her down began to consume me; but I was unable to discuss this with her. Then my libido vanished. Nya and I had made love a dozen times over a span of the last five years prior to coming to The Balsams. I had wanted to hide from Nya, my friends and everyone else. And poor Nya; she didn't know whether I was physically ill or having an affair. But it was neither. So, here we were at The Balsams. And, in all likelihood, this was my last shot at keeping Nya in my life.

Chapter 12

9 P.M. "Just what do you expect me to do, Warn," I asked. While I was trying to appear calm on the surface, I had to sit to keep my knees from shaking.

"I need you to use your instincts to, hopefully, find Mrs. Connor before this becomes a popular topic of conversation throughout the hotel; because, if it does, the results will be disastrous. Just talk with my staff and any guests who may have known Mrs. Connor. You know, snoop around; that sort of thing."

"And how do you expect me to do all of this without making everyone suspicious?" I asked.

"Hell, I don't know Kary. You were a crime reporter; you've had plenty of experience at snooping around without arousing suspicion."

"Jesus, Warn, that was twenty years ago. Besides, I was a writer, not a detective. And, how am I going to explain all of this to Nya. I'm already in hot water for being here with you so long."

"Look, you find out what happened to Edna Connor; and I'll find a way to distract Nya for the next forty hours or so. Just leave Nya to me, Kary."

"And what do you propose to do?" I couldn't help feeling a pang of anxiety about how Nya was going to be occupying herself. That feeling took me by surprise, but it wouldn't be my last before this was all over. I sat quietly for a few moments while I formulated an idea.

"Okay, Warn. This is what we're going to do. Tell your staff that I'm up here to write a book about the resort. Instruct them to cooperate with me fully, including allowing me access to all of the areas that are normally off-limits to guests. If this is going to work, no one on your staff must be suspicious of what I'm really doing."

"With two exceptions," he said in a matter-of-fact manner.

"What . . . who?" I asked. My tone hadn't disguised my annoyance.

"You'll need some help from the inside, someone with access to every nook and cranny at The Balsams."

"I suppose you mean your son Tom."

"I do. Tom will be able to share a lot of information and provide the access you need without raising any unnecessary curiosity. Besides, he's completely loyal to me and the resort."

"Tom will be a welcome addition," I said. Or so I thought.

"John Gray will be your other contact."

"John's a good man; but if you'll pardon me for asking, why get him involved?"

"Remember, John's in a position to see a lot. He already knows what's going on; so he can help to keep a lid on all of this. The way things generally work around here, I'm sure the entire staff knows that a guest has missed her meals. John will help by feeding the staff only the information they absolutely need to know."

"Don't you think it will be tough on John to be holding information back that's going to surface eventually?" I asked.

"He won't be," Warn responded matter-of-factly.

"I don't understand."

"John will share information on a need-to-know basis. Tom and I will carefully prepare what news we'll have him share with the staff." Then he added, "Before you say it, Kary, I realize this may create a few problems. But, the staff is like our family. I've worked with some of these people since I was a teenager. Lucy, the head housekeeper, is Tom's godmother. I can't keep them completely in the dark; I just won't tell them everything until we know exactly what's going on here."

"And what about the guests?"

"I don't want the guests to know anything. This is precisely why I'm involving you before the state police arrive." I could sense bitterness in Warn's tone.

"I've been meaning to ask you . . . why not call in the local guys?"

Warn had anticipated my question. "We're up here in the woods, Kary. We don't have our own police force. Like most of the small towns up here, Dixville counts on the troop dispatch out of Twin Mountain to send help if it's necessary. And, believe me, under normal circumstances, they can get here in a hurry."

Now I understood why we had such a short window of opportunity. With a problem brewing down south and the gendarmes already having been summoned from Twin Mountain, there was little likelihood we would see a police presence until late Sunday afternoon at the earliest, unless Warn was certain Edna Connor had met some untimely fate. My own task was clear: find Edna Connor before the proverbial window closed . . .on Warn Barson's fingers.

★   ★   ★

"Let's get back to your guests," I said.

"What about them?" Warn appeared agitated.

"I understand why you wouldn't want your guests to be privy to an investigation of this nature, but I sense something of an attitude, if you'll pardon me for saying so."

There was a sardonic look on Warn's face. "Do you let all of your students in on important information about college difficulties, troublesome colleagues . . . your family?"

"I share selected pieces of information with a few students who have earned my trust. Why?"

"And, do you like all of your students?" he asked.

"I like the vast majority, the ones who don't make loads of excuses or make demands on my time to ridiculous excess," I responded.

"It's the same in the hotel business, Kary, with one great exception."

"And what's the exception?" I found this dialogue most insightful.

"You have the opportunity to leave your place of employment every day after classes. And, I'll bet there is rarely the need for you to be on campus during the evenings or on weekends," he said.

"That's true. With computers I can do my research at home. And with these new electronic curriculum packages, I'll soon be able to monitor student's progress from my living room."

"The opposite is true of the hospitality business," Warn offered. "We're similar to dairy farming; this is a round-the-clock, hands-on operation." I groaned at my friend's clever play on words. He continued, "You see, Kary, to an extent we hoteliers are the prisoners of our guests. If we serve them well, they leave us alone to do our jobs. However, if something goes wrong, they come after us with a vengeance. And there's no place to hide."

My curiosity was aroused. "If you feel this way, why do you have your office right out here in the open?"

"Two reasons," Warn responded. "First, it's a matter of Balsams tradition. My predecessor and my predecessor's predecessor occupied this office. Second, and more important, the buck needs to stop somewhere. So if there's an irate guest, I don't want my staff or department heads taking the heat. I prefer that they come to me. After all, I'm the one who ultimately makes the decision," he said with a wry smile.

Now, I was really intrigued. "Come on, Warn. Are you trying to tell me that a guest at this Shangri-La would actually be stressed out? After about ten minutes here, I feel too relaxed to give anyone a hard time."

"You're in the vast majority, Kary. The others, thank goodness, are few and far between. But, some people can be very unreasonable."

"Like Mrs. Plessence?" I offered.

"Mrs. Plessence is a pussy cat compared with some of the others," Warn replied.

"Such as?" I was completely absorbed by this conversation. I had naively assumed that the clientele at a resort must be the most docile, pleasant people in the universe. On more than one occasion, Nya and I had discussed the idea of dropping out of our respective jobs and opening a B&B. This was beginning to sound like a very bad idea. Warn was really exercised about this; and I was about to understand why.

"Okay Kary, how would you feel if one of your students came into your office threatening to sue the college because he'd stepped on his shoe lace and fallen on the sidewalk outside of the student union?" Before I could respond, he fired another example at me. "How would you feel if a student demanded compensation for a valuable postage stamp that he'd absent mindedly left in a report he'd submitted to you. Worse, what if he made the demand while pounding on your desk and screaming hoarsely into your face? Or what if he waited until the middle of the night to do all of this?"

I was speechless. But Warn still wasn't quite finished. "Of course, the examples I've just given you are facetious; but we've had guests complain about everything from items their children have lost that have ended up in the hotel laundry, to dentures they've broken because the bathroom floors are too hard, to requests for refunds because a spell of wet weather precluded any opportunity to use the clay courts. And, as zany as some of them are, it's not the complaints themselves that bother us. We realize that, despite our best efforts, we're not perfect. It's the attitude with which they're made. I had a guest walk in here one day to tell me how beautiful everything is, then return two days later to call me an incompetent ass."

I was beginning to be concerned about my long time friend. In twenty years of knowing him, I'd never seen Warn so worked up about anything. "Why do you put up with this crazy business, Warn? With your reputation, you could get a job as a CEO for a major corporation tomorrow."

"Because I love this old place. It's in my blood; it's a part of my soul. And, as I told you, Kary, the people who work here are my second family. But, I have to tell you that I have been thinking about taking a leave of absence."

I was stunned by this entire revelation. In my mind, Warn Barson was the one person in the world who was happy every minute of every day with his work. The idea of Warn without The Balsams, or The Balsams without Warn, was difficult to imagine.

"Gee, Warn. I'm really sorry. I've been so absorbed with my own self-pity that I never considered you might be having your own issues, too."

There was an irony to this entire scenario. Here was one middle age guy who had arrived at The Balsams in hopes of reviving a shaky marriage, looking for a missing guest whose own marital situation, as I would learn, had predisposed her to visit the resort, which was managed by a second middle aged man whose long-term relationship with that property-another marriage of sorts-was in jeopardy.

Too tired to take advantage of any evening entertainment, I remained and chatted with Warn for a while. As I looked at my watch, I realized, to my horror, that it was already 10:30. Then it occurred to me, there really wasn't anything to worry about. Given my track record, Nya would have given up any hope for a night of passion or compassion, and would be in dreamland by the time I returned to the room.

I shook hands and gave Warn my assurance that, as a favor to him, I would be on task bright and early the following day. He seemed satisfied that the extra time he'd spent in the office with me would bear fruit. Before leaving for the night, he had scheduled a department heads' meeting for 8:00AM the next morning; so, the way would be paved for my investigation to begin as soon as Nya and I were finished with our breakfast.

Chapter 13

6:30 A.M., Saturday, July 15th. Nya Turnell is always full of surprises. I had expected her to be angry, or at least very quiet the next morning. But she was neither. In fact, I must confess that I found her extraordinarily cheery mood totally surprising. As always, she was the first to rise, shower, and dress. When I emerged from taking my shower, she greeted me with a smile, a peck on the cheek, and the strict order, "Get a move on, sweetheart; I'm famished." So was I.

Nya wanted to ride the Hampshire House elevator to the main level, so we could peruse the dinner menu that was posted inside. As we rode the elevator down to the lobby level, Nya said, "Oh, Kary, how will I ever decide what to have for dinner? They're serving lobster, black angus steak, chicken Kiev and . . . oh look . . . arctic char. I can feel my waist line expanding already."

Instead of using this opening to tell Nya that I love her waistline, I offered a rather bland comment. "You can eat whatever you'd like tonight, Nya. We'll be here for four weeks." Way to go Turnell, you silver-tongued devil.

Deep down, Nya was probably ready to shoot me, but instead she responded with a cheery, "I think I'll have the char. Yum!"

As we passed Warn's office, to my surprise, the screen door swung open. I hadn't expected Warn to be there at seven thirty in the morning.

"Nya! Welcome back to the Balsams! It's been too long since we've seen you."

Then, as they embraced, Warn added, "Can I talk with you for a few minutes, Nya? I promise I won't keep you from breakfast." As he added the latter comment, he gave me a wink.

"I'll be happy to talk with you, Warn," she practically cooed. "Kary, why don't you get started; I'll be right along."

Well, it certainly hadn't taken Warn long to keep his promise to divert Nya. In spite of myself, I must confess to feeling a little uneasy about leaving her alone. But I was soon at the top of the stairs and entering the dining room. Before long, the lure of French toast and native maple syrup had prevailed over any apprehension I may have felt.

★   ★   ★

7:20 A.M. I was preoccupied with my second cup of coffee and the view of Dixville Notch when Nya arrived at our table. I had planned to avoid any mention of her meeting with Warn, but curiosity got the best of me. "So, what did Warn have to say to you? Did he tell you why my picture isn't hanging on the Wall of Fame any more."

"I'm sorry, Kary, the subject never came up. Warn wants my professional opinion about the latest advertising campaign that Lynn Ride has designed for the resort. I've volunteered to talk with Lynn while he's up here the next couple of days."

I wasn't about to question any of this. Whatever Warn had said to Nya, it appeared that he had cleared my way to "snoop around" for him.

★   ★   ★

After a delicious breakfast of French toast and tomato juice, I kissed Nya lightly on the cheek and left her to eat a breakfast of eggs and pancakes. I had already decided to talk first with Tom Barson. Tom had virtually grown up at The Balsams. According to family tradition, Warn had not pressured nor even encouraged his son to make his living at the resort. Tom had majored in economics at NYU. When he graduated, there were offers from several large financial management firms, including two with firms in the World Trade Center. But Tom had resisted. The two years he had spent in New York while pursuing his MBA had taught Tom all he needed to know: New York was not his kind of place, just as it hadn't been for his great grandfather, Mack. If Tom ever had the slightest regret for his decision to return to Dixville Notch, it was completely eradicated by the events of September 11, 2001. Tom's college roommate, Bill Davis, had taken one of those high paying jobs that Tom resisted. Had he not made an 8 AM appointment to get his hair cut on the lower level of the World Trade Center complex, Bill would have met the fate of twelve of his colleagues. As it was, Bill had run until he thought his lungs would burst, avoiding first falling debris and humanity, then the enormous dust cloud that enveloped the city when the towers collapsed. It had taken Bill numerous counseling sessions and three weeks visiting Tom in Dixville to finally be able to sleep at night. Thus, Tom was eternally thankful that he had decided to move home in 1999.

★   ★   ★

7:30 AM, Saturday, July 15. With Nya absorbed with her breakfast, I knocked on the screen door beneath the thin black and white sign that read "Projects Manager." While Tom's office was situated directly across from Warn's, during the typical day father and son infrequently crossed the narrow hallway connecting the hotel's main entry way to the Hampshire House. It wasn't that the two lacked true affection for one another; rather each shouldered his own responsibilities. It hadn't been nepotism that led the father to recommend his son to the managing partners. Warn recognized Tom's potential value to the resort; and his confidence had been repaid many times. As Projects Manager, Tom Barson had no job description. His role was to work with meeting and conference planners, to serve as a liaison between the business office director, the front desk manager and the head of maintenance. However, his chief role was as a trouble-shooter. If there was an emergency or a strange development at the resort, it was Tom's job to find solutions. He was to use any method at his disposal and to complete his task without attracting attention or the concern of his coworkers. At times, the Scottish temper Tom had inherited would betray him. But, despite these occasional outbursts, he was his father's right hand man at the resort, just as Nancy Barson was at home. The absence of Edna Connor was the kind of problem that was normally assigned to Tom. Only, this job had been given to me. Now, as I entered his office, I wondered if the younger Barson would be harboring any resentment toward me.

"Good morning, Tom." I offered as we shook hands. The one thing that I've always liked about Tom's father is his warm, firm handshake. Warn could be shaking hands with a hangman and it wouldn't make any difference. He'd look the hangman straight in the eyes, flash a friendly smile and welcome him with his strong grip. The father had taught his son well.

The two of us shook hands as though we were preparing to discuss past conquests at a sorority house, rather than investigate a potential disappearance. "How do you want to proceed, Dr. Turnell?" he began.

"How old are you now, Tom?" I countered.

"I was thirty last month," Tom replied.

"Well, then you've just become qualified to call me Kary . . . but just barely," I smiled.

"Sounds good, Kary. What do we do first?"

"The first thing you'll need to do is make certain I have a credible introduction to your department heads. We'll need to convince them that I'm doing background research for a murder mystery that takes place right here at the resort. How does that sound?"

"That should work well. Please remember one thing though, Kary, you mustn't do or say anything that will disrupt the natural flow of things here," he stated emphatically.

"I'm not sure I follow," I replied.

"The Balsams staff is more than a family; it's really an ecosystem of sorts."

"An ecosystem, eh?" I was amused by Tom's allusion to the resort as a natural phenomenon.

However, he was quite serious. "Yes. Instead of plants and animals, we have staff and guests. Instead of a rainforest with trees and flowering plants, we have guest rooms and public rooms and miles of steam and water pipes, electrical wires and other conduits. Instead of the watering hole and wetland vegetation, we have activities and equipment," Tom explained earnestly.

"I understand your analogy, Tom; and I promise not to do anything to disrupt the natural flow of things around here."

"Even if it means you won't be able to find what you're looking for?" he asked. My own look of concern registered on Tom's face. "It's just possible you'll reach a blind alley where you'd have to undermine the staff's trust in us in order to unlock new paths of information."

"Yes, that is entirely possible, Tom."

"Don't you see, Kary, if you do, you'll cause all kinds of problems; it will be difficult for the staff to ever trust my father, John Gray or me again."

"But won't they feel exactly the same way if the state police come streaming in here asking questions after no one has told them anything?" I responded.

This last statement seemed to freeze Tom, if only for a heartbeat or two. Then, after a deep breath, he spoke quietly, "All I can say is we'd better act fast, or this could be a real mess."

Then, spotting Warn entering his office across the hall, Tom asked me to stay put while he went to see his father. Before I could reply he was out the door, had entered Warn's office and closed the door behind him. As I stood in Tom's office I could see, but not hear, the animated discussion that was taking place between his father and him, not more than thirty feet from where I was sitting. It was apparent that the father had had his way this time, as Warn soon guided Tom back to me with the aid of a gentle hand on the younger Barson's shoulder.

When Tom returned to the office, he did not make eye contact, but stated simply, "It's time for the staff director's meeting." As I followed him out of his office, I couldn't help but wonder what had transpired a few moments before. Based upon the body language of father and son, it was likely that the latter had just emerged from a contemporary version of the woodshed. I wondered why.

Chapter 14

There is little to be said about Billy Fenton. To be more accurate, there is nothing positive to be said about Billy Fenton. Billy had been born and raised in Berlin, a pulp mill town on the other side of the Notch. Many kids growing up in a pulp town have felt inferior because of the pervasive sulfur smell and grime. And, having to watch as their parents endured long periods of unemployment and dependence on food stamps made it difficult for teenagers to focus upon the enormous cultural and social capital hidden within the blighted landscape. While the best and the brightest took their educations and skills out of the hinterlands and sold them to the highest bidder in some larger, more desirable community, the Billy Fentons were left behind. This is the unfortunate legacy of company towns everywhere.

When Billy was three days shy of his thirteenth birthday, his mother had shown him the wonders of the town's public library. Billy had responded to this introduction to one of Berlin's cultural icons by throwing a brick through one of its beautiful windows a few days later. Always a poor reader, Billy had misinterpreted his mother's gesture as a taunt, one that needed to be repaid. Unfortunately, Billy had not been caught. As a result, he mistook his luck for cleverness. It wasn't long before Billy and his pals Thirsty and Larry had graduated to petty theft, then to burglary and car theft. Before long, all three had been caught twice, but Billy had miraculously escaped conviction. So, Billy decided that he had outgrown what Berlin had to offer. He began to look for work in a community that was far enough from Berlin to ensure him a certain amount of anonymity, but close enough so he could continue to scrounge off of his mother. After several jobs where his new bosses soon learned to see him for what he was, Billy saw an ad in the Coos County Democrat for maintenance workers. Billy had become very good at doing basic maintenance, including a bit of carpentry. Therefore, when he saw The Balsams ad in the Democrat, he figured he had died and gone to heaven. Owing to a law designed to protect the privacy of honest applicants, Billy was able to get a primary maintenance job at the resort, despite his poor track record. As fate would have it, Billy's first week of employment coincided with the arrival of Edna Connor at The Balsams.

Chapter 15

8 A. M., Saturday, July 15th. The meeting with the department heads and their supervisors went off as planned. I was introduced to the group of fourteen people, two of whom I already knew: Tom Barson and John Gray, maitre d'hotel. Because Warn was occupied with other matters, Tom ran the morning meeting. At Tom's instruction, formal introductions were made by each person sitting at the table: Reg Gill, superintendent of services; Dave Watson, business manager; Sue Nesson, director of personnel; Jay Olds, registration manager; Rolf Vernon, head of maintenance; Jeff Milk, laundry manager; Lucy Laflamme, executive housekeeper; the famous Chef Leonard, at whose introduction I literally quaked; Shannon Parton, director of recreation services; Fran Galloway, longtime orchestra leader and music director at the resort; Jim O'Neil, assistant director of golf; and Bob Clay, director of tennis services.

I told the group that I was doing background research for a novel; it was to be a mystery set at The Balsams. When I asked if I could spend one half hour with each of them to gather necessary background information to ensure greater realism, the reaction was decidedly mixed. Reg, John and Lucy appeared to be very enthusiastic. Unfortunately, my hero, Chef Leonard wouldn't even look at me; and Rolf just glowered. Tom informed those assembled that the general manager had requested each of them to cooperate with me fully. When asked what was meant by cooperation, Tom didn't miss a beat. He said, "Each of us is expected to fill out the sheet that I'm passing around and indicate a time and place where Dr. Turnell can interview you during the next twelve hours."

At this point I thought Tom might have said too much; for, when he emphasized that time is of the essence, Jay Olds asked, "Why is that the case? Dr. and Mrs. Turnell are registered for this entire month."

I was ready with a response. "My wife has made me promise not to spend my entire vacation working on my book." Of course, this was entirely true. I must have been convincing because there were no further questions. However, for some reason, Tom felt that I had shown him up in front of the other department heads. And, when he and I were finally alone, I felt a decided chill in the room.

"You do realize that you're playing with fire, don't you, Kary?" he asked. Well, at least he was referring to me as Kary again.

"I do understand, Tom," I replied. "But as long as I can hide behind this charade of doing research for my book, we'll be okay."

"What happens when you no longer can?" This guy knew how to ask all the right questions.

"Look, Tom. Your dad's welfare means a great deal to me . . . despite the fact he took my picture down." The irony of this last remark was lost on young Tom; so I continued. "I promise you, I'll do all I can to help, not hurt, the situation."

With that, I headed off to the first of many meetings with Warn's staff.

Chapter 16

Early 1993, The Balsams Grand Resort Hotel. It hadn't taken very long for the young assistant head of maintenance, Richard Tomquist, to be fired the first time. Richard was an excellent maintenance man. Even before the ink on his W-4 form had dried, Rolf Vernon had already assigned Richard the important task of repairing broken furniture. He proved particularly adept at replacing broken chair legs and fixing cracked veneer. Rolf and the management team were so satisfied with Richard's work that a master key had been made for him, allowing Richard access to all of the public areas, guest rooms and virtually every other nook and cranny within the resort.

Richard had only one flaw, but it was a doozie. He had a habit of fraternizing with the single, female guests. One of the first things that every new hire at The Balsams is told . . . not once, but several times . . . employees do not mingle with guests. This fact is clearly stated in the employee handbook which is required reading for each and every member of The Balsams staff. Of course, it's not as if Richard were under some form of house arrest after hours; for, all of the resort's employees were given golf and tennis privileges. Employees even had their own swimming beach on Lake Gloriette.

The rules of deportment for the Balsams staff read similar to the strike out rule in baseball; three strikes and you are out. Richard had received strike one during his first year at the resort. One of the housekeepers had observed him holding hands with a pretty, young blond teenager. Richard's explanation was that he had been summoned to fix a jammed window in a guest room on the second floor of the Dixville House. He had followed protocol by leaving the door slightly ajar while entering a guest room occupied by said guest. Richard had soon fixed the problem. But, when the young woman had thanked him, she said that her hands were freezing. According to Richard, he was just warming them for the young woman when the housekeeper had surprised him. The housekeeper had wondered why the open window should have left the woman's right thigh in need of warming as well.

As is the custom when one breaks an established rule at the resort, Richard had received a written reprimand from his immediate supervisor, Rolf Vernon. A copy of the statement, signed by both Richard and Rolf, was then placed in Richard's personnel folder. Thus, his first offense had become a matter of record.

About four months later, Richard had been observed fraternizing with a female patron during the winter season. It seems that the young woman, a resident of Chicoutimi in Quebec, had returned from a morning of snowshoeing, only to learn that the door locks on her car had frozen over night. The young woman had returned to the lobby in a disturbed state. She hadn't been upset about the lock, but was concerned that she would have a problem explaining her dilemma, in French, to someone in a position to do something about it. This is where The Balsams pre-registration interview proved to be her ally. Whenever a prospective guest made a reservation, a good deal of information was gathered. This was stored and shared among vital staff members immediately prior to a guest's arrival. As part of the process for serving its guests, the resort's staff prepared itself to look after the special needs of new arrivals. Thus, when the woman's plight was observed, Reg Gill had been called immediately, not only because he was superintendent of services, but because of his fluency in French. Reg had assured the woman that she was in good hands, not realizing how close to the truth his statement was about to become.

Richard had just finished eating lunch and was sitting in one of the collection of large, red vinyl booths that comprise a part of the employees' dining area. Marge, the attendant of the facility, had called to tell him that Reg was on the phone. Upon hanging up the receiver, Richard was heard to exclaim, "Ooh la la, there is a young damsel in distress who needs me." Marge, knowing her friend's track record, issued a few words of warning, "Be careful Rich; you don't need a second strike."

But that was exactly what Richard got. Dressed in his hotel maintenance parka, he met the woman at her car. Within a matter of minutes the door lock was ice free and the woman said something to Richard in French. Putting two and two together but arriving at six, Richard took the woman in his arms and proceeded to engage in a lengthy French kiss. The woman was at once amused and aroused; clearly she was in no rush to break the embrace. In fact, Richard may well have avoided his second reprimand from the resort's management were it not for the fastidious nature of Reg Gill. The latter had put his parka back on and returned to the parking lot to see if Richard and the woman were having any difficulty communicating, but soon realized they were not.

Richard was spared from immediate dismissal only because the young woman had refused to issue any form of complaint. In fact, her statement to Warn Barson, as translated by Reg, was that she planned to return to The Balsams many times, so good was the service. While Reg had been somewhat amused as he discussed the entire incident with Warn afterward, the latter was not. According to custom at the resort, when a rule has been violated a second time, the resulting reprimand was prepared by Warn Barson himself. In the closed-door session that followed, a red-faced Warn had informed Richard, in the presence of his equally red-faced supervisor, that he was extremely tempted to fire him on the spot. "It's only because Rolf has made it abundantly clear that you are a very valuable employee that keeps me from firing you right now, Richard." Then, after his offer of counseling for Richard was politely refused with a shy smile, Warn sent his handyman with the gigolo bent home on a week's suspension.

Unfortunately, even after the week off without pay, Richard Tomquist's employment at The Balsams didn't last long. Late one night, Mr. Parnell, one of the two night watchmen assigned to keep an eye on things during the hours when guests are asleep, was making his rounds. Uncharacteristically, he stopped in the employees' lounge for a cup of coffee. Then, rather than walk back out through the lobby toward the Hampshire House, he decided to go there by way of the catacombs, the name the staff had given to the large maze of tunnels that lies beneath much of the hotel. Turning left and heading down the large, concrete main ramp leading to the lowest level of the Hampshire House, he heard a distinct, repeated bumping sound, followed by a muffled "shhh!"

"What the heck?" he mumbled to himself as he slowly advanced toward one of the small, clandestine rooms that line the concrete walled passageway. Then he saw them. In a room the size of a walk-in closet that was used to store furniture in need of repair, stood Richard with his bare buttocks now being illuminated by the watchman's flashlight. It was soon evident the handyman was not repairing furniture at that late hour, for wrapped around his waist were a lovely set of female legs. The watchman might have thought he'd discovered two employees with a great hideaway for love making, had he not observed something shimmering in the beam of his flashlight. It was the reflection from an expensive evening bag, the kind carried by guests, not the resort's chambermaids or dining room personnel.

And so Richard was unceremoniously fired that night. It was some time before a craftsman of his ilk could be found again. It was even longer before the suspicion that he had somehow copied his Yale master key prior to turning it over to Rolf had subsided. Every once in a while some object of minimal value would be listed as missing. It had become something of an inside joke with the long-term employees: "Richard's done it again," they would say. Explanations of the source of their levity to newer hirees would follow, with knowing smiles passed among those who had worked with Richard. And the matter would be dropped until the next item was missed.

★   ★   ★

This entire episode would have been meaningless to my story were it not for one detail. On the particularly lengthy July 11th list of new arrivals was a familiar name: R. Johan Tomquist.

Chapter 17

Saturday, July 15th. The next twenty-four hours were going to be crucial. I needed to speak to as many key hotel personnel as possible, while searching for physical signs of Edna Connor. I only had a rudimentary description of what she looked like, but was confident there weren't a lot of bodies lying around waiting for me to find them.

The thing that was going to consume a lot of time . . . too much time . . . was the necessity to interview all of Warn's department heads. For the most part, this was strictly for the purpose of keeping up the appearance that I was writing a book. A look at the schedule which was to occupy my time that morning made me wince:

10:00am John Gray, maitre d'hotel
10:30   Reg Gill, superintendent of services
11:00   Dave Watson, business manager with Sue Nesson, director of personnel
11:30   Jay Olds, registration manager

I had no meetings scheduled between noon and 1PM; someone must have tipped these people off about the lunches at this joint, I mused. However, I groaned when I looked at the afternoon schedule. Because, after lunch, I would be bouncing around the resort like a human pinball:

1:00 pm Rolf Vernon, head of maintenance
2:00   Jeff Milk, laundry manager
2:30   Lucy Laflamme, executive housekeeper
3:00   Paul Leonard, executive chef
3:30   Shannon Parton, director of recreation services
4:00   Fran Golloway, orchestra leader and music director
4:30   Jim O'Neil, assistant director of golf
5:00   Bob Clay, director of tennis services

Looking at this list, it wasn't hard to determine that John, Reg, Sue, Rolf, and Lucy were the people who might help me shed a light on things. The other appointments were mainly window dressing. While it annoyed me to waste valuable time, I couldn't suppress anxiety about meeting my hero-the resort's executive chef, Paul Leonard.

Chapter 18

10:00 A. M. My meeting with John Gray did not take place in the dining room as I had expected. As maitre d'hotel, John occupied a small administrative office adjacent to the elevators on the second floor of the Hampshire House. This afforded him the necessary space to keep track of the complex workings of the dining room. But, as I soon learned, his fiefdom also comprised the coffee shop and the restaurant at the Panorama Golf clubhouse. On a typical summer day, John supervised 125 people, including dining room captains, a hostess, waiters, linen room people, a silver polisher, a uniform room attendant and an expediter.

"What's an expediter," I asked as an icebreaker.

"An expediter is the person who the waitstaff uses to pre-order their dinners; he or she can make a waiter look very good or very bad," John told me.

"So, this is a person who's good side your waitstaff definitely wants to stay on."

"It could mean the difference between an excellent tip or a stiff," he replied.

Now it was time to get down to business. "John, you are one of three people who knows that I'm looking into this Edna Connor business," I said.

"Yes, but I'm one of a dozen or more who knows she's missing."

I was floored. "What?"

"The Balsams has its own built-in communications system, professor." John sat back in his oak swivel chair. With its red leather seat cover and brass tacks, it reminded me of one that had been used by the lawyer who had represented my father many years before. "Each member of the resort's waitstaff . . . the captain and her three waiters . . . knew Mrs. Connor had not shown up for meals long before I did. And there are others who also must know by now."

"Such as?" I asked, while attempting to mask my growing anxiety.

"Well, there's the housekeeper assigned to her room, the person assigned to do her turndown, and possibly others. I suspect you'll learn more about this when you talk with Lucy Laflamme later today."

I had barely started nosing around, and the magnitude of what was facing me already had my head spinning. For a moment I had to question how I ever made a living this way. But, some things are like riding that proverbial bicycle.

"When did your staff notice that she'd missed her first meal?" I queried.

"Let's see." He began to thumb through an elongated loose-leaf notebook. As he did, John mused that he was the last holdout from doing all of his record keeping on-line. Because of his reputation and his length of service at the resort, Warn had not pressed him to abandon the old ways for the new. However, John Gray was aware that change was coming soon. On this day, his notebook didn't betray him. "Mrs. Connor arrived at the Balsams on the 10th of July. She took her first meal in the dining room at dinner that night, which of course is when many guests start their meals."

Computer or no, I figured John could easily tell me what percentage of arriving guests start with breakfast or lunch, as opposed to dinner, but decided it was better not to monopolize any more of his time than absolutely necessary. So, I stuck to the issue at hand.

John soon found the information he was looking for. "Mrs. Connor had dinner on the 10th through the 13th; she had breakfast from the 11th through the 13th. However, we can't be certain about lunches unless they are taken up at the Panorama golf course."

I was confused and told him so. He had anticipated as much. "You see, professor, because we offer a buffet lunch in the dining room, we can not account for specific guests whereabouts, not unless they either request a box lunch or a ticket to eat at the golf course."

"And, I gather she did neither of those two things."

"No, she did not," John replied, while taking a second look at his records.

"But she did return for dinner on the night of the 13th, right?" I asked.

Once again, John rechecked his records. "That's correct."

"Okay, now comes the fun part," I mumbled out loud.

"What's that, professor?"

"I need to know the names of the captain and waitstaff for Mrs. Connor's table."

"That's easy enough."

"That's not all, John. I need to have the names of the guests who were seated adjacent to her . . . particularly any single-person parties."

"But why?" John was clearly perplexed by this last request.

"Because a person seated next to her may have some knowledge of where she is, or where she has gone."

This was clearly more than John had bargained for. "I'll need to clear this with my superiors," he advised me.

"Please discuss this only with Mr. Barson, John." This was fine with the maitre d'hotel, as he was responsible for answering directly to the general manager. I shuddered to think what may have happened if he had another direct supervisor. The chain of command, not to mention the deep sense of trust that he and other employees of the resort have developed over the years, could be undermined irreparably by a single, but significant indiscretion. Were it not for this stroke of good fortune, I probably would have lost his cooperation at that point. Then this entire process would have unraveled.

The next thing I knew, John had picked up the telephone and entered a four-digit number. "Elaine, John Gray here; is Mr. Barson in? May I please speak with him? Yes, I'll hold."

When Warn Barson picked up the telephone two minutes later, John brought him up to date about our discussion. Fifteen seconds after John had concluded, he handed the receiver over to me. "Mr. Barson wants to speak with you, professor."

"Hello Warn."

The voice on the other end of the line sounded quite grave. "Listen Kary, you are treading on some very tenuous turf here; you do understand that, don't you? You need to be very careful about people's right to privacy."

"Trust me, I'll be extremely careful how I gather this information." The truth is, I hadn't the slightest idea how I was going to obtain all the information I needed. There were so many issues to consider that I'd need an abacus just to keep a tally. Besides the obvious need to maintain the status quo at The Balsams, there were other issues that have names like invasion of privacy and potentially interfering with the investigation of a crime. At least I could take some solace in the fact that New Hampshire's prison uniforms no longer sported stripes, which I abhor; they were orange, my favorite color.

Warn asked to speak with John again, so I handed him the phone. "Yes, Mr. Barson, I will." Then following a pause, "Yes sir. Thank you."

When John Gray hung up the phone, he pulled a sheet of paper from his desk. On the sheet he wrote the names of three people who had been sitting alone in the dining room adjacent to Edna Connor's table: Alice Priest (checked out 7/13), Annette Johnston (checking out today), and R. Johan Tomquist (still in the house). As he handed me the sheet, I noticed that two of the guests were women. I soon learned that the former had left on her scheduled departure date while the latter had been offended by another guest and was departing a day early. The third person, the male, was staying at the resort for another night. If it became necessary to question him, I needed to work fast.

Another thing I had noticed was that nowhere on the sheet bearing the three names could be found the seemingly omnipresent logo of The Balsams. "Ecotourism protection insurance?" I mused. Clearly, John was protecting The Balsams from any suspicion that delicate information had been supplied to a civilian such as myself.

★   ★   ★

Thanks to John Gray, I soon had my introduction to Edna Connor's waitstaff. My conversation with the captain and her waiters provided a small surprise. Needing them to tell me about Edna without knowing my real purpose, I continued my ruse about doing background research for a murder mystery. To my amazement, each of them–even the busboys–already had heard about me through the hotel grapevine.

I began my interview by asking each to share any interesting guest stories. Of course, I was running the risk that Grenda, who had been working at the resort before any of her waitstaff was born, would find countless other stories to share before I heard a word about Edna Connor. I need not have worried, for this particular guest remained very much on the captain's mind. Grenda told me that Edna had initially appeared to be a quiet woman. But, before long, she was regaling the staff and the people at surrounding tables with stories about how wonderful it was to be staying at such a beautiful resort. She also remembered having overheard Edna tell the man at the next table that, while she was grateful to her husband for spending so much money on her, she really wasn't missing him at that moment.

The three waitstaff were all internationals. The two males, Stephen, a nineteen year old Polish college student on leave from his studies, and Domingo, a twenty year old Colombian with an interest in eventually being a tennis pro, had not interacted very much with Mrs. Connor. However, Domingo intimated that the lady had called him "saucy." For his part, Domingo indicated that while Mrs. Connor had "very impressive breasts," he regarded her to be much too old for him. "Besides," he told me in his thick Spanish accent, "they are very strict about such things here." He was, of course, referring to the resort's unbending host-guest relations policy. But what if Domingo had pursued Edna Connor; and what if she had threatened to report him? A young man living in a strange land; he could have panicked. I started to ask myself, "Could this young man be our culprit?" But I dismissed this image with a barely noticeable shake of my head. I needed to remind myself that as yet there was no evidence a crime had even been committed.

A young Russian woman, Katyana, had been the most helpful of the three young people. Despite the differences in their ages, not to mention the enormous differences in their cultural backgrounds, the two women had bonded. Mrs. Connor tended to enter the dining room thirty-to-forty minutes before seating ended each evening. At this time of night, there were few if any children present. Katyana wasn't sure why, but she suspected that being around young children had made Mrs. Connor very sad, given the expression she had on her face when a child was sitting at a nearby table. Then there was the matter of the man at the table across from her. Katyana suspected that the two were becoming very friendly, possibly even intimate. She found it interesting that the two arrived for dinner at about the same time, definitely on the night of the 13th and possibly on the 12th; Katyana couldn't be certain about the earlier night. However, when I questioned Katyana further about this, she confessed that it was difficult for her to be certain, given that these two middle age people were speaking a language that was not yet completely familiar to her.

Chapter 19

At 10:30 A.M. sharp, I sat with Reg Gill in the historic Ballot Room. Being surrounded by all of this tradition made me feel special. It was in this very room, every four years, that citizens of Dixville-resident employees of the resort and their voter-age family members-cast the nation's first votes for President of the United States. I had no trouble recognizing Reg. He was one of those people you see time and time again around the resort, if you're observant. Of course, it didn't hurt that the guy had to be easily six feet six inches tall in his stocking feet.

Reg was the youngest of five children whose grandparents had emigrated to New Hampshire's north country, having been pressed south of the border by the Quebec Catholic church's diaspora policy-go forth and multiply. Reg had grown up in the shadow of a pulp mill, where both his grandfather and father had worked before the paper industry experienced one of its all-too-frequent hiccups. Like Warn Barson, Reg had come to work at The Balsams as a teenager; and like Warn, he had stayed. I soon learned that Reg was a man of considerable intelligence. Some people at the resort would tell you that there were three indispensable people at the resort: Warn, Chef Leonard and Reg. Each of these men, especially Reg, would eschew any such claim.

As I had done with the personnel in the dining room, I reminded Reg of my purpose. As we sat there, it occurred to me that if anyone might already be aware of my true purpose, it was the man sitting before me. After all, Reg Gill was a vital cog in the day-to-day operation of the resort. If he were on to my ruse, he was masking it very well from a lifelong reader of faces. Yet, for reasons I couldn't put my finger on, I felt he knew more about my true purpose than he was indicating.

Had I realized prior to our meeting how much Reg could tell me, I would have made a longer appointment with the guy. It was no accident that I had seen him everywhere during the brief time Nya and I were at the resort; his job required him to be nearly omnipresent. Yet, despite these pressures, Reg's smiling demeanor gave evidence to the fact that this was a man who enjoyed his position at The Balsams.

I soon learned that Reg supervises 25 people, including the resort's doormen, bellmen and the people who run the information booth situated along the road across from Lake Gloriette. I asked him what a typical day is like.

"A typical day," he laughed, "let me see. There really is no such thing as a typical day for a person with my job. I spend a chunk of time at the bellman's desk supervisin' the movement of guests and their luggage in and outta the hotel. I meet with the housekeeping staff about a lot of stuff throughout the day, and frequently meet with the front desk staff and the dinin' room folks, also. At lunch time I meet with Jay Olds, Lucy Laflamme, and John Gray, or else one of his staff people. I'm real busy while I'm here but, hey, y'aren't gonna catch me complainin'. No sir. I've gotta a thing about this ol' place."

"So, tell me something you'd know about that others would only learn much later, in the event of a crime at The Balsams. You understand, Reg, we're speaking hypothetically here."

"Hypothetical, eh?" Someone else might have misinterpreted Reg's speech patterns for ignorance; but I wasn't being fooled. In fact, I was becoming increasingly confident that he knew exactly what I was up to. However, because I was a guest of the resort, he wasn't going to let me know what he was really thinking . . . at least not yet. "I talk with about ten percent of our guests on average, I guess; that's more than anyone else except for maybe John Gray. But I seldom see two people in the same place or doin' the same things," he laughed. "Tom Barson and I are the resident trouble shooters, so if there's a problem, it's frequently mine to handle."

"And it's not just us. Tom, Rolf, Lucy and I are all expected to be all over the place. It's important for morale and staff discipline that we be seen a lot."

"Discipline?" I repeated with furrowed brows.

"Yeah, we try to set an example for the new folks . . . show them that we're always hustlin' and ready to take on anythin' that comes along. For the old timers, we've just become a part of their day. They see us; they may ask for an idea or they may want support for what they're doin'; if one of us says it's okay, it makes 'em feel good. And, I'll tell ya' this, because I'm all over the property, there isn't much that gets by me. I have a master key for all of the guest rooms and another for all of the traditional locks in the place. You just never know where ol' Reg is going to turn up," he laughed.

"Traditional locks?"

"Yeah, you know, all of the locks to the storage spaces, to the children's recreation space, to the movie theater, an' so forth use old fashioned metal keys, like these here." With that, he lifted his prodigious key ring from a leather strap that attached it to his belt.

"Holy cow! Do other people have these same keys?" I asked.

"Yeah, but I use 'em the most," he laughed again.

"Who else has these keys?"

"Well, let's see . . . there's Rolf, Lucy, and the head electrician and plumbing chief and, of course, both of the Barsons," Reg replied.

"Are these the only ones who have keys like these?"

"Yep . . . well . . . used to be a fella, Richard, who was Rolf's assistant. He left . . . fired actually. Some say he left so fast he never turned in his badge or keys. After that, Mr. Barson put a strict limit on the number of masters."

"This Richard, why was he fired, Reg?"

"He had a thing for the ladies."

"So? That describes ninety-five percent of the men under this roof right now," I said with a smile.

"Guests," he replied without one.

"Oh." This had been an interesting diversion, but, I wanted to hear more about the keys. "Do any of you ever share your keys with others on the staff?"

"Nope," he replied.

"You seem pretty sure."

"There is a very strong rule against doing that. And all of us who have those keys, well, we take this responsibility very serious."

"One last question, Reg, if you were going to hide a body at The Balsams, with the idea that no one would find it for a while, where would you hide it?"

He pondered this for a second, then laughing, responded, "I'd put it up on the middle of one of the greens on the golf course, maybe the fifth hole. No one ever seems to hit that one in reg'lation." Once again, Reg laughed heartily. But then, pondering some more, he offered, "There's a lot of square miles out there, 'course it wouldn't be easy to take a body out of this place without someone seein' ya . . . even at night."

"Why not?"

"Well, there's the two nightwatchmen and a bunch a staff comin' and goin' from the dorms. Besides, lots of our guests are light sleepers; even up here in this wonderful clean air. So someone's bound to be lookin' out of one them hundreds of windows, don't ya think?" Again, he laughed. It was the laugh of a man who had gained satisfaction from providing an important piece of information. But, Reg wasn't done. "If a person knew the place well enough, he'd know where to hide a body long enough so that he could get far away from this place before it could be found."

"Got any hints, Reg?" I asked.

"Why don't you test that one out on Rolf; you're meetin' with him after lunch, right?"

I had to smile at this man's handle on things. He knew my appointment schedule better than I did. As we shook hands and parted company, it occurred to me that this is the man Warn should have asked to be his investigator. And, for a mere instant, I wondered, "Why didn't he? This man is so loyal . . ." But, now I was off to the resort's business office to continue my education.

Chapter 20

I arrived at the business office at two minutes after 11:00, and found my interviewees-Dave Watson, the resort's business manager and Sue Nesson, director of personnel services-engrossed in a quiet conversation. As I entered, the serious expressions on their faces were replaced by friendly smiles. It wasn't even noon on the 15th and I already was paranoid that everyone in the resort was aware of my real purpose. And what was worse, the time before a missing person report would be filed-and the subsequent arrival of real investigators-was growing short. Edna Connor's absence had been reported to Warn after dinner on the 14th. She had last been seen at about 9:00 on the evening of the 13th. There was still so much information to gather and absorb. The task was daunting.

"Professor Turnell?" The voice of Sue Nesson brought me back to the task at hand. "Is everything all right? You seem upset."

"No, no, everything's fine. I'm just mentally organizing all the information that's been crammed into my head this morning," I lied.

"From what I understand, this morning's meetings are just the beginning," she smiled.

"Well, you know what they say about writing crime fiction . . . every hundred pages you write requires at least as many hours of research."

"Gee, I had no idea," her boss, Dave Watson chimed in. There's a good reason, I thought to myself, I've just pulled that statistic out of my butt.

"What can we do for you, Professor?"

"I'm trying to understand something about personnel matters . . . you know, what the rules are for hiring and firing an employee."

Dave seemed almost relieved. "Well, you really need to talk with Sue," he said, "I'm the cash and insurance guy. While I go over all applications with Sue, this is really her forte'." And with that said, he shook my hand and walked out the door.

After Dave had left, Sue told me, "Dave's an institution here. He's worked at The Balsams for three decades. And he's in the office seven days a week, for as few as 60 or as many as 80 hours."

"Wow, that must be tough on a marriage!".

"Not on the Watsons' marriage it isn't. Dave and his wife both work here; their kids are all grown; so, The Balsams fits into both of their daily lives." Then she gave me a scrutinizing look and said, "But this isn't why you're here is it, Professor?"

"No, not really, but it's always good to hear how different people make a marriage work," I replied. Clearly I wasn't going to hold my own up for similar scrutiny. "Please help me to understand how The Balsams hires people; and then, if you'll indulge me, I'd like to know about any failings of this system. I'd especially appreciate it if you'll give me a few examples of employees who went bad, omitting the names, of course."

"Sure," Sue replied. With that, she explained how the resort sends out ads about job openings, primarily to local newspapers and area employment firms. "The resort accepts applications throughout the year, which I place in a file. Then, if a particular department head contacts the personnel office to say there is a certain opening to be filled, I invite the department head to view the existing files. If the department head decides to interview any of the people in the file, it is my job to contact them. Of course, people have been known to drop in or call for an application form. If a candidate gets through the initial screening process, he or she is invited to interview with the department head and me."

"That sounds simple enough," I said. "Is the system effective in screening out turkeys?"

"By turkeys, I take it you mean people with unsavory pasts, criminals and the like, but not just someone who smells bad or lacks the necessary skills to do the job we're filling?"

I nodded. "Can someone with a criminal record be hired by The Balsams? I'm not thinking about misdemeanor stuff; I'm talking about guys who have committed felonies."

Sue Nesson sighed. "During an interview, we are limited as to the questions we can ask someone."

"Limited how?" I asked.

"Like all businesses, we can only ask an applicant his or her name and address, the date of availability, a record of past employment, whether they speak a foreign language, and whether they have ever been convicted of a felony. We also ask for names and contact information for references, as well as their physical ability to do the job they're seeking. However, we can't ask for information on marital status"

"But you can filter out any bad seeds?" I said. It sounded as though I was trying to convince Sue.

After taking a few seconds to absorb my emphatic response, Sue replied, "Yes, we call their references. But most past employers will only give out information on employment dates and positions held. They aren't going to tell you if Joe is a wife beater or Mary has been suspected of taking drugs. The employers of today tend to be somewhat close-mouthed. I suppose they're afraid of slander suits."

"So, how can you possibly fill all of your employment needs way out here—no offense—in the woods?" I asked.

She smiled ruefully. To The Balsams staff, the resort was the center of the universe. "It isn't always easy, which allows an occasional problem child to be hired . . . but generally not for long."

"Tell me more."

"At one time, most of our employees were transient seasonal people from Florida."

I remembered reading about that in Karl Abbott's treatise on the hotel business in Open for the Season.

"But, for a long time we primarily have hired people from the local area, from Pittsburg to Berlin."

"That must be an advantage," I said.

"Yes, in a lot of ways. The job of advertising for employees up here is much less complicated. And up here someone knows everyone we interview; so we learn a lot about our applicants from our staff and the people we know in those communities. In fact, over half of the local staff is related to one another. Also local adults are very happy to find work here. We have an excellent track record; we treat our employees well; and they can make a decent living here."

"Then tell me, why do I see so many foreigners working in your dining room, bar and housekeeping department?"

"Because, while we are attractive to the local adult population, we have been finding it difficult to find enough north country residents who want to work our whole season from May to October and December through March, particularly at the pace that the dining room demands, and the wages we are able to pay. But, the European kids are a perfect match. Their fall university terms don't begin until November; so, they're more than happy to remain until our season concludes after Columbus Day. And the South Americans work here during the winter season, which falls during their summer vacations from school."

"So that's why I've heard so many Irish lilts since we arrived."

"Yes, and if you listen carefully, you'll hear French, Spanish, German, Italian, and a number of eastern European accents as well," she offered.

"I spoke to a young man from Poland today," I informed her. "There was also a young woman from Russia."

"That's not surprising. We also have people from South Africa, South America, Australia and New Zealand working at the resort every winter."

"That's amazing, but sad in a way," I pondered. Here was a resort offering a number of terrific summer jobs, and they have had to lure college age people from half way around the world to fill them.

Thanking Sue for her time, I rose to leave. As I reached to open the door, she told me that at one time the resort had hired a north country man who, prior to his successful interview had lived as a hermit in the woods north of Errol. Having performed so admirably at the resort for six months, the management had placed a photo of him in the Democrat. It wasn't long before law enforcement officials arrived and quietly lead the man away. It turned out that he'd robbed a bank and had escaped from custody while being transferred to the state penitentiary in Concord.

As I left Sue Nesson's office, I couldn't help but wonder whether history was repeating itself in Dixville Notch at that very moment.

Chapter 21

4:30 P.M., Monday, July 10th. Billy Fenton's meeting with Edna Connor had resulted from her clumsiness. Edna had just arrived in her room on the fourth floor of the Hampshire House. She had stood by while Buddy, the septuagenarian bellman, removed her five matching faux leopard skin bags from his bell cart. Then, after he had hung her endless array of cotton print dresses in the closet nearest to the entryway to her room, had explained where things were to be found in the room, and had showed her which card to bring to the dining room that evening, Buddy slowly turned to leave. At that moment, Edna had stepped forward, and reaching into her purse, handed the elderly bellman a dollar for his labors. As Buddy closed the door behind him, Edna wondered if she'd given him too much money.

She then proceeded to unpack. Having placed her blouses in the drawers of the dresser to the right of her bed, she removed the new, lacy underwear to which she had treated herself at Target. Then, she removed her toiletry kit from the smallest of her cases, and placed all but one of the bags in the closet nearest to the windows. She entered the bathroom with her kit. It was at this point that Edna first spotted the glass étagère with the small bottles of shampoo and lotion. Until that moment, Edna hadn't realized how warm she had become from the excitement of her arrival at the Balsams. Suddenly, she felt the need to cool her self off. She removed the jacket that nearly matched her low cut sleeveless blouse and short, tight-fitting skirt, and placed it on the chair situated just outside the bathroom door. In her haste to get comfortable, she attempted to remove the washcloth lining from the basket containing the shampoos and other bottles of fragrances. Given Edna's chronic clumsiness, this proved to be a bad idea. Within seconds, the basket lay on the floor surrounded by a miniature sea of broken glass. This, of course, upset Edna greatly. She was determined not to make a scene; so, eschewing the telephone, she went out into the hall hoping to spot a housekeeper or maintenance person. As luck would have it, at that very moment, Billy Fenton walked past wearing his hotel maintenance uniform and tool belt.

Edna was pleased to the point of near delirium. Touching Billy's arm, she exclaimed, "Am I glad to see you." The sight of this freshly coiffed, well endowed woman set Billy's male libido into high gear. While Edna appeared to Billy to be nearly twice his age, the young man was instantly turned on by the display of cleavage and her tight fitting, short skirt. So, he willingly followed her into the room, taking note of the apparent intentional display of lacy undergarments on her bed. It didn't take long for Billy to clean up the glass and to request that a replacement for the broken shelf be brought upstairs. However, he appeared to be in no hurry to leave. Despite Billy's unkempt appearance and his nicotine stained teeth, Edna was strangely flattered by the attention this young man was paying to her. After years of being ignored by Al, it was exciting to receive this kind of attention from one so young.

Not knowing quite what to do, she reached out to shake his hand. As their fingers touched, Billy flushed. Then he replied with a smile, "Glad to be of service, m'am."

As he left Edna's room, Billy was convinced that he was "Goin' ta get laid before this broad left an' took those big tits home with her." He didn't know when or where he was going to do it to her. But, rules or no rules, "I'm gonna get me some of that," he muttered as he walked down the stairs in the Hampshire House, running his fingers through his long, greasy, black hair.

Chapter 22

11:30 A.M., Saturday, July 15th. There was to be no rest for the weary on this day. Five minutes after parting company with Sue Nesson, I was sitting in the resort's Sun Room, which is situated at the west end of the Dixville House. I had no sooner placed my tired behind on one of the pastel colored chairs, when Jay Olds, the resort's reservation and front office manager, joined me.

"Good morning, Professor," he greeted me. Clearly Jay was having a much better day than I was. "So you're writing a murder mystery?"

While Jay's query amounted to nothing more than small talk, I could feel my anxiety level rising. "Does he know what I'm really doing, too?" I asked myself. A quick self-appraisal told me I was getting a little out of control. I had a sudden chill when it occurred to me, "Jesus, these people are really counting on me to write a book!"

I replied, "Yes, I thought it would be a great idea to write a murder mystery set in a remote, historic mountain resort."

"Well that's us all right."

Never one to make small talk easily, all of this was beginning to be painful. However, my attitude softened as I looked across the table into Jay Olds' eyes. It was obvious that he wasn't terribly comfortable doing this either. So, to do us both a favor, I got down to brass tacks. "Tell me a bit about your part of this operation."

"Oh, my. I hardly know where to begin. Yes, let's see . . . the reservations department takes all calls for inquiries and reservations. There are three shifts for the desk clerks. They do check-ins, check-outs, process guests' bills, and answer guests' questions."

"That's a lot of work for a few people," I replied, still searching for a comfort zone with this guy.

"Eighteen."

"Really?"

"Yes, eighteen. We have eighteen people in our department. We are the ones who are responsible for introducing all callers to The Balsams. While people are on the telephone, we tell them about the full American hospitality plan, our accommodations, the facilities; then we offer to send them a brochure or to make a reservation."

"From what I have heard, your people are sort of a reconnaissance team as well." I smiled so he would understand my meaning.

"If you mean that we are the ones who gather information about a potential guest's name, address, special needs and that sort of thing then, yes, we are The Balsams reconnaissance team." I nodded and he smiled, obviously pleased at his own importance.

And now switching gears, I asked, "I'm looking for any information about what your department does which could potentially aid me in solving a crime at The Balsams."

It appeared that Jay had been prepared for just such a question, for his response seemed too well rehearsed. "We would be important to such an investigation in two ways. First, no guest can gain entry to the hotel or the dining room without being checked-in by us. Second, of course, guests must check out before they leave."

I smiled. Then, looking directly into Jay's eyes, I asked, "But suppose someone wanted to leave without checking out?"

His reaction was one of surprise and, I felt, a bit disdain filled. "But no one has ever done that. Besides, we have their home address and credit card number. So what would be gained." Then, finding a reason he hadn't thought about before, "I suppose they would avoid tipping the bellman."

To which I added, "And the housekeepers, the doorman and the waitstaff."

Jay was suddenly amused by all of this. "I must tell you, in all my years . . ."

But, I interrupted, "Hasn't anyone ever left early on a whim, or perhaps there was an emergency?"

Jay pondered this and said, "I'm not certain about the whim, but presumably they would receive the emergency call through the central switchboard. Until now, cell phones haven't worked well up here. Calling out on a cell phone can be problematic, for now."

"So, if a guest had decided on a whim to leave, he or she would only have the option of notifying someone outside the area through the central switchboard."

"That's not entirely true," Jay replied. "There are pay phones in the lobby."

"Then a record of any calls would be available through your department."

"Only those using the phone lines in the guest rooms; pay phone records are available through the local phone exchange in Colebrook."

"Hypothetically speaking, if I wanted to have access to the phone records of one of your guests, would I need to go through you."

"Well, first, such records are a matter of extreme privacy, protected by law. So, only the police would have access to such records. But, assuming that access had been approved, each of the Barsons knows the access code to our telephone records. Although, to my knowledge, they have only used it on one occasion, and that was to catch an employee who was harassing a guest."

"That must be an interesting story," I said with a grin that was too large for the moment. Jay wasn't biting. Rising from his chair, he took my hand in his and smiled, "My lips are sealed."

As Jay walked away, I peered at my watch. Then it suddenly dawned on me that I hadn't spoken a single word to Nya since we parted company at breakfast that morning. With all of this Edna Connor business, plus my guilt about leaving Nya alone, I suddenly was anxious to see my wife. Nothing about this vacation was feeling right. While we were packing for the trip, then again while we were driving up here, she had been vigilant, lest I fall back into the neurosis triggered by my failure as an author. But now, since her discussion with Warn, she had been super patient with me. I had been given carte blanche to chase around The Balsams, while leaving Nya to her own devices. Was this because she had been mellowed by The Balsams' ambiance; or was it her involvement with Lynn Ride, and the resort's advertising campaign? Or, was there a third scenario . . . could Nya have finally tired of my sexual lethargy, and sought the affections of someone else at the resort? Hell, in my state, even Warn was under suspicion. I shook my head, at once annoyed with my suspicions and fascinated by this sudden attack of jealousy. Had I discussed all of this with Nya at that moment, she would have been incredulous. After all, what business did I have to feel jealous? Her love has always been there . . . a battery waiting endlessly for a boost, hoping for a hint of vitality. But none had been forthcoming.

★   ★   ★

What was causing me to feel this way? The case? After all, Edna Connor was not much younger than Nya. Like Nya, Edna was married to a man whose priorities had been short-circuited by the rigors of nine-to-five. Each of their men had stopped acting like one in the bedroom, leaving each woman silently, starving for attention . . . if not sex, at least an occasional warm embrace. In lieu of an expression of love, each woman had received a turned back. For both women, The Balsams would be their arena, the place where disillusionments must end. This was their last resort.

Chapter 23

12:00 P.M. I started walking toward our room. I hoped to find Nya curled up on her bed reading a book. As I neared the room, I became conscious that I hadn't used the men's room all morning. During the last five years, I had become a fitful sleeper. Every night, I made intermittent visits to the bathroom. I couldn't remember when my prostate had betrayed me . . . I'd even given up my precious coffee and cut back a little on alcoholic drink . . . nothing seemed to help. It probably had something to do with my nerves.

Arriving at number 264, I inserted my electronic key card into the lock and opened the door. The interior door was ajar, so I could see that Nya wasn't in the bedroom. I checked in the bathroom. She wasn't in there either; so, I stood and did my business.

Another ten minutes passed before I heard the electronic mechanism being activated by Nya's card. She appeared in a pair of yellow shorts and matching top. Yellow has always been Nya's favorite color. She had on no makeup, which is not unusual, but her hair was uncharacteristically messy. The look on my face must have tipped her off because she looked into the mirror of one of the closet doors and quickly fixed it.

"What have you been doing all morning?" I asked, surprising Nya and myself with the concern in my tone.

Nya pretended not to detect anything uncharacteristic about my behavior. "While you were working on Warn's mystery project, I was meeting with him and Lynn to see if I could add some spice to their promotions," she replied. Suddenly I had the image of my wife lying naked on a white bedspread with the two men lying happily next to her. I shook my head to make the illusion disappear. Nya, who had witnessed my odd way of dispelling negative images for years, took notice, but said nothing.

"Are you ready for lunch?" I asked.

"Oh, I'm sorry, Kary, I figured you'd be occupied all day today. Warn said you would be; so, I'm meeting Lynn and Warn." Then, pausing, she added, "Privately." I was nonplused by her emphasis on the word privately; and Nya seemed to be enjoying that.

Nya removed her yellow shorts and top, and prepared to replace them with a white skirt and mauve blouse. As she stood there, I noticed for the first time in quite a while that Nya's thighs were still like those of a young woman; her skin was soft and smooth. The absence of apparent redness immediately reassured my jealous mind. Nya surreptitiously observed me watching her, fighting back the anticipation of what she interpreted as a flicker of interest on my part. I hadn't remembered seeing the blouse before, and mentioned it to Nya.

"That's because it's brand new. See, it's a Balsams shirt. Warn gave it to me." Then, following a dispassionate kiss on the cheek, Nya was off for places, not to mention activities, unknown. It occurred to me, too late, that we hadn't discussed when we were meeting for dinner.

And so, I walked through the buffet line and ate lunch alone at our table in the dining room, reminding myself to ask Warn when Nancy Barson would be returning to Dixville.

Chapter 24

12:50 PM. I heaved a sigh. It was time to head to another interview. On the other hand, my stomach was saying, "Have another chocolate éclair." I sighed again, then got up and walked out of the dining room. I hadn't spotted Nya, but of course she could have been in the Hale Room, the more intimate rear section of the dining room, or the Ballot Room, or the Panorama golf course. "Damn, this just isn't like Nya," I muttered to myself. And, I was right. Nya and I had gotten in the habit of knowing where one another was during the years we were raising toddlers. In the days before cell phones, our itineraries and the numbers of nearby telephones were shared more frequently than affectionate phrases . . . particularly in my case. But now she was acting mysteriously. Or, at least that was my take on things. At any rate, Nya was right, for the next two days I was doing Warn's bidding. But, I couldn't escape the feeling that something was different between Nya and me.

★   ★   ★

1:00 P.M. I didn't have to go searching for Rolf Vernon; he found me. I had seen Rolf all over the resort. As head of maintenance, he was equally likely to be called into the ballroom or the movie theater as the women's room or a guest room. While the typical guest had no idea what Rolf's name was, most had seen him somewhere on the property.

Rolf was about average height, with a shock of blond hair. His build could best be described as muscular, going to hefty. Two things set Rolf apart from most other members of the maintenance staff: the multiple band radio he carried and the enormous set of keys dangling from his belt at the hip. We shook hands, mine consumed by a surprisingly large, meaty one. Once again, I began by reminding him about my work of fiction, the book I had no intention of writing.

"I love murder mysteries," he began. His voice was gruff, almost hoarse from too many cigarettes, if the nicotine on his fingers was any indication. "So, what can I do to help, Professor?" I may have been mistaken, but there seemed to be something condescending about his tone. Whatever; I decided to ignore it because this guy was important to me, at least for the moment.

I really had no desire to discuss all of the repairs and renovations, the plumbing and electrical work, the roofing and landscaping that this man and his 79-man team accomplished for the resort. And, I already knew that he had master keys, both of the traditional and card variety. So I said, "I'd like you to take me to see the nooks and crannies."

"Nooks and crannies?" Once again, there was that note of sarcasm in his voice.

"Yeah, you know, places where a bad guy might hide a body."

Rolf looked at me for a good thirty seconds, then smiled and asked, "Are you ready to take a hike?" And before I could respond, he'd added, "I hope you don't mind getting a little dirty, Professor." Next, he put his radio near his mouth and pushed the talk button. A woman's voice was on the other end.

"Darla, listen, tell Reg I'm taking the professor on a little tour, and ask him to cover for me. He'll understand." I could sense the smile in Darla's voice on the other end of the radio. Apparently I had been the subject of more than one conversation over coffee that morning.

And tour we did. We began in the Dixville House. We climbed stairwell after stairwell until we arrived at a final, narrow set of stairs leading to a door that was held shut by a swinging hasp with a Yale lock through it. Removing the keys from his belt, Rolf easily located the correct one. He placed the key in the lock, turned it, then removed the lock and put it in his pocket. We stepped through the doorway and, to my surprise, found ourselves on the roof. The view was amazing. I peered across the sea of red shingles, first taking in the grounds. Below me lay the ferris wheel shape of the resort's formal floral garden. To my right were the tennis courts and the swimming pool, the contrast of red clay and azure water never more apparent to me than at that moment. In the distance was the pool house and, just beyond, was Lake Gloriette, the lake that had been constructed to satisfy the boating and fishing passions of the resort's guests. In the distance, I could see the piece de resistance, the high narrow granite walls of the notch. It took a few moments, but I soon reminded myself why I had taken this tour, rather than ministering to my fledgling preoccupation with Nya's whereabouts. Thus grounded, or as grounded as one can be while standing fifty feet above terra firma, I scanned the roofline and the adjacent structures for a likely place to hide Edna Connor's body . . . if indeed there was a body to be found.

After about five minutes, Rolf turned to me and asked, "Ready to move on, Professor?"

I was really beginning to feel fatigued as well as frustrated by my lack of any real progress. And my feet were screaming for a rest. But, I forced a smile and replied with as much contrived enthusiasm as I could muster, "Sure."

We went back down the narrow set of stairs after Rolf had replaced the lock. But, instead of walking down to the next level of the Dixville House, Rolf wanted me to have a closer look at the hallway that we were standing in. At first, I didn't understand why we were stopping. But, I soon did. While one side of the hallway was lined with small bedrooms, which I presumed were for housing the staff, the right side of the hallway contained a number of storage closets, large storage closets. In one, there were dozens of chairs; the next contained dressers the same color as the ones in our guest room. The third contained rollaway beds and other reserves necessary for the successful operation of a grand resort hotel. As Rolf closed the last of these, he looked at me and smiled, "There are rooms like this one all over the place, Professor. And, unlike the roof, which requires a master key, there are at least ten keys in circulation that can open these places." Then, as we walked down the hallway, toward a staircase to take us to the lowest levels of the Dixville House,

Rolf supplemented my growing frustration by simply adding, "And wait until you see where I'm taking you next." The s.o.b. was enjoying himself immensely.

Chapter 25

Early July 2003, Cranston, Rhode Island. Richard Tomquist was happier than a pig in the brown, smelly stuff. Having left The Balsams employ under unfavorable circumstances more than a decade before, his dismissal had burned inside him. Here was a man with something to prove. Just as the kid who had been voted least likely to succeed in his high school yearbook can be guaranteed to attend his tenth reunion after he's made his first million, or published his first book, Richard wanted to show Rolf, and especially Mr. Barson, a thing or two. Warn had referred to him as "in need of professional help" after he had been caught fornicating with the rich lady in the catacombs years before. "Well, look at me now, Mr. Barson," he smiled at his reflection in the mirror while dialing the number of The Balsams reservations office. But then, Richard noticed that he was perspiring. "I hope the reservations people don't recognize my name," he muttered to himself. "I'm not ready to let them know that old Richard's back . . . not yet."

When he gave his name, "R. Johan Tomquist," to the woman in reservations, he was relieved that she hadn't recognized him as Richard. Of course, Richard needn't have concerned himself. Young Pamela Bracket was a high school freshman in Homer, Alaska the day Richard had signed his resignation letter. When Pamela had asked him whether there was a specific room that he preferred, he had been aroused by his own response, "Yes, the Tower Suite." She advised him to hold the line, then disappeared and was replaced by some classical music that Richard was not remotely familiar with.

As he waited for Pamela to return, Richard was standing in the raw before his full length mirror. Thoughts of repeated conquests in the suite's hot tub flashed through his brain. Standing there, he was very impressed with the size of the male part that reflected back at him in the mirror. Never particularly satisfied with his facial features or his physique, Richard was very proud of his silo, as he called it. In fact, he was absolutely obsessed with this element of his anatomy. A few years before, he had conjured up an idea after seeing Close Encounters of the Third Kind on the big screen. He had reasoned that Devil's Tower only looked as big as it did because there were no huge trees or hills to block one's view of the monolith; so, he had begun to shave himself from his chin to his ankles.

Pamela's voice replaced the music on the other end of the line, "Mr. Tomquist, are you still there?"

"Yes," he replied, his voice cracked slightly, a betrayal of his excitement.

"I'm sorry to tell you that the Tower Suite is unavailable for the week you have requested. In fact, all of our suites are booked until the middle of August. Can I help you with a different accommodation?"

Richard was crestfallen. But, his work schedule only allowed him to carry out his plan during the third week of July; and, he was not going to be swayed from his intended visit. "Do you have a room in the Hampshire House that overlooks the tennis courts?"

"Yes, there is exactly one room left in that part of the hotel," she responded.

"Then, I'll take it," he said, trying to sound more enthusiastic than he really was at that moment.

A few minutes later, after obtaining his address and credit card information, Pamela informed Richard that his room was reserved.

And so, this is how Richard Tomquist came to be registered in room 168, the corner room right next door to Edna Connor's.

Chapter 26

1:35 P.M., Saturday, July 15th. The next part of my tour with Rolf began in somewhat surprising fashion. We came down the main stairway leading to the second level of the Dixville House. Then, passing the entrance to the dining room, we took a left and walked down the carpeted stairs leading to the main lobby. At the bottom of the stairs, I started to walk straight, toward the direction of Warn's office and the Hampshire House. But Rolf grabbed for my arm and steered me to the left while saying, "No, this way." I had no idea where we were headed. All I had ever noticed before in this corner of the lobby were the restrooms where macabre Far Side cartoons situated over the urinals in the men's room made urination an even lengthier process. Then, of course, there also was the large brass plated scale. This device was used by the more masochistic resort guests, who derived some perverse pleasure in weighing themselves both before and after dinner just to prove that Chef Leonard had succeeding in putting fresh poundage on them. What I had never noticed previously was the small beige door situated immediately to the right of that treacherous weighing machine.

Rolf pulled open the door and held it until I had entered. We took an immediate right hand turn and found ourselves in a totally different world. Here, white walls and chandeliers were replaced by low ceilings, narrow passageways and miles of pipe and conduits. We walked a short distance down a wooden ramp before Rolf paused, turned to his left, then pointed. There was the first in a series of underground catacombs-tunnels, in truth. One of these extended fifty or more feet, its terminus shadowed in black. Other tunnels housed elements of the heating and plumbing systems, a furnace here, a huge water heater there. It immediately occurred to me that a body could be placed in any one of these nooks and remain there, awaiting either a chance discovery by a maintenance worker or until the pungent odor of decaying flesh necessitated that a party be formed to find the source of the offense. Rolf was observing me at that moment and was taking great pleasure at the consternation showing on my face.

From here, Rolf pointed out other alcoves, one that housed the recreation director's office and a second that led to the resort's laundry facility. He pointed to a stairway near the end of the hallway we were occupying and offered, "That's where the other half lives." When he saw the confused look on my face, he elaborated. "This is where the staff eats and hangs out. There's a cafeteria and a lounge with a television and a pool table that are for the staff to use. Of course, the pool table doesn't have leather pockets like the ones in the Dixville House do; but then, we aren't paying several hundred bucks a night to use it, neither."

Next it was time to head down Broadway, which is the name some staff ascribe to the long hallway that connects the Dixville House catacombs with the lower level of Hampshire House. The view along this concrete corridor looked similar to the road leading from a military base or a mining facility shortly after the cessation of all activities. Along the walls were tables, chairs, drawers, desks and file cabinets, all awaiting reactivation, permanent storage or disposal. As we continued walking, the ceiling suddenly rose to nearly twenty feet. I surmised that we were standing beneath the entry way and the Barsons' offices; however, I saw no need to query Rolf.

What Rolf showed me next was interesting indeed. While I hadn't been a guest at the resort in a number of years, I had been something of a regular at one time. In all of the years I had stayed in the Hampshire House, I did not recall seeing, much less hearing, a freight elevator. When I revealed this to Rolf, he said, "It's been here for longer than I can remember, Professor. The thing is, it gets almost all of its usage while guests are eating or out playing golf and such."

I replied, "But they must use it at night sometime."

He shook his head. "No, the guys upstairs are very firm about that. Here, look at the sign on the elevator door, '. . . do not use this elevator between the hours of 10pm and 8am.'"

"I suppose there must be a reason for that."

"There is; let's take a ride, Professor." Somehow, the way Rolf kept using the word "professor" spoke volumes. Clearly, here was a man who ascribed to the adage that professors are a bunch of eggheads with absolutely no common sense. I would have loved to take him back a notch, but that would have to wait until the Connor business was over. So, I resolved to put up with his guff and absorb as much information as possible.

Rolf took me up one level then back down. It only took a few seconds to understand the purpose of the sign; a Harley Davidson motorcycle emitted a more subtle sound than that elevator.

Stepping out of the elevator, we were now in the outer foyer of the resort's movie theater that doubled as its chapel. The door to the theater was open and we entered. As we did, I took note of the fact that a traditional lock graced the doorway. As if anticipating my reaction, Rolf offered, "That lock's going to be replaced with a card key system over the winter." We walked through the theater; and, as we did, Rolf told me about a passage way without floor boards that extended along both sides of the theater. We walked along with a minimum of light, making our way through the entire length of the theater, then up the steps to the back-stage area. Following yet another passageway, we soon found ourselves standing at the rear door of the children's recreation center. Rolf, who was growing weary of this activity, simply pointed and said, "Traditional locks, both doors."

"Both doors?" I queried.

"Yeah, the main door leads out to an indoor stairwell that sets in the middle of all the hallways in Hampshire House." I made a mental note to check this out. Next, we retraced our steps to the rear of the theater. Only this time, we walked along the opposite wall. There, immediately to the left of the backstage area, was a wooden door without a lock. Rolf opened the door about a foot, just wide enough for me to see that there was a narrow, vertical crawl space without floorboards.

At Rolf's urging, we moved on.

Chapter 27

1:55 PM. It was nearing time to meet with Jeff Milk, head of laundry services for the resort. Realizing that it would take between five and ten minutes to get to the laundry by walking around the staff residences and the rubber plant, I opted to use the passageway that Rolf had shown me. Of course, nothing ever works quite as easily as one plans. I opened the door adjacent to the scale in the lobby and stepped into the tunnel. I took exactly five steps before I was stopped by a hostile laundry woman who was returning from her break in the employees' dining area. "Sorry sir, employees only!" she bellowed. However, I had gone too far to turn back. So, I looked her in the eyes and said the first thing that popped into my head, "Mr. Barson sent me." I figured that would hold her. Of course, I had no way of knowing what Warn's response would be, in the all-too-likely event that she informed her superiors. She reluctantly stepped aside to let me pass.

I made my way farther down the corridor and turned left toward the entry way to the laundry facility. I half expected to find a small laundromat at the end of the tunnel, but had completely miscalculated! Instead, I had walked into a small industrial complex that was hard at work. There seemed to be people moving everywhere, loading laundry into washing machines the size of Volkswagens, removing laundry, drying laundry, pressing it, folding or hanging it. My first impression was that there were hundreds of people at work; I later learned there were about fifteen.

"You! What are you going? Don't you know it's dangerous to be in here?" the fast-approaching older man barked. Tall, thin and red-faced, Geof Milk reminded me for a moment of the carnie barkers who had frightened, yet excited me during my youth. There was something about this man's presence that was at once intimidating and compelling. My first inclination had been to turn and run. After all, visiting the laundry was part of my ruse; I really wasn't expecting any help in locating Edna Connor here.

Once I'd identified myself to Mr. Milk, his demeanor softened, at least a bit. I soon learned the cause for his concern. A huge industrial laundry such as this one is a place where water "so hot that it could pull all the skin off a grown man in thirty seconds," blister-breeding chemicals, hot pressing machines, and a contraption called a high velocity rotary extractor together create an environment more evocative of a minefield than a walkway.

Jeff Milk had clear blue eyes that seemed to pierce through me. He asked, "What kind of help can an old laundry man be to a novel writer?"

"Start by telling me about yourself."

I soon learned that Mr. Milk had a most interesting past. For years he had been the right hand man of a major corporate head. Then, tired of working twelve-hour days and logging hundreds of thousands of air passenger miles, he had simply walked away. One year later, during a visit to The Balsams, he had taken the resort's historic tour led by Warn Barson himself. As the tour concluded, Jeff Milk had told Barson how impressed he had been with the resort's history and its efficiency as an operation. A half hour discussion ensued during which Milk imparted a brief explanation of his own background. Before the two parted company, Jeff had surprised himself by asking the general manager if he had any use for an old man who knew how to organize things like a walking Palm Pilot. Two weeks later, Jeff and Edna Milk and their cat Alphonse found themselves as the proud owner of a white, two-story wood frame house one block from the main drag in the nearby town of Errol. A few days later, Jeff had assumed the position of manager of the resort's long-floundering laundry complex. And, within sixty days, he had it functioning like clockwork. During a typical week, the staff and guests at The Balsams managed to soil four thousand bath towels, nearly the same number of hand towels, two thousand table cloths, three thousand bed sheets, five thousand pillows, six thousand napkins, countless rags, not to mention a variety of uniforms.

Given the scale of what Jeff was describing, I was reluctant to bother this busy man with the hypothetical issue of crime solving; but I pressed the issue anyway, if you'll pardon the pun.

"You'd be amazed with some of the things we find in a place like this, and some of the things we're asked to find," he told me.

"What kinds of things?"

"Well, we've found some interesting stains on sheets, pillow cases . . . even on the small bath carpets that come out of the guestrooms."

He had my full attention.

"If a stain looks particularly bad, the better housekeepers will pull it aside so we can give it special attention. In the old days, mercurochrome was the worst; I sure don't miss that stuff. Now, we see a lot of urine, and of course, blood. Also some of the dyes in the candies kids eat these days can really mess up a bed sheet."

Then it occurred to me to ask, "Suppose a person had been murdered in her room and their was evidence . . . uh . . . a stain of some type . . . perhaps blood. Would you be able to identify where it came from?"

Mr. Milk stared at me thoughtfully with those clear blue eyes. "I'm afraid the odds against that would be long ones," he said sadly. Then brightening, he added, "Of course, if we knew that there had been a murder, the police wouldn't allow the housekeepers to come in and remove the linens and towels from the room, now would they?"

His response had made my stomach churn. For a moment I had been hopeful that I'd stumbled on to something. But, as expected, my visit to the laundry had not been terribly fruitful; however, it had been interesting.

★   ★   ★

Our meeting had ended about ten minutes early; so before heading to my next appointment, I asked Mr. Milk to borrow his phone. Once again, I failed to connect with Nya, thus adding to my mounting apprehension. Hanging up, I accepted Mr. Milk's offer to escort me back out of the catacombs.

Chapter 28

I was ten minutes early for my 2:30 appointment with Lucy Laflamme. So, I decided to swing by Warn's office and give him an update on how things were, or weren't going. I also needed to ask him to use his influence to get me some information. Looking at my watch, I realized that we now had less than twenty-two hours to find what had happened to Edna Connor.

As I passed through the lobby area, I could see the large picture window that forms the west wall of Warn's office. A few strides closer and I could make out the familiar profile of Warn. The way he was moving his head, it appeared he was having an animated discussion with someone.

"Damn," I muttered half aloud, "my timing is as crappy as usual." However, as I neared the office he spotted me out of the corner of his eye. He waved at me to come inside. I entered and extended Warn a curt hello.

From beyond me came a familiar voice, "It sounds like someone's having a bad day." I had been hearing that voice for the last thirty years; and I turned to face my wife.

"Nya. Where have you been? I've been calling you from all over the hotel!"

"I've just been staying out of your way, Kary." Her tone sounded patronizing. But, before I could respond, she added, "Besides, you know that I've been occupying myself with Warn while you're busy." Then standing, she moved toward the door and cooed, "Well, I've gotta run . . . kiss kiss."

Kiss, kiss. Had my wife just said kiss, kiss? And, what was worse, she seemed to be looking at Warn when she said it!

I stood there dumbfounded. It was Warn who first broke the silence. "So, my friend, what can I do for you."

I was anxious to bring him up to speed, but had something else on my mind that needed to be said. "Say Warn, I don't mind working on your problem for the next few days; but, you shouldn't feel that you have to keep Nya company while I'm doing it."

"Keep Nya company!" he howled. "Quite the contrary, Nya's been terrific. I've known you two for more than thirty years and I had no idea the level of that lady's talents. Frankly, I'm the one who is thankful that she's here." Then, Warn did something that was very peculiar. He sat there and stared at me, as though he were gauging my reaction. I had the sense he was gaining some form of perverse pleasure from it.

★   ★   ★

"Now, tell me. What about Edna Connor?"

"I don't have much to tell you yet. But, I do need some information from you."

"Sure, what do you need?" Warn replied.

"I need a list of people who received calls from Edna Connor's room, or who may have called Edna from noon on the 11th through late evening on the 13th. And, I have to tell you up front Warn, if that doesn't show us anything, we'll need to access the telephone company's records for calls from the pay phone in the lobby."

Warn did not look particularly pleased by my first request. "Is the telephone stuff really necessary, Kary? Remember what I said about invasion of privacy."

"Look Warn, if we're going to find out anything about Mrs. Connor without turning this place completely upside down, we need to know who she's talked to and spent time with."

Warn had a look of apprehension on his face. But, after taking a minute to ponder the options, he agreed to do what he could about the telephone records. I wasn't finished.

"Oh yes, and there's one more thing, I had asked John for the names of guests who were seated adjacent to Edna. Has he given the list to you yet?"

Warn was looking a little pale to me. "Not yet; but I'm sure he'll work on it before the pre-dinner meal with his staff."

With that, I rose to leave. But there was something I needed to get off of my chest.

"Look Warn, I have a funny feeling you're not telling me everything. If you want me to stop digging, just say so. I can go play tennis with Nya. I've been busting my butt to avoid arousing suspicion. But, the information I've asked for is absolutely essential. I don't think I have to tell you, if the cops get involved, they're going to be a lot less delicate than I've been. Now, is there anything else you want to tell me before I leave?"

"No, if I think of anything, I'll let you know," Warn replied. As his office screen door closed behind me, I wasn't so sure.

Chapter 29

Two minutes later, Warn walked across the hallway and entered Tom Barson's office. He informed his son about the two items on my check list.

"What the hell!" his son bellowed. "Look, Dad, I know that Professor Turnell and you have been friends for years, but I think you should put an end to this business right now. If he keeps digging the way he is, there's going to be a backlash that's bigger than even you are aware."

Warn tried to keep his son calm. "We're okay for now, Tom. John tells me that most of the staff have bought Kary's story about the murder mystery. We may have to take Reg into our confidence fairly soon; because Kary's probably going to need to take advantage of his talents." Warn remained seated, but turned to face his son squarely. "I know you're just worried about me, Tom; but, I'm well aware of the risks. I can't leave this situation as it is. The long term consequences are simply unacceptable."

Tom was concerned about the tension he could read in his father's face. So, in an attempt to lighten the mood he said, "Well, it's your call Dad. But if this idea completely backfires, can I have your desk after Mr. Tillson gets wind of this?"

This unexpected comment made Warn chortle. As he stood up to leave, he gave his son a soft punch in the right shoulder. Once back in his office, he sat for several minutes pondering the forces that had been unleashed the evening before.

Chapter 30

My detour had made me a few minutes late for my 2:30 appointment with Lucy Laflamme. Based on the fact that she had been at the resort for more than two decades, after having completed four years at the state university, I estimated her to be in her early fifties. However, had I met her on the street, I would have deducted at least ten years. The woman sitting before me was a gorgeous redhead, doubtlessly the subject of many men's dreams. Her body was slender with, as they say, her curves in all the right places. All of this aside, I soon learned that this woman was a cracker jack administrator. And, like so many of the other people I had met that day, Lucy Laflamme was responsible for a small empire.

"What exactly is the housekeeping department's responsibility?" I asked her for openers.

"It's simple, Professor," she replied with a big smile, "our job is to keep The Balsams clean. I oversee as many as forty employees each day . . . maids, housemen, and public area people. For my part, I do schedules, keep our budget . . . I generate reams of paper work. You might say I'm a one woman tree killer," she laughed.

"As you know, I'm writing this murder mystery. So, I'm here to find out how I could use the resources of housekeeping to catch my man . . . or woman."

"Well, of course, we keep careful records about people's shifts and their work schedules. And, like the waitstaff stations in the dining room, our people are assigned to specific guest rooms. They don't just walk by a room and say, 'This looks like a good one to clean'. And, before you ask, housekeeping doesn't work like musical chairs either."

I had to smile at the visual of a bellman closing the door to a party's room at check out, just as two maids, each pushing her cart, raced down the corridor to see who could strip the beds first.

Lucy continued, "One of our responsibilities may be of interest to you."

"What's that?"

"The housekeeping department maintains a lost-and-found for the resort. If someone loses an item . . . whether it's valuable or not . . . our housekeepers are required to bring it here for storage and, we always hope, identification."

"I'll keep that in mind," I said. Frankly, I didn't expect that piece of information to be terribly useful; but I was enjoying talking to this stunning woman. "There is something that you can tell me more about, if you don't mind."

"I'll be happy to help if I can."

"Thanks. I've been hearing about the wonders of this new electronic key system. But, I must confess to being something of a skeptic. I thought your old skeleton keys were charming. And I even liked the smaller keys with the room tags on them." Then, reaching into my pocket, I added, "Look, I have a brass reproduction of one of your old oval room tags."

"Oh, I remember when they sold those in our gift shop," she chuckled. "Let me tell you about the new key system. While it isn't as romantic as the old metal key, the card allows us to keep excellent track of things. As a crime fiction writer, you can appreciate that not everyone . . . guest or employee . . . is honest. And we've noted over the years that people can be unbelievably careless when it comes to leaving their valuables around."

"I can relate. I've been known to leave my billfold on my dresser, then go out and play tennis or go swimming. Sometimes I figure, 'Hey, I'm on vacation at a resort; who needs to carry money?'"

"And you're not alone, Professor." Somehow when the word professor spilled from Lucy's lips, it didn't have the same meaning as when Rolf had said it. "By using the key card, we have a record of the date and time, as well as the specific persons who entered a particular area during the course of a day, week or month."

I was impressed. "Allow me to try this out on you. Suppose I was trying to find out who was the last staff person to enter a guest room before a particular item went missing, will the new key system allow me to do that?"

Lucy smiled. "Of course. And the best thing is that it protects both the guests' valuables and the housekeepers' reputations."

"Give me an example."

"Sure. A few weeks ago, we had a very nasty guest here, a woman from Atlanta. First, she called to tell us that housekeeping had stolen her son's small Braves baseball patch. When the patch was described to us, we realized that it must have been about two square inches in size. To make matters worse, the item had been washed numerous times and had faded from a bright azure to a baby blue."

I interjected, "Or the color of the blankets in your guest rooms."

Lucy gave me one of her best smiles, in apparent appreciation for my power of deduction. This caused me to think, "Well heck, I am a mystery writer."

She continued. "So this angry lady, screamed at the housekeeper for losing this tiny little cotton Braves patch. Of course, the housekeeper came to me in tears. So, I went to see the lady. Now, I'll tell you, Professor, I'm paid to listen to guests' complaints, but she was among the worst I've ever heard. The next thing you know, I'm on the phone to Jeff Milk . . . by the way, have you met with him yet?" I nodded. "Well, I tell Jeff what's happened, and he yells to his people to stop everything."

"Stop everything?" Having seen the scale of the resort's laundry first-hand, I couldn't believe what I was hearing.

"Stop everything," she repeated. "So Jeff and his staff went through every blanket, every sheet, every pillow case. But they didn't find anything. I mean, there wasn't a trace."

"So what happened next?"

"Of course, Mr. Barson had to meet with the woman and she singed his ears, too. When Mr. Barson offered to give her son a gift certificate at the

Balloon Store, she snatched it out of his hands, then told him she wasn't coming back to The Balsams ever again."

"That's a great story," I said. "But what does that have to do with the card keys?"

"Oh, yeah, I did get carried away there, didn't I?"

"No complaints on this end." With that, Lucy gave me that smile of hers that should have been served with insulin.

"Well, not two days later, the same woman calls us to say that one of our maids has stolen her wallet. She calls us the most dishonest people she has ever been associated with; then she tells us that the Greenbrier and the Mohonk Mountain House never treated her like that. Of course, I'm not going to mess with something like this; so I call Tom Barson. He talks to the woman and asks when she last saw her wallet. She tells him she had last seen it about two hours before that thieving maid had been in her room."

"Go on."

"Well, I'm leaving out a lot of the details here; but, Tom Barson checks the key entry record only to find that the maid had finished the woman's room one hour before she had last seen her wallet. And . . . here's the funny part . . . the woman says that my housekeeper must have snuck back in and taken it later. Of course, the record shows that she didn't go back to the room; in fact, she was subbing for the pusher at the time of the alleged incident."

"Pusher?" I inquired.

"Yeah, the person who goes around to the various floors of the hotel and brings dirty laundry down to Jeff Milk's shop. So, you can see how the card key had saved our housekeeper's reputation. In the old days, the guest's word would simply have been taken and the staff person's reputation permanently smudged. These electronic keys really are a valuable tool. And," she gave me another one of those smiles, "you should use them in your book."

Promising that I would, I rose to leave when I remembered there was yet another purpose for my visit. "Lucy, I just thought of another question that I need to ask you."

"What's that, Professor?"

"How frequently do your housekeepers come into contact with guests?"

"Not all that frequently, unless you count passing momentarily in the hallways. Why do you ask?"

"I was just wondering if one of your people would take note if a guest were to be spirited away somehow."

"You mean like Edna Connor?" she asked. As she mentioned Edna's name, she looked directly into my eyes. The blush on her cheeks betrayed an obvious concern that she had just committed a faux pas of colossal proportions.

"Who's Edna Connor?" I lied. This was one of those moments that seem to pass in slow motion. My entire effort on Warn's behalf might hinge on the next several seconds. As she held her gaze on me, I was sure that Lucy could see the sweat that was pouring down my back. As we both considered how we were going to extricate ourselves from the discomfort caused by her slip of the tongue, Lucy spoke first. "Oh, it's not important." Clearly, with discretion being the better part of valor, I remained mum. Ten seconds passed before the tension was broken by the sound of the telephone ringing. As Lucy answered the phone, we exchanged friendly waves, and I left her office.

*　　*　　*

Lucy's slip of the tongue had provided me with an answer to my question. She must have learned from someone on her staff that Edna Connor was missing. As John had indicated, the housekeeper doubtlessly had discovered that Edna's bed was not slept in on the morning of the 14th. It would have been her responsibility to report that information to her supervisor, Lucy. I now surmised that Lucy had spoken to Warn about this, probably around the time he had enlisted me to find Edna. No doubt Warn had entrusted Lucy, who he'd known for many years, to keep a lid on things. Did she know about my real purpose? I couldn't think of another explanation for allowing Edna's name to slip in my presence. However, I had no time to worry about this, but made a mental note to have Warn explain Lucy's involvement to me after the fact. For now, I had a job to do.

Thus, as we parted company, I was convinced that Lucy, and perhaps Reg and Rolf, were doing their part to protect the Barsons and the resort.

*　　*　　*

2:52 P.M. I had one stop to make on my way to meet with the executive chef. Warn was sitting alone in his office when I entered. He was looking a bit peaked and I was concerned. "Are you all right, Warn? You aren't looking so great."

"I just had a visit with another satisfied customer," he said with a wry smile on his face.

"You mean another Mrs. Plessence; or was this one more like the woman from Atlanta?"

"So, you've been talking with Lucy, huh?"

"Yup," I smiled knowingly.

"Well, what she may not of told you is that I took care of her personally after the incident with the housekeeper," he said.

"No, she hadn't. And did the woman mend her ways?"

"No, she came back the next year and was as bad as ever. I pity her poor kids."

I was compelled to say, "It doesn't seem that you're having much fun these days, Warn." Then, looking at his full head of silver hair, I added, "It could just be that you're no longer a blond."

Warn forced a smile, but added, "I keep asking myself if I'm really cut out for this anymore, Kary."

"Are you serious, Warn? You *are* The Balsams. It sounds like we need to talk, and I don't mean about Edna Connor," I said. "Look, hang in here for a while, will you? I have five more appointments; but, I'll get back to you about this, okay?" Then, as much as I hated to do it, I added, "By the way, I hate to kick a man when he's down, but I need one more favor, okay?"

Warn looked like he had been kicked in the stomach, or was about to take aggressive measures that would eliminate one good friend. "Sure." But, he didn't sound convincing.

"Now that I've been educated about your key system, I need a list of everyone who used a card key to gain entry into Edna Connor's room from noon on the 12th through the morning of the 14th."

Warn groaned audibly, "I'll get back to you."

As I headed across the lobby, making my way to the Ballot Room to meet with Chef Leonard, I looked back just in time to see Warn unscrew the cap from a small bottle filled with pink liquid.

Chapter 31

3:00 P.M. I approached my meeting with Paul Leonard with a great deal of trepidation. For years, I had read in the resort's newsletter about the culinary awards he had won. He had received enough gold and silver at international competitions to pique a pirate's passion. And, of course, Nya and I had witnessed his artistry first hand, many times, in The Balsams' dining room. So I felt guilty that I was stealing him away from a potentially creative moment to talk nonsense with a total stranger.

I arrived in the Ballot Room promptly at 3PM. There, dressed in white with a black vest stood Katyana, the young Russian waitperson with whom I had discussed Edna earlier. She brightened when she recognized me.

"Professor, the chef has been delayed. He will be here in about ten minutes."

I thanked Katyana, and as she was about to leave, asked if she could answer another question for me.

"Certainly, sir," she replied.

"When we talked earlier about the lady, Mrs. Connor, you told me that you liked her . . . Why?" I asked.

"Because she appeared to be a . . . how do you say(?) . . . lofely person. Vy do you ask me this, Professor?" Her Russian accent seemed to be growing thicker, as though she was fearful that, by talking to me, she might somehow place her job in jeopardy.

"It's nothing really; I'm just looking for a few good characters for my novel." Of course, I was lying through my teeth; and, had she been able to touch the back of my tee shirt, she would have felt the mass of sweat making rivulets toward the waistband of my BVDs.

Fortunately, her concerns had been assuaged. I had to smile to myself. Dating back to my days on the Inquirer, I've always been amazed at the amount of crap people will swallow if they think there's a chance they'll be immortalized in some pabulum that passes for literature. Apparently, even a Russian woman was susceptible to the same trap.

"She vas wery sweet . . . but wery unhappy."

"Unhappy?" Now I was getting somewhere. "Why was she unhappy, Katyana?"

She paused and stared at me. I could tell that she was trying to decide whether to continue or not. Then I had an inspiration.

"By the way, Katyana, how do you spell your name? I want to make certain I spell it properly in the book."

That did the trick. I saw her smile slightly; and the blush on her cheek told me I'd converted her. "It's K-A-T-Y-A-N-A. But use only my first name, please.

"That's fine, Katyana. But, why was Mrs. Connor unhappy?"

"She missed her husband, I think. She said he sent her here to get rid of her."

"What did she mean 'get rid of her' Katyana?" I asked, trying not to sound too anxious to hear her answer.

"He vas always thinkink about his business, and never about Mrs. Connor, I think." Then, reflecting for a few seconds, she added, "I don't think he loffed her."

Then, after a moment of reflection, she expressed doubts about what she'd just said, "Perhaps he luffed her in one way; but, she told me one night after a few wodka gimlets that he didn't . . ."

Katyana couldn't get the words out; but, her blushing told the story. Mr. Connor wasn't having sex with a wife who probably was ready, willing and able. My stomach was beginning to feel queasy; this was sounding too familiar. Katyana, now fully embarrassed, left the room without me taking notice.

I was almost relieved when Chef Leonard came rushing in and announced that he really didn't have time to talk with me. Frankly, I wasn't really in the mood to fill in the clumsy silences with small talk anyway. Before he left, he muttered something about having to supervise one hundred people and needing to speak with his sous chef. And, with that, the great man was gone, leaving me alone to stare at photos of the past several decades presidential candidates, each of whom had trekked north to this quasi village in hopes of earning the first presidential votes that were cast every quadrennium.

★   ★   ★

I had fifteen minutes to kill before I was to meet Shannon Pardon on the veranda of the Dixville House. So, I thought this might be an opportune time to see what Nya was up to. I walked down the steps leading to the lobby and peered across at Warn's office. The office light was off and no one was sitting there. So I picked up the house phone and dialed our room. No answer. Just my luck. Suddenly, I found myself really needing to talk with Nya. This was very unusual; I hadn't ever been one of those sloppy, St. Bernard-type husbands. You know . . . the guys who have to say 'sweetie' this and 'honey' that every two hours or they'll have a coronary. I'd always hated that stuff. But, there I was, standing in the lobby of The Balsams, thinking how nice it would be to hear Nya's voice.

Chapter 32

3:15 P.M., Saturday, July 15th. Nya had completed the evaluation that Warn and Lynn Ride requested during their lunch at the Panorama golf course. The two men had other meetings to attend and were preparing to part company. Lynn, a thin, dark-haired man with a slightly pockmarked face that revealed a bad case of acne during his teens, had excused himself first. He needed to talk briefly with the business manager before driving back to Boston, and was anxious to get started. He shook hands first with Warn, then turning to Nya, he said, "It's a pleasure, Nya. You are one sharp lady. I'd love to see what you're like when you aren't preoccupied." But, when Nya gave Lynn a startled look, he added, "I hope that whatever is bothering you gets cleared up fast. It always pains me to see a frown on a pretty lady's face." Then, turning to Warn, he winked and said, "Now don't you dare tell Janey I said that."

Warn had assured Lynn that he wouldn't, smiling wryly as he did. For her part, Nya said nothing but offered a small smile to Lynn as she took his hand and hugged him goodbye. When Lynn had gone, Warn turned to Nya and asked, "Do you want to talk, Nya, or is this something you'd rather handle alone?"

"Thanks, Warn. You're a dear; but I'm afraid this has to be worked out by Kary and me, if it can be. You've already done so much already by upgrading our room."

"It was the least I could do. I don't really know all that's going on between you two, and I know it's none of my business. You know there are few people on this planet whom I admire more than Kary; but if he doesn't have the sense to see what he's got, then my respect for him is about to take a huge hit."

Nya brushed a tear from her left eye. "I'm not sure that Kary's capable of sorting through this mess, Warn."

"Your tone on the telephone told me as much," he said. "I just figured being up here at The Balsams could help. But, I may have really made a mess of things by telling him about a missing guest."

Nya groaned. "So that's what this luncheon meeting was really about? You had me work with Lynn just to cover a little job that Kary's working on? And, stupid me, I was too flattered by your offer to see through your little deception. Was Kary in on this part, too?"

"No; Kary has no idea what you've been working on unless you've told him. In fact, unless I miss my guess, I think Kary's exhibiting signs of jealousy."

"Kary, jealous? That's not likely."

"I could be wrong, but, I don't think so, Nya. Look, I know things seem to be at their darkest right now, but have some faith in the magic of this old place, will you?" And so, as I later learned, at the very moment I was searching in vain for Nya, Warn was attempting to keep her from tossing me onto the marital scrap heap.

Chapter 33

It was nearly 3:30, and I hadn't found so much as a trace of Nya. And, of course, just as before, Warn was no place to be found either. I'd always felt certain that Nya would never have an affair; she'd tell me to hit the road first. And Warn was an old, dear friend. Besides, on the surface, his relationship with Nancy was as sound as . . . he probably thought mine was. Then, at all at once, I had this illusion that Nya had gone shopping with Edna Connor. There was something about this image that sent me into convulsive laughter; and, as I climbed the steps from the lobby, I was literally howling. At that very moment, a pair of octogenarians were laboring to make their way down the stairs. Their total lack of amusement at the spectacle I was making of myself made the laughter pour forth in an even more voluminous manner.

★   ★   ★

3:30 P.M. I opened the door to the veranda and looked for two Adirondack chairs situated along the outside wall of the dining room. I had arrived ahead of Shannon Parton, so I sat down and watched in amusement as four hummingbirds vied for the nectar stored in the baskets of pink impatiens that hung from the eaves.

I didn't have to wait long, for Shannon was prompt. Just as the previous interviews had begun, we spent the first few minutes discussing the make up of Shannon's staff of 24 and their tasks. I learned that recreation staffers and children's counselors are constantly on the go from 7:30 until the kids have lunch; then the fun begins again until 4pm. After dinner, the recreation staff keeps the children entertained until 9 PM. The program Shannon described was remarkably diverse, and even involved members of the maintenance and culinary staff, who showed the children in the program how to construct, paint, or cook, once the kids had tired of swimming, tennis, traditional kids games, going to movies, etc. etc. etc. After listening to this, I would have been tempted to place a call to tell my mom how deprived I was as a kid, had she still been alive. Of course, her rejoinder would have been completely disarming. "My dear boy," she would have said, "your daddy and I wouldn't have dreamed of spending an entire day without you and your brothers. And do you know why? Because we loved you too much." Terrific. My mother had been dead for more than a decade; and, even from the grave she was laying a pretty good guilt trip on me. However, my mother's point of view not withstanding, what kid wouldn't want to spend his days doing cool stuff and being fawned over by a bunch of attractive twenty year olds?

Shannon didn't have much to tell me that was going to help the Connor case, but she did share a story that sent my mind into overdrive. She told me about an elderly gentleman who, unbeknown to the resort staff, had arrived at the resort with the intention of dying in Dixville. It seems that the gentleman had spent his early years hiking and climbing in Dixville Notch with his father and two brothers. A half century before, the younger of his brothers had lost his grip when trying to scale the north edge of Table Rock, and had fallen, injuring himself mortally. As Warn Barson would later learn, the man had promised his dying brother that his soul, too, would leave this earth from Dixville Notch. So, when the old gentleman's doctors had informed him that he had two weeks left to live, he had immediately made a reservation to return to The Balsams.

The old gentleman had been very honest. So, upon checking into the resort, he had paid his bill in advance, in cash. Then he had left strict instructions not to be disturbed, lest the well-meaning staff would find him alive and whisk him off to the North Country hospital. Finally, after the gentleman had not been seen or heard from for thirty-six hours, the general manager had opened the room door with his passkey. Finding the old gentleman dead, the general manager had to contrive a method for removing his body from the resort without unnecessarily disturbing the other guests or the staff. And so they had placed the man's body into a laundry hamper, covered it with his bed linens and wheeled the body through the tunnel connecting the Hampshire and Dixville Houses, to a hearse waiting outside the laundry room. No one had been any the wiser. Having heard this story, I was tempted to ask whether the man's bed and bed linens were still in use, but decided to keep this query to myself.

While Shannon didn't add to my fact finding effort, she had shared a very interesting anecdote and had reinforced what I had been learning all day: namely, Warn Barson must be one incredible administrator, for he had been successfully manipulating a small army of staff who came to the resort from a wide range of backgrounds, and who had arrived with very different skill levels. I was more convinced than ever that Warn's ability to make important decisions, often under great pressure, was having an enormous impact upon the quality of 400 guests' experiences and, more important, upon the welfare of a workforce that numbered nearly 500. Moreover, I fully believed that Warn's abilities hadn't been diminished one bit; and, I was going to make it my business to persuade him that this was true.

Chapter 34

3:47 P.M. I had a few minutes to spare and had been thinking about trying to find Warn when I saw him coming out from behind the wood and glass door of the dining room. "Warn, do you have a few minutes?" I called.

"Oh . . . eh . . . sure, Kary." The tone of Warn's response indicated that he either had become completely drained by the day's events or was tired of seeing me. At that moment, I was more concerned that it was the former.

"Do you have anything for me, yet?"

"As a matter of fact, I do. Come on down to the office," he called over his shoulder. He sounded more like a man who was glad to be rid of a burden than someone who was enthusiastic about the information he was about to share.

I followed Warn to his office, hoping to be surprised once again by a Nya sighting. But I was to be disappointed. "Sit down for a minute," he instructed. "I have these things stashed away where no one will accidentally find them." He opened the second small drawer on the right side of his large mahogany colored desk and pulled out a manila envelope containing several computer print outs. Handing the envelope to me, he reminded me one more time about the extreme sensitivity of the documents I was holding.

"I understand completely." For an instant, I had a good mind to say, "If you don't trust me, why did you involve me in this mess?" But I thought the better of it. Instead I said, "There is no need for this envelope to leave your office. I can find out everything I need in about ten minutes."

"Here, then, sit at my desk and look things over. Take as long as you need." Then rising, he started to go out of the office.

I called to him, "I'll only be here for a few minutes. What do you want me to do with this stuff if you're not back before I have to go?"

"I'm just going across the hall to talk with Tom; I'll be right back."

With Warn gone, I opened the envelope and removed the three documents from it. I grabbed the first document. It contained a list of all persons who had used a card key to enter Edna Connor's room between noon on the 11th and the time she was reported as missing. Unfortunately, the report contained nothing out of the ordinary. There were several entries showing when Edna had entered and left. Of greatest interest, it appeared that she only left her room to take meals, that is, until the evenings of the 12th and the 13th. On the second night she had gone to dinner, but had not returned until nearly midnight. What, I wondered, was a middle age, married woman traveling alone, doing out of her room until midnight on the night she disappeared from The Balsams? I made a mental note to ask Warn to find out if she had attended the night club that evening. To my knowledge, there would have been no other resort-sanctioned activity that could have kept her out until that hour. All of the other entries in the document were from the housekeeping staff. Based upon the times of day, they represented people coming in to freshen the room and to perform The Balsams turndown service during the dinner hour.

Next, I opened the report listing telephone calls made to and received by Edna Connor on the 12th and the 13th. There were only five. Two calls were from her neighbor, Mr. Tomquist. So, the two had made a connection. But was it an innocent friendship or something more? Had things become passionate, so passionate that they cost Edna Connor her life? The third call was placed by Edna to her husband, Al. It was made at 4pm on the 13th. The return call had been placed from a cell phone registered to Mr. Al Connor. Things were becoming more interesting by the minute.

With the time for my next appointment rapidly approaching, I wanted a look at the print out from John Gray. It indicated that two women and a man, each traveling alone, had occupied the tables nearest Edna Connor. This information corroborated what I'd learned earlier. Both women had checked out of the hotel already, but the man, one R. Johan Tomquist remained. Then I saw it . . . the real blockbuster . . . Mr. Tomquist was staying in room number 168, right next door to Edna Connor's room, number 167! This, in combination with the information in the telephone log, was a very interesting development indeed. As I looked up from the last of the three files, I happened to look across the hallway toward Tom Barson's office. There in the window, stood both Barsons staring directly at me.

Satisfied that I'd made significant progress, I rose to leave. That's when I noticed an open file on the desktop. At first I didn't pay it any mind; for, one thing that I had learned about Warn is that he was extremely fastidious about the disposition of confidential materials. But my curiosity got the best of me. My eyes scanned across the top page of the report, and the words "unfit behavior" and "disciplinary action" stuck out at me. With my curiosity now thoroughly piqued, I quickly looked for the name of this alleged perpetrator. The man's name was Billy Fenton. Shutting the file, I prepared to make my exit. As if on cue, the screen door swung open and Warn Barson entered. "Find anything interesting?" His question seemed innocent enough.

"I was beginning to think I had a prime suspect, but you apparently have other information that may complicate things," I said while staring into Warn's eyes to see if my words had elicited a reaction. If they did, he was playing it very cool.

"What additional information are you talking about, Kary?" I wasn't sure I trusted Warn's innocent sounding question at that particular moment.

"I just noticed the file on this guy Fenton that you happened to leave open on your desk."

"Jesus, Kary, that's a confidential report you just read."

Warn was feigning anger; but for some reason I remained unconvinced. "Please, old friend, spare me the indignation. You are one of the most fastidious characters I've ever known. Hells bells, your office always looks like a housekeeper just left. If I didn't know you so well, I'd swear you never did any work. So, you're just not the type to leave a personnel file carelessly lying around."

If Warn was upset by this accusation, he didn't show it. "But, I was trying to get out of your way so you could work in here. In my haste, I obviously failed to put the report away properly."

"So, do you think Fenton could be our man?" he asked.

"I'm not ruling Fenton out, but there is a heck of a lot of circumstantial evidence here against one of your guests, a Mr. Tomquist. And, I'm also trying to understand why Mrs. Connor would have called her husband at one number, which I presume is her house number, while the husband called her back much later from what appears to be a cell phone."

"Jesus Christ. Did you say 'Tomquist'. Richard Tomquist?" Warn was ashen.

"All I have here is the name he registered under . . . "R. Johann Tomquist."

Now Warn's mind seemed far away.

I placed my hand on his shoulder. "Is there something you're not telling me, old friend."

Without answering me, Warn had turned and kneeled against a file cabinet that was situated in the corner behind his desk. After a minute, he rose and turned. In his hand was a white envelope that had turned yellow with age.

He mumbled, "I haven't looked at these in years." Without saying another word, he handed me the envelope. Then he sat at his desk, his face in his hands.

I opened the envelope and carefully removed several now yellowed newpsaper stories. The stories were thorough, the pictures all-too-graphic. After carefully consuming each word and the photographs, I turned to Warn. "Who . . .?"

"My niece, Sarah; Nancy's sister's daughter. She was the same age as Tom. They grew up together."

"It says here her body was found more than ten years ago, in Colebrook; that's ten miles west of here isn't it?" Warn nodded. "The article also says that Richard Tomquist was a prime suspect, but there wasn't enough evidence to prosecute."

"That's right. Those were the days before CSI's and DNA."

"Were there other suspects?"

"Yeah, but Tomquist used to work here. I had to fire him. And . . ." he paused to compose himself . . . "Tomquist was the last person to be seen with her . . . alive." Warn was fighting his emotions now.

I needed Warn to keep his focus. "You fired him? Why?"

"He couldn't keep his hands off of . . . . ." I was losing Warn.

I shook him gently. "Listen Warn, if R. Joann Tomquist is really Richard Tomquist, he could have something to do with Edna Connor's disappearance, too. But you have to stay focused. Remember, he may not be the same guy; also, let's not forget that we have two other possible suspects who we'd better not ignore."

"So, what next, Kary?"

"I need a few favors.'

Warn had the same tired look on his face. "And what are those?"

"First, I need to know if Mr. Tomquist is the same guy you've been talking about. Next I need to know if Mrs. Connor and Mr. Tomquist reserved tables for the nightclub show on the 13th, together or separately. Third, I need to know if there is anything in the resort's registration records that will tell us something useful about Mr. Tomquist."

"And fourth?" he asked. The look on his face indicated that he'd already anticipated what I was about to ask.

"I want to know whether this Fenton character has anything else in his personnel folder that would suggest he's a potential felon."

Having said that, I rose to leave. I took two steps toward the door, then turned and asked, "When did you last see my wife?"

"Nya and I had lunch together with Lynn."

"Is that business all finished?" I asked.

He looked at me for what seemed like a full minute before answering. "Yeah, it's finished. But . . ."

"But what?" I asked. Warn said no more. However, his face spoke volumes; and, for once, I was listening.

Chapter 35

4:00 P.M. When I arrived at the ballroom, I was no longer in any mood to make small talk with the remaining department heads. There was really no one left on my list who was likely to help me. Fran Galloway introduced himself with a genuine smile and a handshake. He asked me to call him Frannie, something that I was reticent to do, given the fact that he was a male and about twenty years my senior. Frannie explained that the resort employed him and the five members of his band. He went on to say that he always had the greatest difficulty finding good piano players. "Guys who play a decent horn are all over the place," he told me, "but not the ivory ticklers." He told me how some musicians have proven to be real bummers: showing up late, dressing all wrong, or quitting without providing notice. I must confess that I was about to call an end to this conversation when Frannie offered me a real gem.

"We're not like the other employees at The Balsams," he said. "By that I mean we frequently play golf and tennis with the guests. Just a few days ago, I got hooked up at shuffleboard with a lady who said she'd heard terrific things about our show."

This, of itself, was not earth shattering information. But, it gave me an idea that I decided to explore. "Frannie," I asked, "when you're interacting with guests, do they ever say anything negative about particular employees?" In my mind, I figured that this little fishing expedition had about as much chance of success as winning Megabucks. But, happily, Frannie soon proved me wrong.

"It's funny you should ask about that," he began. "Because the lady who was playing shuffleboard with me was really peed off about a young maintenance worker. She said he was making her feel really uncomfortable. At first she was flattered by his attention, but he seemed to be standing there every time she turned around. And, she said his comments were becoming more and more forward."

"Did she do anything about it?" I asked.

"She said she didn't want to make trouble for the young man. It was obvious that she hadn't ever been treated like that before. An', you know, I'm sure she figured if she ignored him, he'd stop bothering her. Finally, she'd told this guy that if he didn't stop bothering her, she would have to talk to the general manager."

"Did this put a stop to it?" I asked.

"Well sort of," Frannie replied. "She said that he got up real close to her and said, 'Okay lady, but we'll see who gets hers'."

"Holy cow; did she report this to anyone?"

"That's what I asked her," Frannie replied. "I doubt she ever did. I guess she figured he'd get smart and go about his business."

"Did she ever tell you this guy's name?" I asked.

For the first time I had aroused the musician's suspicions. "Why do you ask,

Professor?"

I had to think fast. "My wife and I are on vacation. I just want to be ready to avoid trouble. That's all."

Whether or not Frannie was satisfied with my story, he decided to respond. "She called him 'The Phantom', or something like that."

My mind went into overdrive. His name hadn't been Phantom; I'd bet the name she had used was Fenton. So, it had to be him . . . the same man whose file I had seen on Warn's desk. But this seemed like too much of a coincidence. Is it possible that two pieces of evidence would point toward the same man within a matter of twenty minutes? Especially since I hadn't ever heard of this Mr. Fenton a mere half hour before.

It was obvious that, with the clock ticking, I'd only begun to sniff around the edges of what had happened to Edna Connor.

Chapter 36

4:15 P.M. I had foolishly planned to meet with both the golf and the tennis pros at the tail end of the day. This was a bad idea for two reasons. First, it seemed unlikely that either of them was going to be able to shed light on Edna's disappearance; and, more important, I was bone tired. However, if I was to maintain the ruse that I was doing research for a novel, it was important to keep both of these appointments. Before meeting with Bill Head at the bar that overlooks Lake Gloriette, I once again used the house phone to call my room. Two rings, then three. I was about ready to hang up, not wanting the front desk to pick up, when I heard Nya's voice on the other end of the line.

"Hello."

"Nya, is that you?"

"Well who else do you think it would be, Kary?" she replied.

I did not like the sound of this. Nya was in a terrible mood. "You sound terrible; are you okay?" I said, without making an effort to mask my concern.

"I'm fine, Kary. It's so nice of you to be concerned. Where are you; and what are you doing?"

"I'm down near the pool interviewing the golf pro," I replied truthfully. Of course, I immediately regretted my choice of words before they had passed my lips.

"You don't even play golf, Kary. Why in the world are you talking to a golf pro?" She was clearly agitated. "Our first full day at The Balsams is almost over, and I've spent all of . . . what . . . ten minutes with you? Apparently it's the same old thing at a new address, isn't it Kary? I thought coming up here might . . ."

I could tell she was fighting back tears; and, as per usual, I was helpless to find the right words to make her feel better. What had been worse is that she had always found the right things to say when my emotional wounds needed soothing.

Then, out it spilled; I can't tell you how many times I had offered the same tired, benign statement, "Look I'm sorry, Nya. Really. I love you." Had I stopped there, I may have had a chance. But, stupid me, I added, "Listen, I have to go talk to these guys. I'll see you in the room in an hour."

For about ten seconds, there wasn't a sound on the line. And when there finally was, it was a soft click. As I walked down the long set of wooden stairs toward the swimming pool and the cabana bar, it was a miracle that I didn't trip, so completely was my tail hanging between my legs.

Chapter 37

4:30 P.M. Bill Head didn't appear for our meeting. His assistant, Jim O'Neil, had the perfect golf pro look: compact, broad shoulders, a narrow waist and tanned, well-developed biceps, and wavy blond hair. I had to suppress a smile; for, it was doubtful that this guy had to ever worry about his hair blowing in the wind. Given the quantity of mousse holding things in place, it probably couldn't have been moved by anything short of a level-5 hurricane. However, after spending a few minutes with Jim, I began to feel guilty about prejudging pro golfers. Jim and his boss Bill Head clearly knew their business and, like so many of the others I'd met that day, had oversight over a small army of employees and a bunch of really valuable real estate. Prior to talking with Jim, I had had no idea how much work went into running an operation like the Panorama Golf Course. Not only does your typical golf pro need a feel for sales and public relations, but he has to keep abreast of the latest in golf equipment technology and even has to be somewhat conversant with chemical fertilizers and insecticides. If their grasp of any these fields was short of PGA and USGA standards, the outstanding reputation of The Balsams as a golf resort would go down the toilet, and a lot more than the eighteen jobs they supervised might be lost along with it.

It had been a long day. I'd interviewed twelve department heads, one general manager and his projects manager. I had toured the resort's highest and lowest points; and had been trying, unsuccessfully, to make things right with Nya. So, as I had done with each of the department heads who were not going to provide me with clues about Edna Connor's disappearance, I spared both of us from meeting any longer than his schedule and my fading sanity would allow.

I began by saying that the purpose of our meeting was to obtain information that could be used in my novel. In doing this, I had forgotten my own axiom that people will never miss an opportunity to immortalize themselves by getting their name in print. Jim, unfortunately, wasn't any different. While much of what he said had little bearing upon Edna's disappearance, it was helpful to know that his boss, Bill Head, lived in an apartment above the Panorama club house; and, Jim assured me that Bill would certainly overhear anything unusual that might occur 'up on the mountain' where the golf course was situated. After about ten minutes, we shook hands and prepared to part company. As I started to walk away, Jim called to me.

"Oh, one more thing, Professor, if there's anything else you need to know, Bill will be back in a week."

"Thanks. That's good to know. By the way, where is Bill?"

"He's in South Carolina for a week visiting his sister. A friend of his is using the apartment for a few days while he's gone."

"It must be nice to have friends in high places," I remarked with a smile.

Now it was time for my last appointment of the day. So we shook hands again and went our separate ways.

Chapter 38

My last meeting was with Bob Clay, the resort's tennis pro. We met at the small white iron table outside the pro shop at 5 PM, more than twenty minutes after my meeting with Bill Head had concluded. This was the earliest time Bob could spare, as it was right after his last lesson for the day. I had known him for years, for I'd spent quite a bit of time under his tutelage. Bob had been a very patient teacher, working tirelessly with me until I had mastered the rudiments of a topspin serve.

We shook hands warmly, and Bob asked how my game was, which of course, it wasn't at all. I explained that it was impossible to write novels and keep up my game. He responded, "So, you did finish that book you had been telling me about." It had been more of a statement than a question, but I was already down 30-love, and the interview hadn't even begun.

Bob and I reminisced for a while. As I had suspected, he had little to contribute to the Edna Connor business. To be truthful, by this time I was totally preoccupied with thoughts of facing Nya, given the way our last telephone conversation had gone. So Bob and I shook hands again, and he let me go, but only after I'd promised that I would try to get down to the court for a lesson soon. As I made my way back up the steps toward the Hampshire House, I realized that there were more important lessons in life that I needed to master first.

Chapter 39

5:15PM. While I really hate riding in elevators, and almost always opt for the stairs, I decided that it would be wise to carefully study the dinner menu posted inside the Hampshire House elevator before meeting Nya. This would give me something to use to break the ice. As usual, the menu was simply out of this world. Black Angus, Boiled Lobster, Chicken Kiev, Arctic Char; each item was more mouthwatering than the previous one. And this was not all. There were interesting salads and a choice of soups, including my personal favorite, chilled strawberry soup with a touch of Grand Marnier. Armed with this list of delicacies, I slipped my key card into the lock and opened the outer door.

"Nya!" There was no answer. "Nya!" Again, no answer. I was concerned. It was already close to six. And, based upon our conversation at breakfast, Nya had really been looking forward to being pampered at another of the resort's incredible evening meals. I thought about leaving, figuring that she had dressed and was waiting somewhere in the lobby, or perhaps the library, for me to show up. I was convinced that she was no longer in the room, as the lights were out and the shades drawn. Although it was more than two hours before dusk, the room was surprisingly dark.

For my part, evenings were the best part of an experience at The Balsams. Men and women dressed for dinner and an evening of light entertainment. I always felt as if I were on a land cruise during evenings at the resort. I was anxious to spend time with Nya at dinner. But, where was she? Turning to leave, I had nearly reached the door when I heard a low moan. "Nya?" I called again, this time with a noticeable tone of concern in my voice.

"I'm over here." It was not the voice of someone who was happy to see me. I flipped on the overhead light which engendered a muffled, "No, turn off the damn light." Ignoring her, I made my way over to the double bed she had slept in alone the night before. I sat down on the bed and searched for her forehead with the palm of my right hand. "No, get away from me!" she screeched. "Can't you see that I'm not feeling well, not that you give a damn."

One of us had to remain calm and, well, passionless. And by this time, if you haven't already guessed, I qualified as an expert in being passionless. "It's okay now. Please tell me what's bothering you."

"Uzzz.," she replied.

"I don't understand what you're saying."

"Us . . . you and me, Kary. We're what's bothering me.

I sat down gently by her side, trying not to shake her or upset her further. "We're what's bothering you? But you're the best part of my mundane life, Nya."

"And mundane is good enough for you; isn't that true Kary?"

Having successfully seated myself on the bed, I realized that Nya hadn't spent the afternoon alone. Something heavy nudged my knee as I sat down.

I reached under the sheet and soon found the neck of an oval shape glass bottle. Nya's companion had been the contents of a large bottle of 2001 Rose Grenache. I was shocked. Nya had been something of a party girl back in our dating days. But ever since I'd become a slave to the bottle, she had eschewed anything stronger than an iced tea.

"Nya, I don't understand. I . . ." Holy shit, she smelled like a winery.

"Just go-o-o-o, Kareeee . . ."

"God," I muttered to myself, "she is really sloshed."

But, Nya was in no way, shape or form finished with her monologue. "I've given you the best years of my life; I've shared my love, my money, my friendship, my . . ."

"I know, Nya. I know. Please, be quiet now. You need some rest."

" . . . and what did you give me? AND, don't you patronize me; I'm trying to tell you what's wrong with us!"

Fearing that Nya was going to say something she or, more likely, I would long regret, I grabbed her by her shoulders and said, "This isn't the time, Nya. You have just consumed more alcohol in the last hour than I've seen you drink during the last five years."

"Thaas, right, Kary. It . . . it's more than you've seen me drink."

These last words really stung. It's not easy to hear such a candid expression of your failings from the one you love, even if you deserve every single sound bite. But, for once, I realized that my own pain could wait. I had to calm Nya down and get her to sleep before she hurt herself. Holding her firmly but gently, I whispered, "Please, Nya. You must listen to me. You need to rest now. I'll stay here and hold you until you fall asleep. We'll talk about this tomorrow, I promise." The combination of the alcohol and her outburst had apparently worn her battery down. There was no response when I asked her if she wanted me to help her on with her nightgown. So, for several minutes, I held Nya in my arms and watched her sleep, all the while relecting on how I'd made such a mess of things.

Chapter 40

With Nya incapacitated for the evening, it might seem like this was the perfect time for more private investigating. But I was exhausted and really wanted to slip into bed. Something was bothering me. I couldn't help thinking about what Katyana, the young Russian waitress, had told me. Edna's husband had lost interest in her. He'd been indifferent toward her, but for how long? And then, there was the information from the telephone log. Edna had received two telephone calls from her husband; but what about the two from the man in the next room, Mr. Tomquist? Putting two and two together, it was apparent that Edna Connor had arrived at The Balsams a lonely woman. And–as I had just learned from a front row seat–when a wife has been spurned by her husband for too long, she can be driven to drastic measures. In Nya's case, so far as I knew, she had found her measure of relief in a wine bottle. But, what about Edna? Had she been driven by loneliness into the waiting arms of another man? And, had it cost Edna her life?

★　　★　　★

7 P.M. Entering the dining room, I caught John Gray's eye. Using the combination of a few hand signals and an urgent expression, I conveyed to him that we needed to talk right away. He whispered something in his assistant's ear, then asked loudly enough so she was able to hear, "So, how's the research on that book coming, Professor?" Saying this had been very clever of John, as it provided him with an excuse for diverting his attention from the guests lining up at the doorway. After all, by this time, most of the staff knew that there was a novelist in the house.

"I have to make this quick, Professor," John said, never taking his eyes off of his assistant and the growing number of first day arrivals who were waiting to be assigned their tables.

"This won't take a minute, John," I said. "I need a favor. My wife won't be joining me for dinner this evening."

"That's unfortunate. Is she ill?" he interrupted.

"She's just a bit under the weather," I offered. "I'm sure she'll be feeling much better in the morning." Yes, but would our marriage?

"You may feel free to sit at your usual table. We'll simply inform the waitstaff," he said.

"That's just it. I want you to reseat me." I replied. John looked at me as though he'd been gut shot. "I don't know, Professor. Look over at the entrance; it appears we're going to be nearly full this evening."

"I know it's asking a lot, but I'd like to sit at Mrs. Connor's table. It hasn't been reassigned has it?"

He looked at me for a few seconds pondering his next words. "No, we have kept it until you . . . er . . . we know more of Mrs. Connor's disposition." That,

96

I thought to myself, was an unfortunate choice of words. Then, because he needed to get back to his position at the dining room door, he offered, "I suppose that it won't present a terrible imposition on the waitstaff if you sit there. After all, the table is still their responsibility."

"Thank you, John. Do I need to tell you why I'm doing this?"

"No sir; in fact, I'd prefer that you did not." Then John added, "You can be seated. I'll inform the captain that you have been moved for the evening." Following his instructions, I had started toward Edna's table when I felt a hand on my shoulder. It was John. "Oh, there is one more thing that Mr. Barson thought I should tell you."

"What's that?"

"Brian, one of my waitstaff, was in the staff cafeteria when he heard one of the new maintenance people bragging how one of the guests has the hots for him. It was Brian's distinct impression that he might try to do something stupid, so he told me. I, of course, reported this to Tom Barson."

"Hmm, this is interesting. Was the young man's last name, by chance, Fenton?"

John seemed a bit nonplussed. "How did you know that, Professor?"

"Just an educated guess," I replied. "Do we know if the woman in question was our missing friend, Edna Connor?"

"Not definitely. But the description that Brian overheard makes this a distinct possibility," he offered." "But, please sir, be careful how you use this information."

Chapter 41

7:15 P.M. Fortunately, the table to which Nya and I were assigned and the one Edna Connor had occupied were at opposite ends of the dining room. This lessened the likelihood that my former waitstaff would see me ingratiating myself to the older woman and the middle age man sitting at the two tables adjoining mine. I sat down nearer to the woman, said hello and initiated a dialogue.

"I wonder if I might ask you a few questions?" I was speaking a little too loudly for intimate conversation. But there was a method to my madness. It was really the man seated at the table to her left who I wanted to engage.

"I suppose so," she replied.

"Great," I began. "I'm writing a novel about people who stay at a grand hotel similar to this one." I thought it best to alter my story slightly for these two people. It seemed like bad form to tell a potential murder suspect that I was writing a murder mystery. Actually, I'd like to interview you, too, sir," I said while looking directly at Mr. Tomquist.

"Me," he said. "Why would you be interested in talking with me?"

Using the instincts that had made me an excellent crime reporter but, alas, apparently a lousy husband, I formulated a quick fib. "Each of you represents a different gender, a different generation and, I'm guessing a different motivation for visiting The Balsams." I was willing to wager that I'd been correct about all three.

"I'm willing," replied the woman, who identified herself as Mrs. Seligman. This was another example of my old axiom at work. Here was a woman who was thrilled at the prospect of having her name in print. It didn't matter that my "novel" could turn out to be a Harlequin romance. After about ten seconds had passed, the man also agreed to participate, albeit somewhat more reluctantly. That was a relief, for this would not have been a good time for my axiom to be disproved.

Before long, Tomquist was having cold feet. "Say, could we possibly do this after dinner; or, better yet, how about tomorrow morning?" But I wasn't letting him off the hook; so I countered, "Why don't we eat our dinner, and then we can talk during dessert and coffee. Does that sound good?" Mrs. Seligman was so willing to participate that she had unwittingly helped me trap Tomquist into going along.

We ate dinner without any conversation. Although, periodically, Mrs. Seligman would break the silence by saying to one of her waitstaff or to no one in particular, "Isn't that a lovely presentation," or "my that is a delicious dish." For his part, Tomquist was completely silent during his meal.

After we had ordered our dessert, I said, "I think this would be a good time to begin. So, if you don't mind, I'll ask you three questions to which I'd like you each to respond in turn."

"I'm ready," Mrs. Seligman blurted. "This is really exciting, young man."

"Okay then, my first question is, 'How long have you been coming to The Balsams'?"

Mrs. Seligman didn't waste a second before she answered, "I've been coming up here for more than seventy years. My grandparents and parents first took me here as a little girl. Then, after I married my husband, he and I came every year together until he died in 1990." With that she removed a white lace handkerchief from her evening bag and dabbed at the corner of her eyes.

"And what about you, Mr. . . ?

"Tomquist." he said. "My name is Richard Tomquist." So, the R in R. Johan stood for Richard. This was the same guy Warn had told me about. By now, Warn would also know that this was his former employee and possibly, just possibly, the man who had escaped justice for murdering Warn's niece. I had to suppress a cold shiver that had designs on my spine.

"First time," Tomquist said.

"First time?" I repeated.

"Yeah, this is the first time I've been here." And then, after thinking about whether he should continue, he added, "I used to work here."

It was Mrs. Seligman who registered surprise. "You did? What did you do here, young man?"

"I was in maintenance."

This was a huge disclosure, one that I'd need to act upon before turning in for the night. I really wanted a look at his personnel file.

"Did you work here a long time ago?" I asked. I had to be careful lest I drive him away before I had the chance to ask a more important question.

"I left about ten years ago," he replied matter-of-factly.

I felt it best to change the subject. "Okay, here's my second question: 'Why The Balsams?' Each of you could have spent your money on any other property in New Hampshire or, for that matter, at a resort anywhere. Why did you come here?"

Again, Mrs. Seligman responded first. "This place is a tradition for me. Each part of the hotel ilicits wonderful memories. The people who run this hotel have done a marvelous job of keeping this place much as it was years ago. Yes, they've modernized a few things. . . those new keys and such. But, the important things have remained much the same: the beautiful maroon carpeting with the cabbage roses, the Captain's Study with the books and all of the wonderful memorabilia, the portraits of past owners, the chef's medallions . . . it's simply wonderful here. But, of course, I'd be lying if I told you that the food wasn't an important reason I come here. I've stayed at five-star resorts and they've been wonderful. But, to me, the food here is every bit as good and I'm always made to feel comfortable. Besides, the price is right. Let's face it, I'm an old lady on a fixed income." Then smiling, she added, "It may be a large one; but it is fixed." Smiling, I looked at Tomquist out of the corner of my eye and could have sworn I'd seen him drool. "Paying two to three hundred dollars a night for two months may seem like a lot, but it's all about quality and value. Quality and value . . . that's what my grandfather always said." At this point, Tomquist made an audible groan and, unfortunately, failed to stifle what he was thinking.

"Holy crap, lady. I'm not believing you. You're whining about a fixed income, and you can afford to stay here for sixty nights at three hundred per?" Then Tomquist let out a loud, obnoxious whistle. But, he wasn't finished with his commentary. "How much is that, Professor?" But, before I could respond, he'd figured it out for himself. "That's almost twenty G's after taxes. Lady, you must have more money than Ft. Knox."

I needed to come to poor Mrs. Seligman's rescue. So I pressed him for his own response to my question. "And what about you Mr. Tomquist . . . er . . . Richard?"

"My story sure ain't the same as this old lady's. I came here because I wanted to see if it's as good as it looks on the other side of the tracks. I worked for snooty people like her, day after day, until I was fi..." He paused, and appeared to be admonishing himself for what he had nearly allowed to slip. "I wanted to see if it was as good as it looked. I wanted to see if the . . ." Then, inexplicably, he stopped talking.

But, why had he stopped? Tomquist certainly hadn't been shy about speaking his mind up to this point. I wanted to prod him, to get him to open up to me; but, I needed to be careful. "Wanted to see what, Mr. Tomquist?" I asked. Then, using the first principle of interrogation–namely flattery–I added, "You are a very interesting person, sir. I'd like to pick your brain some more."

"Not in mixed company," he mumbled, as he looked at Mrs. Seligman out of the corner of his eye. "What I have to say isn't for the ears of a lady like her." The inflection in his last phrase reeked of sarcasm.

Mrs. Seligman, for her part, was beginning to feel very uncomfortable with the younger man's comments. And who could blame her. Now the prospect of being in my novel had been completely overpowered by her primal urge to escape from a man who, if not dangerous, was certainly too crass for her tastes. Rising as fast as her eighty year old joints would permit, she thanked me for a most interesting evening, then walked slowly away without so much as a glance in Tomquist's direction.

Before Mrs. Seligman was completely out of earshot, Tomquist bellowed, "I hate people like that!"

"Like what?" I asked, trying to mask my repugnance for his rude behavior, while swallowing the feeling of self-loathing I had for encouraging this worthless jerk while Nya lay alone in our room suffering from my lack of attention toward her.

"You know, born rich . . .a real concern with class." He offered the last while pushing his nose into the air and extending his pinky finger. "She probably never worked a day in her life, and she's got more money than God. Besides, I'll bet her husband died of boredom."

At that moment, I found myself briefly reflecting again on my own marital situation. Could Nya die of boredom; was I slowly killing my wife with my own self-absorption? Certainly tonight's episode had been Nya's final cry for help. But, was there a cure for our marital woes; or, were we about to simply dissolve everything?

Tomquist's next words snapped me back to reality. "You want to know why I really came here? You got a few minutes? 'Cause I've got a story that will really juice up that book of yours. They say that truth is better than fiction, don't they?"

"Close enough, Tomquist, close enough," I thought, as we left the dining room in search of a quiet place to talk. All I wanted was an opportunity to take full advantage of the effect of the after-dinner drinks I'd been plying him with. But, my feelings of guilt had not been suppressed completely. "What am I doing? Nya's going to have a fit when she sees this tab." That is, if she would ever speak to me again after the day's events.

Chapter 42

From all reports, Billy Fenton couldn't shake his obsession with Edna Connor. The question was how far he'd take it. I had only seen the man briefly; but, he was one of the sleaziest guys I'd ever set eyes upon. I asked myself how this guy could have possibly slid under Sue Nesson's radar. Sure, she didn't have all of his records, but look at this guy! Then I remembered an incident that had occurred in my department at the college. Three of us were interviewing applicants for a secretary position. The final interviewee arrived dressed conservatively and handled questions as if they'd been scripted for her. I remembered thinking that it was time to start engraving the secretary of the year award. She was a slam dunk, a real pro. So, we offered her the job, which she'd accepted. A week later, when I walked into the office to get my mail, the senior department secretary greeted me with a shrug and a roll of the eyes. I was completely without a frame of reference for her actions . . . but not for long. Our new hiree had changed from Dr. Jeckle to I Want to Hide. The composed woman we had interviewed a week before had become loud, obnoxious, even surly. So, in this frame of reference, I offered a silent apology to the Susan Nessons of the world. Personnel work, in this day and age, is no walk in the park.

★   ★   ★

Billy was still obsessing about the woman in 167 when he took his lunch break on July 11th. "Jeezus, but her tits are big!" he had told his partner Tony in the cafeteria. While Billy really didn't know Tony very well, he was obsessed with Edna Connor and had to share it with someone. Tony and Brian, who Billy called the wussy waiter, were the only ones in earshot as he drank a coke and picked at his hamburger and fries. "I really want her; and she wants me, too," he had told Tony. "Why else did she wink like that at me?" Tony had shrugged, "Be careful man; you know what the brass around here thinks about us even talkin' to the tourists. An' what you have in mind is a lot more than talking." But Billy wasn't looking for Tony's advice, or anyone else's. He was going to have her. "No freakin' doubt about it. The only question is where and when. And you better keep your mouth shut to the brass, Tony. You, too, asshole," he had said to Brian.

Chapter 43

Billy continued to stalk Edna during the next two days, until his chance arrived. He was on call on the night of the 13th when his quarry and the big guy from the room next door had arrived back at their adjoining rooms in the Hampshire House. Standing in the hallway outside the service elevator, Billy could see them and hear some of what they were saying. At first, he had thought the two seemed a bit uneasy with one another. The big guy had been trying to get close, even whispering something in her ear. But she began to relax more as they stood there. She had laughed and had given him a push. It hadn't been a defensive one; it was more flirtatious than anything. But then she had whispered something in his ear, and the two had laughed. While their voices were muted, given the lateness of the hour, Billy thought he'd heard the big guy say something like, "Are you sure, darling?," and the woman had nodded. The big guy had said, "Now don't you go anywhere; I'll be right back." And the two had laughed and kissed. In Billy's mind, it was the way a man and a woman acted before they were going to do the deed.

Next, the big guy made his way back toward the elevator. He'd had too much to drink to negotiate the stairs; so he pushed the elevator button. As he stood waiting for the elevator in the Hampshire House to arrive, he muttered in a voice that was just loud enough for Billy to hear, "Please be open; please." With that, the elevator door closed and the big man disappeared. With the way clear, Billy looked back toward room 167. The hallway was empty. "She's gone into her room to get ready. I guess it's now or never." So leaving his tool belt and jacket behind the door leading to the service elevator, he quietly made his way toward her room, his heart beating like a conga drum.

Billy knocked. The woman's voice betrayed amusement. "That was fast Richard." Without looking through the peephole to verify her assumption, she opened the door, and Billy Fenton, wearing his yellow toothy grin, stepped inside and closed the door behind him.

Chapter 44

9 P.M., Saturday, July 15th. Warn Barson was sitting in his apartment that abuts the Dixville House. He was like a bachelor for the two weeks that Nancy had been away. Sitting in a pair of pajama bottoms, he had to smile in spite of the mood he was in. "Look at me sitting around like this; I'd never do this if Nancy or your sister were here." The person he was saying this to didn't need convincing. Tom Barson couldn't remember the last time he had seen his father without his shirt on. But now, as the two men sat, each sipping a glass of Johnny Walker Red on the rocks, neither man was in the best frame of mind.

"I'm telling you, dad, this business with Edna Connor has disaster written all over it. What if your buddy Kary screws up? He's not a detective, you know."

"I'm well aware of what Kary Turnell is and is not," Warn lectured his son. Then, sensing that his tone had been too harsh, he added, "But you're right to be concerned."

"Why are you handling things this way?" Tom asked.

Warn paused and took a long drink of his scotch before answering his son, as he groped for the words he wanted. Then, placing his glass on the cork coaster that protected the teak table he and Nancy had bought during their honeymoon in eastern Africa, he said, "You'll have to trust me on this, Tom."

"But, why involve him at all?"

"Look Tom, I shouldn't need to remind you, once the state police show up, no one around here will have any privacy. I know we're taking a risk by not reporting this now, but it's a chance we have to take."

"But, why not just check things out ourselves?" Tom asked. "Why involve Kary?"

"Can you imagine trying to dig up any information around here ourselves, Tom? Think about it. You were in diapers when a lot of these people were hired. You told Grenda about your first crush two months before mom and I knew about it. These people are like our extended family. So tell me, how do you think people would respond if you and I went around asking a bunch of questions, and then clammed up when they wanted to know why we were asking?" And before Tom could say anything, Warn added, "Frankly, I'm more concerned about protecting The Balsams family than I am about anything else. There are a lot of households that depend on the stability of this place."

"But, what do you think will happen if the professor comes up empty and then a body is found. Aren't you worried that our employees will see this as a betrayal of their trust?"

"I guess I'm prepared to take that risk," Warn replied.

Then Tom looked his father square in the eyes and asked, "Is there something else you're not telling me, Dad?"

"Look Tom, I do have another reason for handling things as I am; and, I promise I'll tell you everything when the time is right."

"Okay Dad, I'll have to trust your judgment." Tom Barson was having difficulty masking his concern for his father's welfare. In all the years he could remember, he hadn't seen his father looking this melancholy. Warn Barson was a born fighter, the same man who had convinced a wealthy corporate head that he was the man to run The Balsams, despite the fact that formal training in resort management was lacking. However, Tom also knew that Warn Barson was a sensitive man, one of those rare people who really could feel the pain of a loved one, or an old friend. If he was being cryptic and a bit glum, he must be worried about someone, or something. But who or what? Perhaps the answer lay in his relationship with the professor. Tom tried one more time to find out. "Dad, I have to admit that I still don't understand why you haven't asked the security guys to help Kary."

"Don't sell Kary short, Tom. Remember, he spent years as a crime writer, and he teaches criminology. He has the investigative skills and, unlike anyone else who's in Dixville, we can trust him to keep confidence with us," Warn said.

"But, how can you be sure?" Tom asked.

"Because he's one of my oldest friends and, besides, he doesn't have all of the built-in loyalties that that everyone else has. Now please, Tom, let's drop this."

Tom sat for a few minutes and sipped his drink, while discreetly monitoring his father. Warn seemed to be a million miles away. When Warn failed to respond to one of Tom's barbs about the latest collapse of the Fenway gang, the latter's concern for his father's well-being had been augmented. "Dad." No response. "Dad!" Finally, the father looked up at his son. "Is everything all right . . . I mean, are you and Mom okay?"

Warn laughed softly at his son's last query. "Yes, Tom, everything is fine with your mother and me. Except, of course, that I miss the heck out of her."

But Tom was not to be discouraged. "Then what is it, Dad?" No response.

"Okay son, if you must know, I don't know if I'm still the right man to run this place." As tough as it was to say this, for now, it was better than telling Tom that Richard Tomquist was back at The Balsams.

Chapter 45

9:15 P.M., Saturday, July 15th. I felt as though my head were going to explode. Richard Tomquist wasn't the sleaziest jerk I'd ever met, but he was certainly a medallist. As tempted as I was to go up and check on Nya, I just had to follow through with this. I'd taken things too far, even spent about twenty bucks to get this guy in a talkative frame of mind. Besides, Nya had been fast asleep when I left for dinner. I'd quietly said goodnight as I'd left. But the only sound I'd heard was the tall pole fan that was circulating the air in our room.

Tomquist was a large man, but did not appear to be particularly fit. He was about six feet three and maybe two hundred sixty pounds. With his sports jacket open and his tie askew, you could see that he was sporting a fairly large gut. Nonetheless, he was certainly big and strong enough to handle a middle age housewife with ease.

"Okay Professor, so you want to know why I came here. I used to work here, d'ya know that?" Richard emptied his glass as he finished speaking.

"Yes, you just told me that," I replied. Clearly Richard Tomquist was feeling very little pain. I was concerned, lest he pass out without allowing me to complete my questioning. "Earlier you told me that you'd come here to see what it was like on the other side of the tracks. Is that all there was to it?"

"Other side of the tracks. Ha ha ha! Other side of the tracks. Yeah, that's it Professor; the other side of the tracks." Tomquist was becoming loud and even more obnoxious than he had been while sober. I was concerned, lest he'd attract the attention of a guest, or worse, a staff member. If that had happened, they would have insisted upon taking him to his room to sleep it off. I didn't have time for that. It was nearly 11PM; I had only thirteen hours to try to figure out what had happened to Edna Connor.

"Truth be told," Tomquist was now speaking with his eyes closed; he was rapidly giving in to the effects of the alcohol. Given his size, I was a bit surprised. I had been careful to cut him off after three glasses of booze. He should have been able to handle that. Was this a ruse? Or perhaps he wasn't normally a drinker. Maybe this had been the first time in a while. I decided to find out.

"Geez, Richard, you can sure put the booze away; you must go drinking a lot."

"Nah! Would you believe that's the first alcohol I've had in about a year? Other than two nights ago," he offered.

Now we were getting somewhere. "Really," I asked, "did you go drinking two nights ago?"

But he was on to another subject. "Broads," he said in an even louder voice than before. "I came here to feast on rich broads. People don't realize that they're even easier than the poor ones. Only the rich ones take a guy into the sack, and they think it's all their idea. If a guy plays it smart and acts like he's being led, he can have a field day at a joint like this."

This was just the information I had been hoping to pull from Tomquist. But now, I wanted him to get back to two nights before. Had he been drinking with Edna Connor?

"So what happened the other night, Richard?" I queried.

"When?" he replied.

This wasn't looking very promising. "Come on Richard, you know, you said that you went drinking with some woman two nights ago. What was that all about?"

He was practically in a stupor. I had to do something. I opted to slap him upside the head.

"Ow, shit! Whadya do that for?"

"Sorry Richard. But you have to stay with me, at least until you finish your story."

He was becoming increasingly disoriented. "Sure, Professor, but what story?"

"The one about the woman you were with the other night," I prodded. Clearly this was my last chance.

"Oh yeah . . .the woman next shtoor." His speech was becoming increasingly slurred.

"She was staying in the room next to yours, Richard?" I asked.

"Yeah, table nesht to mine, too."

"Tell me about her." I shook him. "Richard, I said tell me about her!"

"Nice lady. Lonely. Big tits." Richard slumped over and nearlt hit his head on the bar.

"Damn!" I said out loud. This sure hadn't been my day. Now, what was Tomquist about to tell me? Had he done anything wrong? All I had was questions with very few answers. Tomquist had had dinner with Edna. They had, according to his story, been drinking a lot. He had wanted to seduce her and may well have. But did this make him a killer?

Chapter 46

11:30 P.M. I was really wired. There was no way I was going to get to sleep. The combination of alcohol and coffee was working like a stimulant. I decided to go to the billiard parlor just down the hall from where Richard, now snoring loudly, was found by a passing night watchman. At that late hour, there certainly would be no problem getting a table. In fact, I expected the place to be empty. To my surprise, there was someone else shooting pool. I couldn't see who he was because he had his back to me, but it was obvious he had been practicing. Ignoring him, I pulled about five balls from the leather pockets of the first table to the right of the entrance and simply picked up the stick that someone had left lying on the table. By luck it was a twenty-ounce cue, my weapon of choice. I moved the cue ball down to the far end, leaving my back to the other shooter. I lined up on the yellow, number one ball and missed the pocket by two inches. As a further indignity, I had scratched on the cue ball. I walked along the left side of the table, when I heard a familiar voice, "I didn't know you were a pool hustler, Professor." It was Tom Barson.

"Not hardly," I replied. "I used to play a lot, but my game took leave with my eyesight."

"You want to play a game?" he asked. But I wasn't interested. "Me either; I'm actually pretty tired," he said.

"I know the feeling," I replied. "This has been quite a day, hasn't it?"

"For both my father and you."

"Warn? He sure has his hands full," I offered. "Of course, you can hardly blame him. This Connor business has to be weighing very heavily on his mind. Yours too, for that matter." For the time being, I'd elected to keep my interrogation of Tomquist to myself.

"Yeah, I'm concerned about her disappearance, too." Tom's voice betrayed a deeper anxiety. He looked at me and, for an instant, it appeared he was going to unburden himself. But when he spoke, he said, "Dad really cares about this old place, Professor."

"And I'm sure you do too, Tom," I said.

"Yeah, but it isn't the same. This place is like an elderly relative to my father; and the staff are like . . . like his aunts, uncles, nieces, and nephews. I worry that it would kill him if anything happened to The Balsams."

There was a lesson to be derived from his delivery of this message. "Listen Tom, I can't promise you that I can solve Mrs. Connor's disappearance, but I can promise you that I'm not going to do anything to make the situation worse. Your dad's friendship is too important to me."

Tom stepped closer. I couldn't read from his face whether he was going to hit me or hug me. Instead he simply extended his right hand. When I accepted this gesture, he placed his left hand on my shoulder and said softly, "I know that, Professor."

This was probably the one bright spot in my entire day. Unfortunately, Tom had more to say: "Professor, there's more." I didn't grasp what Tom was saying at first. Realizing this, he continued, "Dad is second-guessing himself. I'm afraid he may walk out of here."

"You mean quit . . . Warn's thinking about leaving The Balsams?!"

Tom whispered, "Shh!"

I immediately looked around to see if anyone had overheard; but we seemed to be alone. "I know he's been really upset about all this. But, shit, we all feel that way at some time in our lives. Some more than others. How could he have reached this state?" It was meant as a rhetorical statement.

"I'm not sure. But, I think it would be a tragedy, for both my dad and The Balsams."

"Tom, I want you to know I'm here to do anything I can for Warn. I hope you'll call on me."

He said that he would. Although, I'm not certain he really meant what he said. As I turned to leave, he called to me, "Professor, I almost forgot. I have a message for you."

"Message?" At that late hour, I couldn't guess what the message could be about.

"Yeah, my father said to tell you that both the male guest and Mrs. Connor had made table reservations at the night club last night."

"Interesting. Separate reservations or a single reservation?"

"They sat together," he replied.

"That's helpful, really helpful, Tom. I'd better grab a few hours of shuteye, because I'd wager that tomorrow is going to be an interesting day.

★   ★   ★

11:54 P.M. I opened the door to our room and undressed in the dark. I was glad that I'd had the presence of mind to leave my pajamas laid out on the second bed. I finished dressing and reached for the covers. Something small slid from the bed and hit me in the foot. "What the heck," I said to myself. I reached down and picked up a shiny object about the size and shape of an old half dollar. Instinctively, I smelled it. "Chocolate, oh no," I said aloud. This was a hell of a time to realize that I'd forgotten to put the Privacy Please sign into the key card slot when I'd left. This meant that the turndown service had arrived and, seeing one bed occupied, simply turned down my bed. I wondered if Nya had been awakened by their intrusion. I was tired. And, as I drifted off to sleep, I wondered if the housekeeping staff was, at that very moment, discussing the dysfunctional couple in room 264.

Chapter 47

According to Katyana, Richard and Edna had remained seated at their own tables during the dinner hour, both on the 12th and the 13th. Edna was concerned about appearances; besides, she'd just met this large man with the nice khaki suit two nights before. And, of course, there was Al. While Edna knew she still loved her husband, it had become increasingly apparent that his idea of marriage was about having a clean house and three square meals. Al would come home late six nights a week after spending each day in the seven by six room he called his office. He'd give her a peck on the cheek or the forehead, but never on the lips. They would sit down to dinner and he'd read the paper; and perhaps they would discuss what each of them had done that day. Edna had never been sure whether Al was listening. He'd nod and mumble things like "umm hmm" or "that so?" One night, Edna had said, "Al, don't you find me attractive anymore?"

Al had replied, "Of course you're attractive, Edna. You know I enjoy looking at you."

Exasperated, Edna had growled, "Well, I'm tired of just being looked at, Al Connor!"

To which, Al had replied, "umm hmm".

For his part, Richard instinctively recognized that there was some reticence on the part of his latest quarry to submit to his "charms." As he had gotten older, he'd begun to regard the chase as more fun than the actual act. Now in his late thirties, Richard's very average looks hadn't improved. His hair, although still dark black, was thinning, making it more and more difficult to disguise his bald spot. He was especially troubled by the hair growing in places where it shouldn't, and went to great pains and expense to purchase gadgets and creams designed to remove his unwanted body, ear and nose hair. While Richard's enthusiasm for the chase had escalated, his ability to deal with rejection had diminished. The last time, he'd even scared himself. Now, as he waited for Edna to arrive in the dining room, he shuddered at the thought of how close he had come to really losing it. "That was terrible," he muttered to himself. Richard had been chasing his favorite quarry, a redhead, for more than a month. Finally, the woman, a thirty-five year old secretary, had agreed to have dinner with Richard. They'd gotten along fine. She seemed to find him very interesting; and he'd been very interested in her. After dinner, they had taken in a movie, a remake of "Roller Ball." Richard had really enjoyed the original, but the two were equally and vocally disappointed in the newer version. However, when his date made comments like "That one character's pants were so tight you could plainly see his privates," Richard began to smell an opening. When he offered to take her for a drive to a place where "it's dark enough to see the city lights," she had consented. As they drove, Richard began to quiver slightly, so sure was he that he was nearing a conquest. When they stopped the car, she had permitted him to kiss her on the lips. Soon they were both participating enthusiastically. However, when Richard tried to slide his hand between her knees, she had pulled back and said, "Whoa partner, we're moving just a little too fast." But Richard wasn't about to take no for an answer. Besides, from his distorted point of view, she really wanted it, too. She wasn't wearing a bra nor stockings; and the top she wore was low cut . . . what else could he think? Despite the fact that it was a hot, humid night, Richard figured there was only one reason why she was showing him so much of her skin. So, using his size and strength, he had attempted to pull her onto his lap. But the woman had kept her wits about her. For a moment she had pretended to submit; but, when he let his guard down briefly, she buried the spiked heel of her shoe into his shin. Having temporarily disabled Richard, the woman got out and ran away.

Then, another thought that he had long repressed resurfaced without warning. But Richard shook his head to hold it at bay. Now he could feel the sweat on his brow as he walked. "Cool it, Richard," he told himself. "This one will be different. From what I heard Edna say to that young waitress, her husband's been ignoring her. If I play my cards right, this will be easy; she's really starving for it."

★   ★   ★

Their evening together on Thursday, the 13th had started quite well, at least as far as Edna was concerned. Richard had acted like a real gentleman. They continued to talk about some of the things they had spoken about during dinner the previous night. Edna learned that Richard had never been married, but that he had been born into wealth. He told her he was a very successful businessman whose holdings included mineral rights in Alaska, Norway and the Middle East, all of which he visited frequently. When Edna asked if Richard was married to his work like her husband, he had replied, "No. And if I'm ever fortunate enough to have a woman like you in my life, I won't be foolish enough to leave her alone for very long." Edna felt as though she were in the company of a man who knew how to treat a woman. And, even when Richard fed her the line, "When I look at you, I can see a woman whose passions have been bottled up; surely there must be hope that your husband will open his eyes and discover them," her enthusiasm had not diminished one iota. Later that night, they had strolled arm-in-arm from the dining room to the ballroom. Here they had sat and talked. As Richard purchased first one bottle of wine, then a second, they began to hold hands, then to dance very close, the tips of his fingers resting on her firm, generous bottom. Others around them, spying her wedding ring, were convinced they were a loving, married couple. They were the last to leave the ballroom that night. It had taken them a while to negotiate the stairway leading up to the nightclub's entryway; for, by this time, the dual effect of fatigue and alcohol had impacted their navigation skills. These, after all, were not habitual drinkers. Richard had not taken a drink in more than a year, while Edna had seldom consumed more than an occasional glass of sherry to help her sleep. Next, Richard had suggested that they walk up one flight of stairs then traverse the hallway that led to the Hampshire House. The corridors were completely deserted, save for a solitary maintenance worker who appeared to be fixing something near the service elevator. Neither Richard nor Edna paid him any mind. Richard's hand had become attached to Edna's butt like a barnacle. At the same time, Edna was holding Richard's arm and laughing at the suggestive remarks he was making in her ear. As they arrived at her door, Richard had looked into her eyes and announced his intentions. However, the pronouncement of what he wanted to do had an immediate sobering effect upon Edna. She had to think fast, because, while she was tremendously flattered by Richard's attention, she needed to reflect upon his proposition for a moment. It was clear to her that her escort had other expectations. While Edna needed to think, she did not want to lose the attention she had been receiving. Then, at once, she had a plan. "Richard, darling, I'd like to have some champagne; and I really could use some aspirin."

"Champagne! Aspirin!" he blurted. Then calming himself forcibly, he added, "We've already had two bottles of wine, my dear. Don't you think that was enough?"

"Please. You would make me so happy," she giggled.

It was only when Richard remembered that he had forgotten to purchase a package of condoms that he agreed to Edna's errand. So, he sighed and made his way to the elevator. As the elevator came up to meet him, Richard muttered aloud, "Please be open; please, please."

Chapter 48

6:20 A.M., Sunday, July 16th. I was awakened by the sound of drawers opening and closing. The next thing I knew, the door to the bathroom was being closed sharply. I groaned softly. After all of these years of marriage, if I'd learned anything, this was a signal that my wife was not happy with me. It always had been easy to tell when Nya was in a good mood, which has been most of the time . . . but certainly not this particular morning. Normally, she walked around the house as though her feet were swathed in cotton. Doors and drawers were gently opened and closed. However, when Nya became angry, she moved around like a storm trooper. Furniture would be dragged, doors banged, and the expression on her face could make Arnold Schwarzenegger cower. July 16th was looking like one of those mornings. Having finished in the bathroom, she stormed out, the door banging hard against the doorstop. I sat up in bed but was being ignored.

"Good morning, sweetheart." That was way too cheerily.

Silence.

"Good morning," I repeated. Less cheerily.

"Oh yes, hello, Kary." Her tone was ice cold.

"Are you feeling better this morning?" I foolishly asked.

Her response was indistinguishable; so I asked again.

"Yeah, I'm feeling just terrific," she said.

"Listen, Nya," I began, "I'm really sorry about . . ."

"Don't!" she said. Now she was looking me square in the eyes. The expression on her face was positively threatening. "Don't you dare!"

I didn't know whether to be scared or relieved, although the former appeared to be the more sensible response. As strange as it may sound now, I was relieved. Knowing Nya as I do, the fact that she was this angry meant that there was still some feeling left for me. It may have been an "I'd like to kill this stupid bastard" feeling, but it was all I had to go on at that moment.

"Won't you please listen?" I asked. Shit, I was whining.

"Look, Professor Itsallaboutme, I know you are working on something for Warn and I know that you feel that this must come first, because of your terrific sense of loyalty to your friend."

"That's true, but . . ."

"But, when does your loyalty extend to your marriage . . . to your wife? You knew perfectly well when we came up here that I was hoping we could recapture what we once had. But then you went to visit Warn and just disappeared."

"But you were busy, too."

"Bull shit, Kary! Bull shit. You and your friend concocted something to keep me busy while you had a chance to do whatever your old friend needs. I feel like a fool having poor Lynn come all the way up here just to baby sit me." Nya was absolutely fuming. However, I still felt the need to explain.

"I had nothing to do with you working on . . ." I offered.

". . .You know what, Kary, it doesn't matter. It just doesn't matter any more. What does matter is how I'm going to feel later today, tomorrow, and for the rest of my life."

The way she emphasized the word *my* had scored a direct hit. "Don't you mean *our* lives, Nya.

"Right now, I just don't know, Kary. I've waited, how long now, for you to start being the kind of husband you promised to be on our wedding day. I've put up with your drinking, the sulking and, worst of all, your inattention. But, I'm tired. You've worn me out, Kary. Your preoccupation with yourself has beaten us both. You gave up long ago; but I've been a bit slow. It's taken me longer to see that this is a battle I can't win."

"Please, Nya," I tried to say more, but the words just wouldn't come. I reached for her arm, but she pulled away. She was dressed now. I was still in my pajamas, and was unable to stop her before she opened the door and stepped into the hallway, closing the door behind her.

As I stood alone in the room, I became aware of something I hadn't experienced since I was a boy. Tears were streaming down my face.

Chapter 49

4 P.M., Thursday, July 13th. When the telephone in Al Connor's office had rung, he'd expected it to be Grady Fraser from the landfill. Grady and Al had agreed to discuss a project they were working on, and this was the one time they could actually get together. Al and Grady were the two hardest working stiffs in western Massachusetts, at least to Al's way of thinking. The two had respected one another for years, but had never had the opportunity to work together on a special project. Sure they had discussed things plenty of times, but this was a once in a lifetime opportunity. They had learned about the project two weeks earlier, but Al had decided to wait until Edna went to The Balsams, so he could devote all evening to the project without worrying about Edna. When the phone rang, Al was prepared to answer with his patented, "Hey! you buzzard," which he always used when he could be sure it was Grady calling.

Only, it wasn't Grady on the other end at all. It was Edna; and she sounded overwrought. When Al told, rather than asked Edna, "Hey, I'll bet you're having a good time up there," he hadn't been prepared for Edna's response. No, this was the last thing he'd expected when he packed his wife up and shipped her to such a nice resort. It was true that Edna had been spending time with another man. But, because she still loved Al, Edna couldn't suppress the guilt she was feeling about the attention she was receiving from the man staying in the room next door. So, she told Al how the large man in the nice suit had been bathing her in attention and how they had made plans to have dinner together that evening. No, she had said, he hadn't been anything but a perfect gentleman . . . at least up until then.

★   ★   ★

There's nothing quite like the attention of another man, or woman, to suddenly awaken one spouse to the virtues of another. Al Connor had been without a rival his entire married life. But, as he sat in his office, he was in a brand new place. Now the important deal with Grady Fraser was the farthest thing from his mind. All he could think about was the woman who he had always relegated to the background. Al Connor had been an analytical man. It was his ability to carefully analyze that led him to make decisions that resulted in profits. He had used these same skills to select a serviceable woman like Edna. And, as the years passed, she became just one element in his life's plan. But never, at least before ten minutes ago, had Al thought about Edna as flesh and blood; never had he paid heed to her desires. As was his nature, it didn't take Al long to decide a course of action. He let the phone ring a second time. Then he arose, shut off the light in his office, locked the door and walked to his car. Opening the car door, he sat in the driver's seat and put on his seat belt. Before starting the car, Al checked to see if the glove compartment contained what he needed. He immediately felt the flashlight; removing it, he checked to be certain the batteries were still working. They were. Feeling around once more, he removed a small heavy object from the compartment and placed it on the seat next to him. Satisfied that he still had the old New England road map, he closed the compartment. Then Al realized that he hadn't put the heavy object away. He again unlatched the glove compartment door and replaced it, but not before being certain that he'd checked the safety on his small revolver.

Chapter 50

7:20 A.M., Sunday, July 16th. I must admit that I was feeling lower than whale crap when I left our room. I walked down a flight of stairs, then cut across to the Dixville House. If my picture was still absent from the Wall of Fame, I must confess that I didn't notice. My head was swimming and my stomach was churning. Thoughts of Nya were interspersed with those about Edna Connor. As I walked along past Hogan's Alley, where some of The Balsams staff resided, I was being torn apart from the inside. What was eating at me was that Nya was absolutely right. Just throw good old Kary Turnell an assignment to feed his ego, and he'll send his wife off to play second fiddle. The last several days had been a microcosm of our marriage. I'd been an idiot for years. I was the one who forgot to call Nya the night we were supposed to announce our engagement because the Inquirer had a juicy assignment for me. And I'd forgotten her birthday more than once. Was it my indifference that she'd found interesting all of these years? I remembered something her mother once told me: The more the boys chased, the more Nya ran away. But I hadn't chased after Nya; I'd been too busy worrying about Kary Turnell. I sure had taken good care of myself; I'd married a wonderful woman, someone who was committed to loving and being loved. Standing there on the staircase, I was beginning to see that Nya hadn't married such a wonderful man. But, was I was overreacting? Why had Nya waited thirty years to say anything? The answer was obvious; she hadn't waited at all. She had been sending me signals that I just wasn't reading. After a while, she must have been caught in that place between inertia and the outside chance for a miraculous change in personality on the part of her mate. Nya's situation wasn't all that dissimilar to that of a battered wife who keeps coming back for more because she thinks things will change. By coming back, these women are enabling the worthless bums they've married to do the same things all over again. Was I really any better than a wife beater? After all, neglect is a form of abuse. As I walked along, I had to ask myself if Edna Connor's disappearance had been some kind of sign. Perhaps this episode was actually the turning point Nya had been seeking. But where was the turn taking us?

Chapter 51

7:30AM. Warn's morning was off to a similar start to mine. As he covered the one hundred yards from his apartment to The Balsams' main entrance, Warn felt a compelling urge to turn around and go home. This feeling had frightened him; in all of his years working at the resort, or anywhere else for that matter, he had never lacked the motivation to do his job. Even the army had not brought out such feelings. The fact is, Warn Barson had always loved the idea of going to work and, to his lasting good fortune, had always taken jobs that he enjoyed. Throughout the years, he had questioned on more than one occasion whether Mr. Tillson had made a mistake by putting him in charge. Because he was such a kind, sensitive man, one might presume that a person like Warn lacked the thick skin necessary to deal with the everyday trials and tribulations incumbent in such a responsibility. But Warn was special. He had an IQ that would be the envy of most academics; and, unlike some of the latter, he'd been blessed with extraordinary common sense.

Long before the circumstances of that July, Warn had divided the principle tasks of running a resort into three categories. First, of course, were the everyday issues of running The Balsams; Warn had labeled these his compulsories. Compulsories included staying on top of general wear-and-tear, being proactive about the demands of a fickle travel industry, marketing, and the countless other activities that any resort hotel-or, any business for that matter-must tackle. For Warn these were a piece of cake; the people he had hired as department heads were the best in the business. He had worked with the majority of these people for more than two decades, and some even longer. Each was fastidious about his or her responsibilities; and Warn himself had natural organizational skills that seldom failed him. So, no, the compulsories were not what Warn was wrestling with on the morning of July 16.

The second issue was a two-headed dragon that Warn had called staff comportment and staff welfare. With very few exceptions, comportment was seldom an issue at the resort. New hires were screened as carefully as the letter of the law would allow; and each had been well trained in the do's and don'ts of staff behavior. It was expected that a staff member would be well informed, helpful and courteous-both to guests and fellow staff. Then of course, there was the ironclad rule that forbade fraternizing with guests. Warn was aware that a substantial percentage of the waitstaff were young, single people who had given up their summer vacation to work at the resort. He was also aware that a number of them had no intention of returning during the following season. However, each had to understand that no exception would be made to that rule, even for administrators. For his part, Warn had been the perfect example. His long marriage and well-adjusted kids were a living testimonial to the behavior The Balsams espoused. Throughout the years, whenever he and Nancy had been apart, Warn had missed his wife terribly. Despite occasional temptations that may have surfaced, Warn had remained faithful; and, he presumed, Nancy had been no different. As for the resort's staff, there had been a handful of behavioral problems over the years; but only one person had really been a blatant abuser, and that had been more than ten years before. Just a few days earlier, Warn had wrestled with that young maintenance worker's name. Finally, it had been Rolf Verdue who had remembered that the walking paradox was named Richard Tomquist. Yes, the same Richard who had been so capable with his hands, but so careless about where he'd put them. Amazingly, comportment had not been an issue at the resort for an entire decade. However, the name of Billy Fenton had been surfacing too frequently during the short time the young man had been employed at the resort. It would be Rolf's responsibility to rein in young Mr. Fenton. The comportment issue was on a number of minds following July 13. As Warn thought about Edna Connor's disappearance, his attitude swung between hope and conviction that none of his staff was remotely involved.

The other head of the dragon was concerning Warn greatly. Staff welfare was about more than providing a decent wage and good health benefits. The Balsams was like a small city, or more like a community. Because the staff of 500 seemed to know a great deal about one another's business . . . and the department heads had been counseled about rumor mongering . . . Warn feared that a moment's indiscretion could cause mass hysteria, just as it might engender unfounded, mass elation. Either scenario could undermine the working environment and the productivity of the entire staff. Therefore, Warn regarded both as threats to the performance of the resort. In this context, he regarded the Edna Connor situation as a time bomb waiting to go off. And, if it did, the working environment at The Balsams would be a shambles. Now, as he walked into the hotel, Warn said so only he could hear, "Kary just has to find something." Then looking at his watch, he added, "in only four and a half hours."

As Warn entered his office, his thoughts turned to the third principle of running a resort. With this, he felt a growing ache in his stomach. "Our guests," he said audibly. Although Nancy had always called Warn a people person, there had been days during his tenure at the resort when he'd questioned the veracity of such a statement. The normal day-to-day problems that any business has when serving the public were exacerbated ten-fold at a resort hotel. People generally arrive at The Balsams in need of relaxation. They come to the resort to escape the rat race or the hum-drum of their everyday lives. Upon arriving, in the vast majority of cases, people relaxed and let The Balsams atmosphere sweep over them. One guest had told Warn that he never knew how tight his neck muscles were all of the time until he started vacationing at The Balsams. When Warn had asked him to elaborate, the man had said, "Because the only time they don't hurt is when I'm up here." However, for every fifty contented guests, there may be one who finds it necessary to complain about things. For every ten of these, there is someone who is never satisfied; and, if the slightest detail is not just what he or she wants, that person will try to take the nearest staff member's head off. Of necessity, it had become Warn's responsibility to assuage the guest's angst, while protecting the oft fragile emotional state of his staff member. On occasion, a frothing guest has burst into Warn's office, leaving the latter to curse himself for maintaining the resort's open door policy. And on several such occasions, the offended party would employ either foul language or a loud voice, or both, while airing a complaint. In reality, when push came to shove, these visits were not really about principle, but about money. The words, "I want my money back" or "I think you should knock something off of my bill" have been spoken at least as often as, "I just wanted you to know." From Warn's perspective, there never had been a problem great enough to warrant giving a guest his or her money back. As Warn had learned years before, despite the fact that the "food didn't taste the way it looked on the display table" or "the neighbors were too loud," every guest who has ever stayed at The Balsams received more than the value purchased. So, while he might offer the complaining party an alternative solution, anyone who thought Warn was a soft touch was going to be disappointed.

Warn's office was open to the public. Therefore, it came with the territory that guests wanted to knock on his door with a complaint or, as occurred much more frequently, high praise for The Balsams' service. The occasional guest who grabbed him as he was passing through one of the public rooms was quite another matter. As any person in a service-oriented profession will tell you, when he or she is in the office or standing at the service counter, the customer has every right to make demands on your time. However, when service people are running errands or are on break, their personal space must be honored. So it is with Warn. Javy Olds told me a story about an irate guest who lay in wait and badgered Warn every time he made a visit to the registration desk. The way Javy told me, Warn was very pleasant for five days. Finally, he couldn't take it any more. After the sixth day of receiving the same treatment, he called the man in his room at one o'clock in the morning. When the man asked Warn why in hell he was calling him at that hour, Warn had calmly replied, "I apologize sir. I must have forgotten an old rule." The man had thought about this for a second before asking, "And what rule have you forgotten?" To which Warn had replied, "There's a proper time and place for everything." Needless to say, Warn wasn't badgered again by this guest for the duration of his visit, nor during the next ten years of his visits to the resort.

A few pests aside, Warn always took guest satisfaction very seriously. Like most successful tourism industry executives, he understood that the traveling public can be fickle. One small change in travel preferences or one piece of negative publicity could leave a business outside the loop. He was wise enough to see that the roadsides were littered with vacant hotels, restaurants and amusements that had failed to perceive that tastes had changed, or where customers had not been satisfied. Warn always remembered how the Chinese restaurant in his hometown had closed when an unsubstantiated rumor about using cat meat in the pepper steak had become widely circulated.

Unfortunately for the owner, Gemmy Wong, the mayor's missing pet cat had last been seen wandering in the vicinity of the restaurant. Wong's reputation never recovered, even after the stray returned home a few weeks later. Knowing how an obvious urban legend had contributed to the downfall of his favorite childhood restaurant, Warn wondered what the fallout from the Connor business would be. At the same time, he was beginning to think that it might be better for someone else to oversee the resort's future operation. All of these thoughts were playing on Warn's mind as he sat awaiting my arrival on that Sunday morning.

Chapter 52

12 A.M, Friday, July 14th. Billy Fenton could not get out of The Balsams fast enough. "Shit, oh shit. I've really done it now. I've screwed things up big time. Forget this job; forget this place; forget everything. When they find out what I've done, there won't be a big enough boot to kick me in my ass with. Well, I ain't hangin' around long enough for them to find out. I'll scram now, before anyone knows what happened. I know, I'll head up north. I can get into Canada and stay there for a month or so."

He was reaching for his car keys when it dawned on him. "Oh shit, no." Billy remembered the jacket he'd left upstairs near the service elevator on Edna Connor's floor. "I got no choice," he said aloud, "I gotta go back up there an' get my coat." He knew from his brief time working at the resort that the two night watchmen would be circulating about now. If they saw him or, worse, if they found his jacket, then he was screwed. He made his way toward the employees' entrance, on the north side of the Dixville House, hoping to avoid detection by the registration desk staff. He pulled on the door to the employees' entrance. But, it was after midnight and the door was locked. "I can't go back through the main entrance; I'll have to take my chances that one of the doors near the laundry will be open."

So, Billy walked all the way around the staff dorm, past the gift shop, and made his way to the laundry entrance. The door was open. So he made his way through the darkened laundry facility. From there, he entered the catacombs. As he started to walk, he heard one of the night watchmen coming. Muttering "Shit!" under his breath, he was forced to wait for more than twenty minutes until he could be sure that the coast was clear all the way into the basement of the Hampshire House. Finally, as he reached the basement of the Hampshire House he could hear the service elevator moving up. "What the hell?" he asked himself. But there was no time to investigate. He opted to use the stairs, but by the time he'd reached the third floor, the combination of his nervousness and a two-pack a day smoking habit had conspired to leave him heavily winded and perspiring profusely. Ten more strides and he reached the door outside the service elevator. But would his jacket still be there? He turned the corner so fast that he slipped and pulled the hamstring muscle in his left leg. Grabbing his jacket, he removed his keys. Billy was ready to bolt, but was stopped short by the sound of a door opening and then, two seconds later, being closed quietly. He peeked surreptitiously around the corner and glanced down the hall, in time to see the big guy going into his room. There was something large draped over his shoulder. Upon closer inspection, it appeared to be a large green, plastic trash bag. The big man had to face the other way as he opened his door, so Billy figured this was his chance to escape. Holding his sore leg, Billy made his way toward the stairs as fast as he could. The pain was excruciating, but he had to move and move fast. With his keys in his right hand and his left busily supporting his injured leg, Billy had unknowingly dropped his jacket near the entryway to the service elevator. By the time he realized the jacket was missing, it was too late to go back for it. The last thing he could afford was to call further attention to himself.

"What if the big man sees me? To hell with that damned jacket anyway," he muttered; "I gotta split." So, Billy made his way down the stairs, out the main entryway, across the guest parking lot, toward the employee parking lot. Only with considerable pain and some difficulty was he able to negotiate the column of wooden steps that led to the lot. Once there, he started his car and, using the delivery road that took him behind the resort, made his way to Route 26 toward what he hoped would mean freedom.

Chapter 53

6:45 P.M, Thursday, July 13th. Al Connor drove on, as if in a trance. His world had seemed so simple until four o'clock that afternoon. On a typical day, Al woke up at 6:30 in the morning, had breakfast, went to work, skipped lunch most days, stayed at work until six, came home to dinner with Edna, read his newspaper, watched the early news, then went to sleep. He had to admit, after all these years, he'd come to count on Edna to be there. Edna had never been terribly demanding. She hadn't been at all extravagant; in fact, she rarely ever bought herself anything new. Since she rarely got all dressed up, stockings were a rare item, too. Edna had seemed happy enough; although Al had to admit that he hadn't ever asked her. Of course, there were those times when she'd gotten all mushy with him. The fact was that Al was one of those men who was totally consumed by his work. As he liked to put it, "I work to live and I live to work." After a day at work, he was simply too tired to do anything but eat, relax a while and sleep. "Besides, that stuff should be the man's job to initiate, not the woman's," he said to himself. So when Edna had been slightly aggressive with Al, it had only made things worse for her. This behavior had intimidated Al and would turn him off completely.

The result was that Edna became more and more frustrated. As time went by, she had become reticent to rock the proverbial boat. Al had been good to her as a provider. She could have anything that she wanted, and he was almost always kind to her. If the truth be known, over the years Al Connor was becoming the big brother Edna never had, nor wanted. For those reasons, she stayed despite her frustration at Al's lack of affection.

★   ★   ★

"Excuse me," Al said to the attendant at the Hooksett highway rest area, "should I continue north on this road to reach The Balsams Hotel?" The map in Al's glove compartment depicted the six New England states; therefore its scale was too small to provide the detail he needed to plan the remainder of his trip. At closer inspection, Al noticed that it had been published in 1979. The attendant smiled when he saw Al's map. "Things have changed quite a bit since that one was published, Mistah."

"I know. But it's all I have," Al said matter-of-factly.

"Well, I have just the thing for you. Here's a new state road map. It has roads that didn't exist when that one came out."

"Thank you," Al replied.

"Look, heah, I'll outline your route for you with this yellow marka."

"That's just what I need. Thank you. One more thing, if you don't mind, how long will it take me to get from here to The Balsams?"

"Well, traffic's not gonna be a problem today. You should make real good time on the intastate. It's seven o'clock now. I'd say you could be there by eleven if you limit your stops."

"I'll do just that. But I haven't had anything to eat since this morning. Are there any fast food places near here?" Al asked.

"Go up the road about ten miles. At exit fourteen, get off. Take a right at the stop light. Go up the hill about a mile. You'll find all the fast food joints you could ever want."

With that, Al was on his way. As he exited the rest area, he opened the glove box, placed the new map on top of the revolver and closed the lid.

Chapter 54

8:00 A.M., Sunday, July 17th. I reached out my hand to knock on Warn's screen door. "Come on in Kary," he called. Apparently, he had been anticipating my arrival. "Do you have anything for me?" he asked.

"Not yet," I replied.

"Damn!" he said. "I knew it was too much to hope for. Well, I guess I'll have to call Twin Mountain."

"Not so fast, Warn," I replied. "I've made a lot of progress in a little over twenty-four hours. Besides, time isn't up, not yet. I think there's a good chance I'll have something for you fairly soon."

"Will you be able to find out what happened to Edna Connor?" he asked.

"I honestly don't know. But, at the very least, I think I can get a better sense of what's been going on here."

Warn looked me in the eye. "I want you to know that I really appreciate what you're trying to do, Kary. I'm sure this hasn't been too easy on you."

I smiled wryly, "You have no idea."

His response took me aback. "I think I do, old friend." I must have had quite a look on my face, because Warn felt the need to explain his remark. "During the last day or so, I've gotten a sense that things are not great between Nya and you."

"But how...?"

"Look, there's no time to discuss this right now. Let's just say that I've spent time alone with each of you . . ."

"Yeah, I've noticed," I snapped back and immediately regretted it.

Warn was too much of a gentleman to show any reaction to my childish outburst.

"I've worked with each of you during the last two days; and I'm not oblivious, Kary . . . especially when dealing with a couple I care about very much."

Reflecting upon my earlier suspicions, this statement made me feel like a bigger jerk. "I'm afraid that I've made a big mess of things the past couple of days, Warn. Nya has been such a trooper these past few years; but I've been such a jerk. We came up here with the hope of finding something. And then . . ."

"And then I asked you to get involved with a problem I should have solved by myself," Warn interjected.

"Come on, Warn. How could you have handled a guest's disappearance without everyone on your staff and every guest in the place becoming suspicious? Besides, it seems to me that you've been under a lot of extra pressure yourself. Hell, I've known you how many years?"

"A lot of them," he interjected with a forced smile.

"Right," I continued, "and I've never, ever seen you so despondent. Jeez Warn, if there's one thing I've learned this weekend, it's that I'm not the most sensitive person when it comes to others' feelings. And even I can see you're miserable."

"Well, I suppose that's a step forward on your part, Kary."

"Yeah, one step in twenty years," I replied sardonically.

"One step at a time," he offered. "But I do think there's hope for you yet, old friend."

"Thanks, Warn. But I'm afraid it will take more than sweet talk to undo the damage I did right after I learned that my portrait was missing from the Wall of Fame."

Warn groaned. "Listen, Kary. Let me explain about that. I took . . ."

At that moment, there was a knock on the screen door. It was Tom. "Dad, Vermont Highway Patrol wants to talk with you." Forcing my curiosity aside, I stood up as Warn picked up the receiver. I'm sure he didn't even notice that I'd left the room.

Chapter 55

Midnight, July 13th. Richard exited the elevator and made his way to the lobby. "Shit!" he exclaimed, "Nothing's open! The whole damned place is shut down." Richard was desperate; but then, an idea struck him. "If I can just find some champagne, I'll have one out of two . . . that may be enough."

"Can I help you sir?" It was a woman's voice. Richard realized that he had caught the attention of the front desk clerk. She looked very familiar to Richard. "Obviously someone who worked here when I did," he told himself.

"Sir?" she repeated.

"Why yes, you can. I'm entertaining a special guest in my room and I'm wondering if there is some way I can get a bottle of champagne."

Leonette Dubois had spent enough time waitressing and working front desks to know a man who'd had a few too many when she saw one. "Well, I'm sorry but there is nothing open right now. However, if you want, I can have room service bring you one." Leonette had no intention of calling room service. However, she hoped that by getting the large, inebriated man back to his room, he might simply lie down and sleep it off. "Does that sound like a good idea, sir? May I have your room number?"

"No, that won't do me any good. Just forget it; I'll get what I want without it." In his inebriated condition he had not even tried to disguise his aggravation. As he turned and walked back toward the Hampshire House elevator, he became angrier and angrier. Watching him, Leonette commented to no one in particular, "He looks very familiar; but what is his name?"

Richard took the elevator back up to the third floor. As the elevator rose, a plan had come to him. "That's just what I'll do," he grinned menacingly. Richard opened the door to his room. He slipped off his clothing and underclothing and put on a nylon windbreaker jacket and pants. Next, he took a water bottle and wrapped it in a towel. "Now, I'm ready," he told himself. Richard was absolutely quivering with excitement as he knocked on the connecting door between his room, number 168, and Edna's, number 167.

"Who is it?" Edna asked. She'd even put on her brand new nightgown, a long, silky, red one with spaghetti straps. But then, there had been the telephone message-the message that had changed everything.

Richard was no longer in the mood for games. He'd come for what was his. He'd been eyeing Edna's cleavage all evening and had felt the firm ampleness of her derriere. Now he wanted a full serving of each. "Come on, Edna, open the door." With that, he turned the brass knob and unlatched the lock on his side of the door.

Edna was confused and a little frightened. During the last several minutes, everything had changed. She just couldn't go through with it. Richard had been very kind to her, and had indulged her in a manner that she had never experienced before. He'd treated her in a way that had brought out feelings and emotions that had lain dormant within her. Part of her wanted to open the door and release them. But, she couldn't.

"Come on Edna . . . please . . . open the door," he pleaded.

"Richard, please, lower your voice. You'll awaken the whole hotel." Edna was beginning to feel anxious. Her parents had raised her to avoid making a scene. She realized in the heat of the moment that this same upbringing had impeded her from taking more decisive measures with Al. This was something she vowed to rectify.

"If you think I've been loud up until now, just wait."

"Oh, Richard, no. Please, leave me alone and go to bed," Edna said, her voice so soft that it was barely audible on the other side of the door.

Richard had gone too far to turn back. His libido was piloting his ship now; he was prepared to do anything it took to achieve his ends. He began to bang on the door, at first soft, then progressively louder. "Please, Edna, let me in." Then, he had an idea he was sure would work. "Listen, Edna, if you'll just let me in, I promise I'll be back in my room in five minutes. I just want to talk." As Richard waited for her response, he was practically frothing. "In fact, I can be back in three," he said to himself with a sneer.

"What should I do?" Edna said to herself. "If he goes on like this much longer, everyone will wake up and . . ." The mere thought of the potential consequences brought tears to her eyes. Finally, she capitulated. "All right, Richard," she said in a whisper, "if I open the door, do you promise to stay no more than five minutes?"

"Yes, Edna. I promise. Now please, open the door."

The clicking sound had been like the opening of the lid on a coffee can. Richard flowed into the room with a swiftness that belied his size. Immediately, he began to paw at Edna.

"Richard, you promised that you would leave in five minutes," Despite her fear, or perhaps because of it, her voice was only slightly above a whisper.

"Just stop resisting me and I'll be outta here sooner than that," he sneered, as he reached to grab a handful of Edna's nightgown. There was a moment of silence as he closed the little remaining space between them. Edna could feel things growing black; and, as she was falling into a state of unconsciousness, there was the sound of a knock on the door.

Chapter 56

8:30 AM, Sunday, July 16. This had turned into the investigation from hell. At the center of the maelstrom was a missing middle age woman who, for all I know, could be lying at the bottom of Lake Gloriette. The so called investigator, namely yours truly, had no business nosing around in an investigation that, at the very least, belonged in the hands of the state police. In addition, my attention was being diverted by another "minor" detail, namely my very own marital crisis. To make things more confusing, my client-if that's what you want to call Warn Barson-was experiencing serious issues that, at that moment, smacked of a mid-life crisis. As I looked again at my watch, I figured it would be late morning before Warn would be calling the cops. Given the travel distance between Twin Mountain and Dixville, this gave me until early afternoon at the latest before the cavalry rolled into The Balsams. There was so much left to do, my stomach was beginning to ache.

As I left Warn's office, I noticed a very familiar looking derriere moving slowly toward the stairs leading to the swimming pool. I could count on the fact that Nya would be lying by the pool until lunch. This meant that a major hurdle had been removed from my investigation for the next several hours. Of course, I still had a lot of explaining to do to aforesaid hurdle. For reasons I couldn't begin to fathom, Nya had been taking control of my brain; and now, I was seeing her as a walking, talking metaphor for Edna Connor. As I walked toward the bellmen's desk to meet up with the ubiquitous Reg Gill, I couldn't shake the feeling that there were now two people who needed finding, Edna Connor and Kary Turnell.

★   ★   ★

As I walked through the double doors that separate the hotel's entry from its lobby, I was relieved to see the larger than life presence of Reg Gill occupying his perch at the bellmen's desk. "Mornin' Professa." His greeting had been pleasant as usual. If this man had a worry in the world, he certainly wasn't letting on. However, I was about to increase his concerns considerably.

"Good morning, Reg," I replied. "I am really happy that you're here because I need to talk with you whenever you have the time."

"For you? I have the time right now," he smiled.

"Terrific. Can we go some place where we can talk in private?"

Now the look on Reg's face was changed from one of relaxation to curiosity. "I've gotta go down to the theater. Why don't you walk with me?"

As we passed the Barsons' offices, I noticed that father and son were immersed in their respective labors. "No rest for the weary, not even in the Elysian Fields," I told myself. Passing the offices and the boutiques for what seemed like the hundredth time during the last two days, I turned and put my hand on the superintendent's shoulder. He stopped walking and faced me.

"So, what's goin' on Professa?"

"A lot, Reg; a whole lot," I replied.

He looked at me with what I'd describe as a bemused expression on his face. "Wanta discuss your novel some more?" he asked. His inflection on the word novel and the look on his face confirmed my earlier suspicions. Reg was on to me.

"How long have you known, Reg?"

"Why . . . known what?" he replied, while grinning broadly.

"You know that there is no novel; and you know exactly why I'm really asking all of these questions. You sly fox." Now I was the one who was grinning. It was the same expression I'd worn during those times when students had solved one of the clever problems I'd designed to trap them.

"I probably known 'bout the lady's disappearance 'fore you did. 'Course, I'm a man who keeps his mouth shut. Durin' the last thirty years, I've become pretty darn good at hearin' rumors and stoppin' 'em. I learned about the Conna' woman missin' meals on the thirteenth. Then, when you started askin' your questions, I figured the Barson's had called the cops . . . figured you was one."

"What do you think now?"

"You don't act like no cop I've ever seen. So, my guess is you're some friend of the boss who has done some investigatin', but probably not a badge-wearer."

"You are correct on all counts, Reg. I used to write a crime column for the Philadelphia Inquirer. But the part about my being a professor is true." Then as we continued our walk, I asked if I could count on him to keep our conversation between us. He nodded his affirmation, and I gave him an abridged version of all I had learned through my investigative efforts.

When I'd concluded, there was another big smile on his face. "You've done pretty good, Professa. 'Course you could have learned most of that information from a single source," he offered, with his ubiquitous grin.

"A single source, but who . . . YOU?" Now I was feeling foolish. I could have saved myself hours of time by simply asking this clever giant of a man for his help earlier. And, for the second time, I wondered why Warn hadn't simply turned this investigation over to Reg. Surely that was what Tom wanted him to do. This must have been what they were discussing in such an animated fashion the morning before. But, of course, there had been the resort's ecosystem or apple cart or grapevine to consider. And no one understood this better than Warn Barson.

Reg simply smiled and we continued walking. When we reached the Hampshire House elevator, we turned toward the right. Rather than walk toward the elevators, we continued along the lowest level of rooms in the Hampshire House. Passing the service elevator, I remarked that the builder had been very clever to locate such an important piece of infrastructure in such an inconspicuous place.

"There's lot's of hidden areas in this ol' hotel," he replied.

After my investigations during the past couple of days, I had developed an appreciation for the veracity of his statement. We continued to walk along the hallway. Through the door at the head of the hallway, I could see how the land sloped abruptly toward Lake Gloriette. But the lake itself was not visible to me. About halfway down the hall, we came to a set of stairs with a white banister and balustrades. As we walked down the stairs, Reg removed the enormous key ring from his belt, found the correct key among what looked like thousands, and unlocked the door to the children's recreation room. Once inside the rec room, with the aid of the same key, he admitted us to an expansive dark area where theater props had been stored. In the dark he guided me toward the right until we were approaching the backstage of the theater. This seemingly innocent walk, through an area that I'd visited with Rolf the previous afternoon, now had my imagination working overtime.

Chapter 57

1 A.M., Friday, July 14th. Richard Tomquist did not clearly comprehend the events of the past sixty minutes. Whether it was the alcohol or his mind repressing the past hour's events, the man felt a sense of urgency as he opened the door to leave his room. The bag he was carrying was awkward but, in relation to its size, not terribly burdensome. After all, Richard was not a small man. He looked one way, then down the hallway toward the elevator. Not a soul was stirring. "A freakin' miracle," he thought, given the noise that he now remembered making. His memory was returning in dribs and drabs. As he looked again toward the elevator, he was relieved to see that the maintenance kid was no longer there. Then he had a start. "What's that on the floor near the service elevator?" he said to himself. "It's that kid's jacket." Realizing that he'd better wait until he was sure that the coast was clear, Richard waited near his door in case the kid came back. But he hadn't. Finally, after what seemed like an eternity, Richard shouldered his burden and made his way along the hallway toward the service elevator. He knew that using either the main elevator or the adjacent stairway was out of the queston. "Some insomniac might show up, and that's all I'd need," he told himself. Next, he entered the storage area outside of the service elevator and closed the outer door. He would be hidden here while he figured out what to do. One possibility he had considered was to take the bag down the service elevator to the basement level. Richard didn't need to read the sign on the elevator that warned employees not to use it during night hours. After all, he'd ridden that elevator countless times during his days as a maintenance worker at the resort. He frowned as he thought how much he'd loved that job; and how crushed he'd been when Warner Barson had fired him. Reaching into the pocket of his windbreaker, he found the key. It had been a Pyhrric victory that he'd succeeded in leaving The Balsams with the duplicate master key. And now he was going to put it to good use. Despite his temporary fuzzy state, he went through his plan one more time. He would take the service elevator to the basement. It was a stormy night; so, he felt sure that the thunder would drown out the sound of the descending elevator. "And, if it doesn't, who cares?" he told himself. "Unless the watchman hears the elevator and catches me coming out of it, they'll never know who used it until I'm long gone." So, Richard again adjusted his load, entered the elevator and hit the button that would guide him to the lowest level of the Hampshire House.

Chapter 58

9:45 A.M., Sunday, July 16th. "You okay there in the dark, Professa." Reg's voice had brought me out of my musing. "Just stay put; I'll only be another second. I just need to get a few of these lights on; then we can sit here in the theater and talk. That'll do 'er," I heard him say. And with that, he had provided enough light to guide me around the stage and into the theater.

As I walked past the very same doorway that Rolf had opened just to tease me during the previous day, I couldn't suppress my curiosity any longer. Instead of opening the door, I called to my guide, "Reg, what's with this door anyway?"

"Oh, that's just an old crawl space," he said. Then, with a laugh, he added, "Ya' thinkin' we'll find the Conna' woman in there, Professa?"

"No, I suppose not." But, I really wasn't so sure.

Putting this perfect hiding place out of my mind for the moment, I rejoined Reg and we sat in the front row of the theater. It was light enough in that cavernous space to have a conversation, but dark enough to cause me to look for someone lurking in the shadows. The action was not lost on Reg. With yet another hardy laugh, he said, "You been watchin' too many of them spy flicks, Professa." This made me smile.

Satisfied that we were indeed alone, I said, "I hope you have a few more minutes because I need to tap into that information resource of yours." As I said this, I pointed toward his head. The expression on Reg's face indicated that he appreciated my obvious effort at flattery.

"I'll do what I can. Fire away."

"I need you to tell me about two employees, one presently working here and the other a former employee who left here about ten years ago, possibly under less than favorable circumstances."

He stared at me for about ten seconds. At first, I was afraid that I'd stumped the master. But then he said, "I can only guess who the first guy is, but the second one's easy. You must be talkin' about Richard Tomquist."

"That's right!" I exclaimed. "But how did you know?"

"If memory serves me correctly, Richard's the only one who fits the description, that is, if the man you're talkin' about was fired."

"I believe he was," I repeated.

"That would be Richard. He was a real good maintenance man. But, he just couldn't stay away from the ladies. Didn't matter whether they was staff or guests. If a woman had a good figure, Richard's radar would go off. He'd been warned by both Rolf and Mr. Barson that, if he ever messed around with a guest again, he'd get canned. I'm the one who caught him the second time, but the guest seemed more pleased with his attention than she was bothered. So he got one last chance. Too bad it didn't work out. Like I said, he was a great help around here. He was some furniture repairman, that Richard."

"And a pretty good locksmith from what I hear.".

This engendered another of Reg's ubiquitous laughs. "Looks like someone's done his homework," he said. So, why are we talkin' so much about poor ol' Richard?"

"Because he's a guest in the hotel."

"So, that was him," he responded with a whistle. "Have you met Leonette Dubois . . . works the night shift on the registration desk?"

I shook my head no.

He continued, "Great gal; been here a long time. She told me this mornin' when I came in about some guy who was looking for champagne for his little turtle dove last night. She sent him back to his room . . . a bit miffed, I might add . . . but was certain that he looked familiar. There usually isn't much action at night at the registration desk, and the paper work was particularly light. So Leonette started thinking about who he could be. She'd wracked her brain for an hour or more until it dawned on her that it was our old friend Richard. Just to be sure, she looked at the registration list; and there it was in black and white. R. Johan Tomquist."

"Interesting," I replied.

When I didn't say anything else for several seconds, Reg asked, "What's interesting, Professa?"

"Think about it, Reg, we have a missing guest. Then there's a former employee who had been seen in said guest's company, in both the dining room and the Wilderness Lounge, and who later was looking for champagne at a fairly late hour." Then, before Reg could say anything else, I added, "And who may have a copy of the resort's master key in his possession."

Again, Reg let out a whistle.

"One last thing, Reg, do you think Tomquist killed your boss's niece?"

"I guess it wouldn't surprise me none. But the cops weren't able to prove it back then."

Chapter 59

1:15 A.M., Friday, July 14th. As the service elevator carrying Richard and his large bundle set heavily and noisily down at the lowest level of the Hampshire House, its single breathing occupant was sweating slightly. He took a deep breath and pulled back the accordion-like inner gate and then pushed open the heavy, mint green outer door. He peered slowly around the corner and listened very carefully for the footsteps of either the night watchman or some late-night maintenance worker. Silence. He shouldered his bundle and spied the theater entrance at about two o'clock from his position. Sometimes, Igor, the ancient projectionist left the door to the theater ajar, either having fallen asleep or simply forgetting to lock it when he left for the night. However, not on this night. As soon as he'd left the alcove that housed the elevator, Richard could see that the door had been shut tight. "No matter," he said to himself as he reached into his pocket and once again claimed his magic key. But something was wrong. "Damn!" he said out loud. The last thing Richard had counted on was that the management had replaced the traditional lock with one that demanded one of the new card keys.

Richard had little choice. He considered for a moment the option of returning to the service elevator, going out its back door, then carrying the increasingly heavy weight up the concrete catacomb to one of the rooms along its periphery. But, this would be too chancy; for, staff frequented this area at all times of night, as did the night watchman. He considered taking the Hampshire House elevator back to his floor, but ruled out that option for the same reason he had earlier. The storm outside had probably abated, but he felt that his only option was to retrace his steps by means of the noisy, yet efficient service elevator. Now sweating profusely, he entered the elevator, pushed the button and began to travel upward. Reaching the third floor, he exited. After checking the hallway, he walked to the door of his room and opened it. Once inside, he set the bundle, which now seemed to weigh a thousand pounds, on his bed and went to the bathroom, where he relieved himself and washed his face. Thus, temporarily rejuvenated, Richard hoisted his bundle, carrying it across his outstretched arms. He closed the door to his room as quietly as possible, took a left turn and walked to the stairway situated halfway down the hall. Here, he took a left turn and descended the three flights of stairs that led to the children's recreation area. As he reached the last few steps before the entry, he looked heavenward and said aloud, "Oh please; please." Richard had not been praying for forgiveness; rather, he was asking that the lock on the recreation area door could still be opened by his master key. Richard was now nearly completely exhausted from his ordeal. The combination of the alcohol, his altercation with Edna, the mysterious knock on her door, and the weight of his burden had worn him down. Relieved to see that the original lock had not been replaced, he laid the plastic bag and its contents on the ground, used his master key to open the door, then dragged his burden along the carpet to the next door and repeated the process. Once inside the second doorway, he fumbled his way in the dark toward the passageway along the side of the back stage area. By this time the storm had passed, the clouds had lifted and a full moon was shining its light though a small window. He walked step-by-step carrying the bag until he reached a doorway that he knew from experience led to a long crawl space along the east wall of the basement of the Hampshire House. With considerable difficulty, he entered the space, using his left hand for balance while he draped the bag over his right shoulder. Then, when he'd gone as far as the protruding pipes and narrow walls would permit, he carefully laid the bag down, smoothed its contents as best he could, and crawled out of the area. As he was about to close the door behind him, he looked back and said, "It would have been easier for both of us if you'd just given me what I wanted, Edna."

Chapter 60

10:00 A.M., Sunday, July 16th. "Tell me, Reg, do you think we're jumping the gun?"

"Well, you met Tomquist, Professa; what do you think?" he replied.

I had already given this a great deal of thought after parting company with Tomquist the previous night. "I'd say he felt that it was his God-given right to chase skirts," I replied.

"You're right about that," he said. "But, what probably kept him outta jail back then is he never was the violent type 'round this place, anyways. 'Sides, back in his younger days, he didn't have to," Reg smiled.

I thought about this for a few seconds before answering, "Yes, but life changes all of us. He left here under less than favorable circumstances. He's aged . . . maybe he isn't quite the chick-magnet he once was . . . if he ever was at all."

"Oh, he was all right."

Changing the subject back to Edna, I said, "Well, it would appear that Mrs. Connor was interested in him."

"Yep, one of the bar waiters told me they were all over one another on the dance floor." Then Reg added, "She said he had his hands in places that indicated they weren't having a brother-and-sister relationship."

"So, when they left the ballroom, it would appear that each of them was equally anxious to take things a step . . . a big step . . . farther."

"It appears that way," he replied.

"But what could have happened? If Richard got what he wanted, why would he hurt Edna? And, if he did hurt her, has he already left The Balsams?"

"I can't answer the first question, but I can sure do the second," Reg said, as he pulled a two-way radio from his belt. "Dining room, come in please." Reg had placed a call to John Gray, who kept a similar walkie-talkie on the shelf of his maitre d's stand. It didn't take long for John to respond.

"Go ahead, Reg."

"John, I'm here with the professor; and we had a question for you."

The word, "Yes" crackled over the radio.

"We were wondering if Richard Tomquist has arrived for breakfast this mornin'."

"Grenda's right over here. Give me a second and I'll have your answer."

But it had taken more than a second. Apparently, at the very moment we had called, there had been a last minute rush, and John needed to greet and seat a large party of new arrivals. Then, with a crackle, Reg's two-way radio came back to life. "Reg, you there?"

"Right here, John. You find anythin'?"

"Sorry about the delay. We got very busy toward the end of breakfast. I have the information you wanted. Just give me one second." There was a pause as John moved away from the earshot of guests and other staff. "Your man is eating breakfast right now."

"Richard?" Reg questioned.

"The same," came the response.

At that moment I interjected, "Reg, ask John if Grenda or he noticed anything out of the ordinary when Richard came into the dining room." Reg repeated the question to John who placed us on hold while he talked with his captain. "Grenda says, now that you mention it, she did." Hearing this over the two-way radio, I asked for an elaboration. "Reg, tell the professor that he had what looked like a nasty scrape, or possibly a burn, on his cheek."

Reg thanked John, and returned the radio to its carrier. Reg and I looked at one another for a full minute before either of us spoke. He said calmly, "Well, so our man is still in the hotel. An' the folks in registration say he checks out tomorrow."

"My head is spinning right now," I said. Then after thinking about this new information for a short time, I did what anyone who engages in induction might do. "Let's get this straight, Richard was clearly interested . . . make that very interested in Edna Connor. He took steps to seduce her; it's obvious he had given her quite a bit of alcohol with exactly that in mind."

Now it was Reg's turn. "Right. Sometime last night, they walked back to their adjoinin' rooms. Then, based upon what Leonette told me, he returned to the lobby in search of champagne."

"But they'd already had a lot to drink. Why would he be looking for champagne when he was so close to getting what he wanted?" We sat and thought some more and then, in unison, it hit us, "Because she sent him to get it."

This revelation hadn't required an Einstein. "Apparently our boy Richard took the bait and went back downstairs," Reg offered.

"But, why would she send him at all?" I asked. Then, in answer to my own question, I offered, "Unless she was having second thoughts and wanted time to gather her courage . . . after all, she is, or was, a married woman."

"Or, she may have been tryin' to ditch him," Reg countered.

"That's true. Either way, by the time he returned, he would have been in no mood for screwing around." Reg looked at me and grimaced at my faux pas. We sat for a few more minutes, then a thought occurred to me. "Reg, can you get a record of the times of entry into Tomquist's room on the 13th." He nodded. Then, I added, "Can you get it without the Barsons knowing you did?" I could see he was reluctant to consider this, so I added, "Warn's already allowed me to look at the record for Edna Connor's room. The way I see it, this is just a natural extension of that one."

He smiled at my devious twist on things. "But why not just ask Mr. Barson for the other one?"

"He's been feeling a little under the weather the last couple of says. I'm afraid it will only upset him if I do."

"And it probably would," Reg replied. "You're right, Professa', he has been a bit out of sorts lately." He thought about my request for a few seconds before saying, "I can get the information for you right away, unless you need a paper copy."

"No. That's not necessary."

This seemed to make Reg feel better. Taking his two-way radio in hand, he said, "Lucy, you there?" She was. Reg explained that he needed the record for room 168 in the Hampshire House. Whether it was something in Reg's tone or an understanding between two people who had worked together for decades, Lucy had not asked him why he needed the information. As he listened, he removed a pencil and a small pad of paper from the breast pocket of his shirt. When the voice crackled on to the other end, he began to scribble a few notes. When he had finished, he said, "Thanks, sweetheart. See you at lunch." There was no lust in his tone; it had been a platonic greeting for an old friend.

"What did Lucy tell you?" My interest was piqued.

"She says the record shows that the turndown service was there at 8:10PM and that Tomquist entered the room at 6:00 and midnight. But here's the interesting part, it appears that he reentered just before 1:00 and at 1:15AM."

"Huh? Why would he have left at such a late hour?"

"Could he have been next door?" Reg asked.

"I suppose it's possible. As you know, I've looked at Mrs. Connor's room record. But, unfortunately, there's no record of a second key entry after Edna herself entered for the night at 11:30."

"But, if she'd opened the door for him . . ." Reg allowed that thought to dangle.

"You know, Reg, I've been wrestling with a thought and your last remark is making me anxious to check something out."

"Yeah, what's that?" he replied.

"From what I understand, Edna's room is being held open until further notice. It must be the resort's standard procedure, just in case she returns. Am I right, Reg?" Reg nodded. "Then, I'd like to see it, if you don't mind."

"Whoa . . . wait a minute, Professa. That's a potential crime scene. Even housekeepin' has been told to stay clea' since the afternoon of the 14th."

"Yeah, it's a good thing your friend Lucy knows how to keep a lid on things. Otherwise the brown smelly stuff would have hit the fan by now." Then I added, "Believe me, I understand your concern, Reg. I promise not to enter into the actual room, just the entry way."

I could see that Reg was confused, not to mention more than a little skeptical. But when I explained what I was after, he agreed to let me into number 167.

Chapter 61

10:15 A.M. My entry into Edna Connor's room was going to have to wait. The sound of static was an indication that someone wanted to talk with Reg over his two-way radio. It was Tom Barson. Tom had been looking for Reg and needed to see him right away. "Can't say as I'm surprised," Reg said after breaking off the connection. "You and I've been down here jabberin' for more than a half hour."

I looked at my watch and emitted an audible groan. "Oh my God, it's already ten after nine. I've guaranteed Warn some type of answer by noon." That left me less that three hours; and I wasn't even close to providing one.

Reg and I walked up the stairs toward the Barsons' offices. On the way we agreed to meet again outside the door to Edna Connor's room at 10:30 sharp. As Reg walked into Tom Barson's office, I peered inside of Warn's; he was sitting there. When he saw me, he immediately waved at me to come inside. I opened the screen door and started to say something, but realized he was talking on the telephone. So I sat down in one of his small, hand carved wooden captain's chairs and waited.

"Yes, yes, captain. I understand," he said into the telephone. Then as Warn listened, I couldn't help but notice that his telephone was red. I found this very appropriate under the circumstances. After another thirty seconds he added, "Three o'clock. Yes. Sure. I had hoped to see your man at noon, but I understand." Then after listening some more, he looked across at me as he responded to the caller, "Believe me, we hate to see something like this happen, too."

When he placed the receiver down, Warn looked across at me with empty eyes and said, "They're going to be here a little late."

"What else did he say?" I inquired.

"He said not to allow anyone in Mrs. Connor's room and to keep any suspects at the hotel. We may need to call in the night security men early if necessary."

"Anything else?"

"Yeah, he said he felt bad about all of this and hoped it wouldn't damage our reputation." There wasn't much I could say. I really didn't have much information for Warn, and he knew without asking about it. My silence was speaking volumes; and so was Warn's. The expression on his face at that moment was a veritable monument to something every one of us fears: the realization that some significant factor in one's life . . . something we hold dear . . . could be washed away within an instant. Warn finally broke the silence between us. "So nothing at all?" It was more of a statement of resignation than a question.

I tried to sound optimistic, but doubted that I was successful. "I have a couple of interesting leads. We . . . I've made a lot of progress considering I only learned about all of this about thirty-six hours ago." My face felt flushed, as I had nearly let on that Reg was helping me. This was information that I planned to share with Warn and Tom; but this wasn't the proper time.

"Thirty-seven, actually," he smiled.

"What . . .?"

"You learned about it thirty-seven hours ago." You have to appreciate a guy who's able to keep up with his integers while his world may be sliding away from under him.

There was a knock on the screen door. Warn invited Rolf Vernon to come in. "Mornin' boss; hello Professor. How's the book of yours coming?" I was really beginning to dislike that man. But rather than give him the pleasure of knowing he was getting to me, I just shrugged. Rolf needed to tell Warn something about a guest room the management was planning to remodel. I blanked out most of their conversation, but overheard him say something like, "I hope we don't disturb any of the ghosts." He laughed when Warn suggested they channel them into a certain Atlanta woman's guest room. Then as Rolf turned to leave, I called to him.

"Rolf, can you give me a few minutes of your time. I know you're busy, but this will only take a short time." With that, I rose from my chair, gave my good friend a supportive hand on the shoulder and followed Rolf out of the office. At that time of morning, there wasn't anyone in the garden terrace; so Rolf and I sat there.

"What's on your mind, Professor?" His tone had lost all trace of the cordiality he had exhibited in Warn's office.

I was tempted to ask this guy what his beef was, but lacked both the time and any concern about the source of his attitude. However, I had to find a way to ask a question that was sensitive, even under less hostile circumstances. So I decided to concoct a story. "I have a good friend whose nephew works maintenance here. He asked me to look the kid up, but our paths haven't crossed."

"Maintenance, huh? What's the kid's name?"

"Billy Fenton," I replied. "Billy's uncle served with me in the military." Of course, all of this was a complete fabrication, but I didn't know what else to do.

"Well, your buddy's nephew is a real beauty, Professor." I feigned surprise and chagrin at his remark, from which Rolf seemed to gain enjoyment. It was soon clear that he was going to enjoy telling me more about Billy. I surreptitiously glanced at my watch, not wanting to miss my meeting with Reg. Rolf continued, "That kid's a mess. He's been late for work, who knows how many times, and always shows up looking like a bum."

"Oh my." I held my hand over my mouth, hoping it would have the desired effect. It did.

"Shoot, that isn't even the worst of it. The resort grapevine says he's been stalking one of the female guests. From best I can tell, he thinks she wants to have sex with him. Can you believe it . . . some wealthy woman wanting sex with that greasy little jerk?"

Based on Rolf's remarks to that point, I couldn't be certain whether he was aware that Edna Connor was missing. Time was running short, and I wanted to end this conversation; so I stood up and acted as though I needed some air. But Rolf had one more jab to throw. "Wait a minute Professor, I've got more."

"What else could there be?" I said in a tone that was akin to a boxer offering his chin to an opponent.

"He was arrested late last night for speeding in northern Vermont. It appears he was going to duck out on work and spend the day in Canada." So, this was what Warn's telephone call from Vermont had been about.

Chapter 62

10:22AM. I went back to Warn's office where he and Tom were just finishing a brief conversation. Tom was gearing up for a busy conference season and was telling Warn about a new floor plan for the exhibitors. I knocked on the door.

"I'll be right with you, Kary," Warn called to me. I noted that his tone sounded a bit more cheerful which pleased me. As Tom rose to leave, I nodded to him and said to his father, "You seem to be in a bit better mood than you were a short while ago."

Warn forced a smile. "Yeah, just a bit." To which Tom added on his way out of the office, "Sure, he is; Mom just called. She always knows how to make Dad feel better." I understood very well what Tom meant. "Nya has the same effect on me," I offered. Having said that, I could feel an ache in my stomach, as I wondered whether Nya was going to hand me my walking papers before day's end.

"It's amazing how wives can bring husbands back to earth and make us understand what's important and what isn't," Warn replied.

"Yeah, but it never seems to work the same way in reverse. I can never seem to find the right words to take away Nya's pain."

This is when my dear friend Warn taught me a lesson that I should have learned long before. "Life doesn't work like a television show. We can't always find the right words; and, let's face it, the harps and violins don't start playing at just the right moment. But, I've found that I communicate my feelings to Nancy as clearly through my actions as words."

"What do you mean?" I asked.

"If Nancy is feeling really down and I can't find the words to make her feel better, I try just holding her hand or holding her in my arms . . .anything to show that she isn't facing her problems alone. I try to show her that she has a partner . . . a friend . . . who's there for her. And I really believe it makes a difference. The longer Nancy and I have lived together, the more automatic it has become to offer help, but unobtrusively. The best part is, it doesn't take as much to make a bad mood go away . . . for either of us." I didn't say a word because there was nothing I could offer in return. Hell, my relationship with Nya was one hundred and eighty degrees from what Warn had just described. On second thought, it was more like ninety degrees. After all, Nya was the kind of partner Warn had just described. Only, our marriage had turned into a solo act.

★   ★   ★

"What's on your mind Kary. It's already mid-morning; so I can't imagine you came in here for lessons on the foundation of a successful marriage."

That hadn't been my purpose; but his words had not been lost on me. "I'm here to talk about Billy Fenton." Upon hearing Fenton's name, Warn's demeanor darkened noticeably.

"What about Billy Fenton, Kary?"

"I've just learned that he was stopped for speeding near the Canadian border, in Vermont. Is that true?"

"Who told you that? I just learned that myself."

"Rolf told me while we were meeting out on the terrace," I said.

"He did, eh? So, do you think this has anything to do with Mrs. Connor's disappearance?"

"I can't be sure. But it sure would be nice to question him."

"I don't know if that's going to be possible, Kary. The only reason they've held him this long for a speeding violation is his impressive arrest history popped up on their computer. I'll tell you this, had I been aware that Billy was more than just a misguided little boy, he wouldn't have set foot inside this place."

"From what little I've seen and heard, I can see why you feel that way."

But Warn was growing a little defensive. "Well, you're a lot more experienced at spotting these characters than we are up here in the Great North Woods."

"You also weren't privy to Billy's full story at the time you hired him."

"Couldn't be. The damned laws coddle these guys," he said.

But I needed to convince Warn that Billy might have vital information, information we needed; and it needed to be obtained without delay. "Warn, I have an idea how we might be able get some information out of this guy."

"How?" he replied.

"Look, whether Billy had a part in this mess or not, he was awfully anxious to get out of here, and in a hurry. And my guess is that he'd be very happy if he never has to come back here."

"You're right about that. Billy tried to deny ever working here, but his maintenance shirt gave him away.

"They must have recognized the logo," I replied. "Of course, if the kid had half a brain, he'd have changed his shirt before he left . . . but I guess he was in too much of a hurry. Now, by any chance do you know the chief of the Vermont police department that arrested him?"

"Of course I do. We graduated from high school together."

"Perfect, because we'll need him to help in a little charade." I explained to Warn how he should use his connection to our advantage. He was to have the police chief tell Billy that there was some valuable property missing from a guest's room at The Balsams; and, the guest was missing, too. Also, the chief was to say that Billy was the leading suspect; and remind him that, with his record, the term for grand larceny would cost him twenty years plus, with the possibility of a life sentence if he was found guilty of murder. When I was finished preparing Warn to make his call, he turned to me and asked, "What exactly do we really expect to gain from all of this deception?"

"I'm playing a hunch here, Warn. I have a feeling that this kid has some information we need. We know he's been stalking Edna Connor. Just maybe he was outside of her room and saw what was going on that night."

"Or, maybe he's the one who killed her."

"I don't think so, Warn. From what I've heard from some of your staff, the kid is a creep and something of an opportunist. But my experience tells me that young guys like him are afraid of direct confrontation. When they do become violent, it's generally against property, rather than people."

Warn placed his call. Unfortunately, the chief was in a meeting; however, the switchboard operator promised she would have him return Warn's call when he returned in about fifteen minutes. I looked at my watch. It was already nearly after 10:30; time to move on. I walked out of Warn's office with the promise to return in time for the chief's telephone call.

Chapter 63

10:40 A.M.   Having missed my 10:30AM appointment to meet Reg, I'd have to find him and explain what had kept me. That was going to have to wait. The tension had become almost too much to bear. I needed to take a walk. I pushed open the glass door and stepped out onto the terrace, then walked past the resort's beautiful floral gardens and toward the long wooden stairway. At first, I had no particular direction in mind. As I walked, I felt myself being drawn toward the swimming pool, to Nya. Her fresh tan was in perfect contrast to her yellow two-piece bathing suit. She was wearing her hair up to maximize exposure to the sun's rays. From where I was standing, she had never looked more beautiful. I had been staring at her for about twenty seconds when she awakened from her nap. She was startled to see me standing there.

"Kary! How long have you been standing there?"

"Just a minute or so. I thought I'd come down and see how you were doing."

"Oh." Her tone was a few degrees above icy. "I thought you were working on Warn's project."

"Just for another hour," I told her. "I've taken a short break, but I have to head up to his office and talk with someone in a few minutes. Then Tom, he and I are supposed to meet and wrap this thing up a little before four."

"I see." She still seemed distant. Of course, what did I expect, a brass band and confetti?

"Well, I suppose I should get back." I started to walk away, but then a small voice inside my head told me to stop. I turned to look at Nya; but she had already put her head down and closed her eyes. "Nya." I touched the back of her suntanned shoulder, suddenly aware of how beautiful she still was. "I'd appreciate it if you would come to Warn's office for the last part of the meeting." She didn't say any thing, didn't even question why I had made the request. Having received no response, I said, "It would mean a lot to me."

Although I was only about three strides from where Nya was lying, her voice was barely audible. "I'll see, Kary."

Chapter 64

10:58AM. I returned to Warn's office without much time to spare. Warn looked up at me from his desk, a concerned expression on his face. "You sure cut that close. Is everything okay?" When I told him that I'd been down to the pool to see Nya, he smiled and said, "Good." We sat in silence, the tension building to the thickness of midday air in a rainforest. One minute passed. Two minutes. Finally, the telephone rang.

"Hello, Carl. Yes, this is Warn. It's good to hear your voice, too. Yes, I am planning to go back for the reunion next month. In fact, I've already sent back my response card. How about you? Good."

Jeezus. Time is running out and these two guys were tiptoeing down memory lane. "Warn!" I whispered sharply, circling my hand in a clockwise direction for emphasis.

Warn nodded to me. He listened patiently for another second before saying, "Listen Carl. I have a problem over here. I can't give you any particulars right now. But we've got a possible felony on our hands and the guy you're holding . . . yeah, that's right, Billy Fenton . . . he may be involved up to his eye balls." At that point the chief must have asked how he could help, because Warn repeated the scenario I had laid out for him, practically verbatim.

After Warn finished explaining to the chief, there was a long silence while Carl responded. When he was finished, Warn turned to me with his hand over the telephone. "He's not buying it," he said.

"Damn!" I responded.

"Easy, Kary. Look, he can't interrogate someone on our say so."

"So, now what?"

"Carl has another idea. He'll allow us to interrogate Billy over the phone. He'll put Billy on an unmonitored line and will strongly advise Fenton to talk with us; then he's leaving the room."

"Your friend's a smart cop." If this incident was going to be investigated by real law enforcers, it would be best for all concerned if Captain Carl could testify under oath that he knew nothing about the particulars of the alleged telephone conversation.

There was no time to plan how we were going to handle this mock interrogation. Initially, Warn suggested that he do the interviewing. But I dissuaded him by saying, "If he isn't planning to come back to work here, why would he want to talk to you?"

"Do you have a better idea?"

"Yes, I'll get on the line and tell him I'm a special prosecutor. I'll tell him that I'm giving him an opportunity to tell his side of the story. Then I'll warn him that if he doesn't cooperate, he'll be his mother's age before he sees the outside of a prison cell again."

"But, what if he tells the authorities later on that he was duped by you? You could get into serious trouble impersonating an officer of the court."

I smiled. "So who are his witnesses going to be? The chief won't be in the room. He's not recording this. I can't imagine that you're going to turn me in. So, what's to lose?"

Warn removed his hand from the telephone. "Carl, let's set it up. But, we're really running short on time here." There was a pause. "Really! That's great. Thanks Carl." Then, placing his hand over the telephone, Warn turned to me and said, "It's a small police station; there's only one other officer there. Carl will send him out for donuts, then it will take some time to convince Billy to talk with you. Carl says to be ready."

"Terrific." Now I had to prepare myself to sound convincing to a man who had spent a lot of time dealing with the criminal justice system in northern New Hampshire, and now in Vermont. I quickly laid out a plan in my head. There wasn't even enough time to spell it out for Warn.

Whether five or ten minutes had passed I couldn't be sure. When at last Billy had agreed to be cooperative, Warn handed me the telephone and nodded. I cleared my throat and removed my hand from the mouthpiece. "Am I speaking with Billy Fenton?" I lowered my voice a couple of octaves in an effort to sound very professional . . . not to mention threatening.

"Yeah, this is Billy."

"Has the chief of police explained why I'm willing to talk with you," I said in my deepest tone.

"Yeah, sort of."

"Well, let me go over it for you a bit more thoroughly, Billy. Shall I call you William or Bill, or do you prefer Billy?"

"My name is Billy; that's the name my ma gave me."

"Okay then, Billy, I want to know what time you left The Balsams on the night of July 14th."

"I dunno. I can't remember," he replied. I could almost see the sneer in his voice.

"Okay Billy, let me make something clear to you. You can either cooperate with me or I'll have the chief remand you over to the New Hampshire State Police. They are very interested in talking to you about a possible kidnapping. So what's it going to be, young man?" This was a total bluff, and as I finished, I was praying that Billy hadn't received a hands-on course in extradition procedures. Because, if he had, I was dead.

There was a pause of about ten seconds that seemed more like ten minutes to me. "Wait a minute!" I said nothing. "Hello, you still there? Mister?" I continued to be silent in the hope that it would really make him sweat. Finally, I uncovered the mouthpiece. The gamble was working. Billy wasn't at all eager to be sent away for a long term in the state penitentiary. He had enough familiarity with the pecking order in smaller corrections facilities to know that a person who is sentenced for doing bodily harm to a woman is in deep fecal matter.

"Okay, mister, I'll answer your questions; but I want immunity," he said. This time, I detected a smile in his voice.

I needed to think fast. Fortunately, this was one of those days when I was able to spin a tale and make it convincing. I explained to Billy that there were no formal charges against him. Therefore, if he provided evidence that I found valuable in helping us solve the case, I would personally see to it that he be granted immunity from prosecution. What a crock!

He thought about it for a surprisingly short time, no more than thirty seconds, before he came back on the line. "Okay, I'm in. What do ya' wanta know first?"

"Same question, Billy. What time did you leave The Balsams on the night of the 13th?" By the time we were finished, Billy had told me how he was up in the third floor hallway late on the night of the 13th. He admitted that he had the hots for that older chick. But he swore that he hadn't laid a hand on her, as much as he'd wanted to. When I questioned him further, Billy admitted that he had, indeed, been following her around. But he claimed he'd given up on the idea of making his move when saw her with the big guy. When I asked him to describe the big guy, his description matched Richard Tomquist down to the color of his suit. When I asked him what he had seen Edna and the man doing, he replied that they were all over each other. Then he described the big man's odd behavior. "He practically had her in the sack, but then he turns around and goes running to the elevator. I guess he forgot to pack his rubbers or something. What an asshole!"

During Billy's description, he neglected to offer anything else about his own whereabouts while all of this was transpiring. When I reminded him that he'd left his jacket on the floor outside of the service elevator . . . a revelation to Warn . . . he admitted that he'd tried to gain entry into her room, but had bolted when Edna threatened to scream if he didn't leave immediately. He then told me how he tried to leave the hotel but foolishly had left his keys behind. All of this questioning was making my throat incredibly dry. So, as Billy spun his story, I quietly asked Warn if he could possibly have someone bring me a bottle of water. He offered to get me one himself, then disappeared by way of the screen door.

"What happened next, Billy?" I asked. He told me how he'd been forced to enter the hotel through the laundry facility and then had to wait until the coast was clear. When I asked if he heard or saw anything throughout this ordeal he said, "Yeah, the service elevator." Upon further grilling, I learned that Billy had heard the elevator climbing when he'd first entered the basement of the Hampshire House. He estimated, based upon the time it had been running, that it had traveled several floors. When I asked him whether he had seen anyone else moving about in the building, he told me the only one he saw was the big man coming out of his room with a large plastic bag over his shoulder.

This was indeed a revelation. "Do you have any idea what was in the bag?" I asked.

"No, but it was something pretty big."

"How big?"

"I dunno. Maybe the size of a bunch of coats or possibly a . . ."

"Body?" I added.

"Well, could be . . . I guess. I wasn't real close; and I didn't want him to see me," Billy said. "I was afraid he'd kick my butt. He was a damn big dude."

"In which direction was he headed after he left his room?" I asked.

"Toward the other end of the building."

For clarification, I asked, "Away from the elevator?"

"Yeah."

"One last thing, Billy," I asked. "Are you sure it was his room that he was coming out of?" Having seen the key card records, I had a pretty good idea what his response would be. But I asked the question to test whether Billy was being straight with me. And, of course, the possibility remained that Tomquist had exited from Edna's room with her body in the plastic bag that Billy had told me about.

"I can't be sure," he said, "but I'm pretty sure that it was his room."

After telling Billy that he'd been a huge help to our investigation, but that he should plan on remaining in the area in the event that the police should want to question him, I hung up the phone. I don't want to imply that I was anxious about my performance, but this would have been a good time for a change of underwear.

Chapter 65

11:30 AM. It wasn't Warn who returned with my bottle of water. It was Tom. "Dad's been called away for a few minutes, Kary. Here's your water." As I drank, he said, "Well, it looks like time's just about run out. Do you know what happened to Mrs. Connor?"

"Not yet, Tom. But I do have a premonition that may yet pay dividends." Tom just stood there staring at me. I'd had about enough of Tom's negativism; so I changed the subject. "Do you know if Reg is at the bellmen's desk?"

"I don't have any idea. Call him if you'd like," he said offhandedly.

"No thanks, Tom. I'll just take a quick walk over there."

"Suit yourself," he grumbled, then returned to his office, shaking his head as he went. It was apparent that Tom had not yet developed his father's easygoing manner. Nor was he a member of the Kary Turnell fan club at that moment.

I saw Reg standing at the desk talking to one of the new bellman. He was finishing what appeared to be some instruction about the proper way to assist a guest during check out when I arrived. "Now, don't be afraid to ask for help if you aren't sure what to do," he called after the young man who looked to be all of eighteen years old. Then, as he spotted me, he said, "Professa, so how's the game going?"

"We're down a couple of runs and it's the bottom of the ninth. But, I've held my best pinch hitter in reserve," I said with a slight smile.

"I s'pose that'd be me," he replied.

"You're the only one I have left on the bench, Reg."

"Sounds good, Professa. You ready to roll?"

"I'm ready's uncle. Sorry about standing you up earlier." I had been anxious about not keeping our 10:30 appointment.

"No sweat, Professa."

Without much time left to spare, we headed directly to the Hampshire House and climbed the stairs to the third floor. Then standing outside of room 167, I looked both ways as Reg removed the master key card from his breast pocket. Satisfied that there was no one else in the hallway, Reg applied the card to the lock; and, as he removed it, we heard a click indicating that the room was unlocked. I already had explained to Reg he needn't worry that I was going to do anything to spoil what was a potential crime scene. "Hey, I was a crime reporter. I can handle myself in here," I said once more. In truth, we were both taking a real chance by entering Edna Connor's room. But we'd gone too far to turn back now. Reg was actually better prepared than me. He pulled two pairs of latex gloves, made right there in Dixville Notch, from his pocket and handed one of them to me. I placed a glove on my right hand, then stepped toward the door that connected room 167 with its neighboring guest room, number 168. I held my breath as I tried the handle; but to be truthful, it didn't come as a surprise when the door immediately opened.

Then, as I reached for the handle of the second door, I felt Reg's strong grip on my wrist. When I looked questioningly at him, he shook his head back and forth and then nodded toward the door to the hallway. As much as I didn't like the idea, I acquiesced to Reg's instruction to leave Edna Connor's room and wait for him in the hallway.

Once we were both back outside the room again, Reg closed the door. With his voice low, he said, "Jeez, Professa, you nearly blew it in there. Just what were you gonna do if ol' Richard was in his room?"

"But, Reg, we have to find out if Tomquist's side is unlocked, too!"

"Even if it was unlocked, I doubt that it still is, Professa. But, I've got a way of findin' out that should keep our butts out of jail. Now you take a walk down to the service elevator and wait for me there. I'll catch up with you in a couple of minutes."

I did as Reg asked. I'd no sooner reached the outer door to the service elevator when I heard Reg knock on the door of room 168. There was no answer; so, after about thirty seconds, Reg knocked again. When there still was no answer, he used his master key to open the door to the room. Hearing no sound from inside the room, he called out, "Superintendent heah; just checkin' your radiatas". No one was in the room; so Reg put on one of the gloves and tried the connecting door to Edna Connor's room.

A minute later he joined me at the service elevator, meeting my anxious look with a shake of his head. "Didn't see any sign that Mrs. Conna' or any other women have been in Richard's room, neitha." Based upon what we had just learned, it now appeared highly probable that Tomquist had been inside Edna Connor's room and then had left through the connecting doors without locking her side. Yet, why hadn't he simply locked it from Edna's side and then returned to his room through his front door? Could it be that someone had interrupted him? If so, who was it and where was Edna Connor, or Edna Connor's body?

★   ★   ★

11:35 A.M. Having completed our nerve-wracking foray into Edna's and Tomquist's rooms, I now explained to Reg how I had passed the same vertical crawl space near the backstage area of the theater on two occasions, once with Rolf and the second time with him. And, each time I did, I'd had a feeling, a premonition, that something was behind that door, not more than a few feet from where I had been standing.

"You thinkin' Mrs. Conna's in there, Professa?"

"I don't know, Reg. It could be completely empty. But if we don't find out, and Tomquist heads to Brazil or someplace, I'll never forgive myself."

"I hear ya," he said. "I've got my key, so we should get moving."

"Not we, Reg. I need to head to my meeting with the Barsons." Then, looking at my watch, I added, "And it's starting in five minutes. Could you please go down there and take a look?"

"No sweat. If I find anything, do you want me to bring it to Mr. Barson's office?"

"Maybe that's not a great idea," I said. "If you do find something, just come to the office and let us know. We'll figure out where we can go to take a better look at it."

"I'm on my way."

"Just be careful," I said. Reg didn't reply; he just fired a salute into the air and strolled toward the Hampshire House stairs.

Chapter 66

Noon. If it's possible to feel dread and relief at the same time, that is exactly how I felt as I walked the last ten yards leading to Warn's office. The dread was predicated on the fact that, for all my hard work, I still didn't know what had happened to Edna Connor. But the last couple of days had been a revelation of sorts. For one of the first times in my life, I had devoted a large amount of time thinking about something besides my own neuroses. I was much too concerned about what the public's awareness of Edna Connor's disappearance would do to Warn to be worried about myself. If I'd learned nothing else during these last hours, it was to appreciate the value of those few people closest to me. Now, as I prepared myself for this inevitable meeting, I hoped that this enlightenment had not occurred too late. At that moment I was like a drowning man who uses every ounce of his remaining strength to reach a lifeguard's outstretched hand. The last two days had put a measurable strain on a number of people, but none more than Nya-beautiful Nya-who, having experienced so many years of disappointment, had gambled one last time that she could rescue her drowning marriage. And, like that swimmer, I was now consumed with the need to reach out to her.

★　　★　　★

Warn and Tom were already sitting in the office when I arrived. My pants had barely touched down into the chair when Warn asked, "So what do we have, Kary? Do we know where Edna Connor is and who is responsible for her disappearance?"

"No, we don't, Warn." My response hit both Barsons hard, especially Warn, who had gambled, against his son's advice, on my ability to find Edna Connor. Tom sat looking down at the floor. But Warn looked like someone who had been gut-shot. Thirty seconds passed before Tom arose and threw his hands in the air, "Well, that's that." His tone betrayed exasperation. Frankly, despite my displeasure with Tom's attitude during the last two days, I couldn't fault his reaction.

"No, it's not, Tom," I replied. "I've actually found out a good deal about what happened on the night of the 13th. But without the ability to question people openly or to enter Mrs. Connor's room . . . I chose not to reveal what Reg and I had just done at that particular moment . . . I can't say for certain what happened to her."

"That's great, Kary. Except now the cops will be all over the place." Then looking at his father, he added, "Everyone's going to know, Dad! Everyone!" For the third time in the last two days, Tom was having trouble controlling his anxiety. And, while I felt compassion for him, this was not the time for histrionics. We needed to pool our collective brain power and take a cold hard look at the facts.

"Please, give me a chance. I'm not finished explaining." But Tom was beginning to pace and rant under his breath. Not surprisingly, Warn had maintained his composure. "Tom, please, sit down and let Kary talk. We enlisted him in this situation. He's given it his all; and he's risked plenty."

"Risk . . . what the hell has Kary risked?" Tom blurted.

I gave Warn a look that said, "Please don't say any more." But he ignored me.

"Kary is up here trying to save his marriage. He put that on hold for us, Tom. His risk far surpasses ours, and his gain will be far less. If you and I lose this resort, we still have our family; we have each other, Tom. But Kary's loss could be much greater than anything you or I, hopefully, will ever be able to comprehend."

Leave it to Warn to put everything completely into focus. Why had it taken something like this weekend to help me see it? Why hadn't I been able to reach this conclusion for myself years before? All of my adult life, I had been striving aimlessly to achieve goals that had been shaped by editors, deans and corporate heads, but not by Kary Turnell. If I live to be a hundred, I'll never understand why had it taken me so many years to learn what Warn had clarified for his son in the heat of that moment. At last, I understood that accomplishment isn't about receiving promotions, writing award-winning novels or earning fame and fortune. It is about building warm, honest, unselfish relationships with family and a few good friends. For his part, Warn had taken these values one step farther, making them part of what he was as a husband, father and friend, and also as an employer.

Tom's voice brought me back to the issues at hand. "I'm sorry, Kary. I had no idea."

I really didn't want to belabor this point any more. In fact, I still wish that Warn had kept this extremely personal information to himself. But there was nothing I could do about it at that moment; so I changed the subject without responding to Tom. "If you'll indulge me for a few minutes, guys, I think you'll agree that we really know quite a bit about what happened that night."

"Go ahead, Kary. We won't interrupt you again," Warn said. I nodded, then reminded them that two possible suspects had surfaced, Billy Fenton and Richard Tomquist.

"Tomquist; that lousy bastard." Tom cried. But remembering his promise to remain silent, he ducked his head, and seethed.

I continued with a discussion of Billy Fenton, telling them about Billy's shenanigans with Edna Connor. I tried to leaving nothing out, beginning with his bragging that he was going to have his way with Mrs. Connor.

Now it was Warn's turn to interrupt. "That guy is despicable! How did he meet Edna Connor in the first place?" I searched my notes to refresh my memory, then told them how, according to information I'd obtained from Rolf, Billy had called from Mrs. Connor's room to report a broken glass shelf. Upon hearing this, both Barsons looked at one another and simply shook their heads.

Now it was Tom's turn to ask, "So, Rolf knows about this, too?"

"Look Tom, you're well aware of the grapevine effect around here. Once the housekeepers and the dining room staff heard that Mrs. Connor was missing, word was probably starting to spread before I first met with you yesterday morning." Both men nodded at one another and smiled wanly. Hearing no immediate opposition, I continued. "In answer to your question, I did speak to Rolf, about two hours ago. He provided me with this information because I convinced him that I was looking into Billy's welfare for an old army buddy."

"Army buddy . . . you?!" Warn scoffed. Ignoring that reference to my civilian purity, I said, "Yeah. Good old Rolf took particular pleasure in making me squirm. I had to put on quite a performance to sell him on the idea that hearing anything bad about poor little Billy was painful to me. He was enjoying it so much, I'm surprised he didn't give me the kid's underwear size. The short answer to your question, Tom, is that I don't think Rolf has the full picture . . . yet."

"Pretty soon everyone will know," Tom said.

Returning to my story, I told them that Billy had been waiting outside of Edna Connor's room late on the 13th. He had witnessed Edna and Tomquist returning. "He told me on the phone that Edna had talked Tomquist into going downstairs. I learned from Reg that he had. . ."

"Ye gods," Warn blurted, "Reg knows about this too?" I figured that this was as good a time as any to tell them that Reg had been an important cog in my investigation. I told them how it was Reg who was able to obtain a wealth of information for us without being anywhere near as conspicuous as I would have been. When I had finished, Warn said, "If you needed a confederate, at least you chose a person who can be counted on to keep this information to himself." As he said this, he glanced over at Tom for confirmation.

Tom simply nodded and said, "A regular Fort Knox."

Their interruptions were beginning to unnerve me. "As I was saying . . . I learned from Reg that Tomquist had gone down to the lobby looking for a bottle of champagne and a box of condoms." This made Warn and me laugh in spite of the pressure of the situation. But Tom simply shook his head and said, "That's Richard all right. He obviously still thinks he's quite the ladies' man."

"To cut to the chase, next Billy went to see Edna while Tomquist was downstairs."

"Oh no, did she let him into her room?" Warn asked.

"You know, for a couple of guys who weren't going to interrupt, you've sure perfected the art." Both men smiled at this remark and vowed to keep silent. "Sure you will," I said. Billy tried to put his best moves on Edna, but she wasn't having any of it. When she threatened to scream, he took off like a bat out of hell."

"So, was that the end of that?" Tom asked. I simply looked at him, bared my teeth and growled. He got the message.

"Billy went to his car and was ready to leave but there was one small problem . . . he'd left his keys in his jacket sitting by the service elevator." I thought the Barsons would wet their pants when they heard this. Two elderly guests walking past the office tried to see what the raucous laughter was about. They probably felt that they had eavesdropped on a small party. But this had been a light moment in the face of a coming storm.

"So he had to come back into the hotel, but couldn't get in the easy way. He finally made his way in through the laundry room."

"In the dark?" Warn asked. "He's lucky he wasn't beheaded in there."

"Next, he went through the catacombs without being seen. But he was delayed when the night watchman decided to take a detour through the catacombs. When Billy finally made it to the Hampshire House, he heard a familiar noise. It was the service elevator."

"At that time of night? But who(?) . . . Bill Norman would never use the elevator at night!" Tom nodded his agreement to his father's assessment.

"Who's this Bill Norman?" I asked.

"He's one of our night security people," Tom replied.

Continuing, I left out the part of how Billy, in a rush to hide in the alcove, had hurt his leg. After all, how much body shaking laughter can two grown men endure. I did tell them how Billy had arrived in time to see Tomquist return to his room with a bundle over his shoulder.

"A bundle?" they said in unison.

"Just wait, that's coming," I replied.

Warn interrupted yet again, "For the sake of time, let's cut to the chase, shall we, Kary. Is Billy Fenton a suspect or isn't he?"

"Based on what I know, the only crime that Billy committed was being an obnoxious young jerk."

"But," Tom added, "he did force his way into Edna Connor's room."

"Technically, Edna let him in and then threw him out. I don't see him getting any more than a slap on the wrist for doing that."

"He'll get a lot more than that if he ever shows his face around here again!" Warn said scornfully.

Chapter 67

12:20 P.M. "Are we ready to discuss Mr. Tomquist, gentlemen?" Warn looked queasy, while Tom grunted, "That bastard."

Warn didn't do anything to make my job easier. "Tomquist is here, Tom."

"What are you talking about, Dad?"

For the sake of time, I filled Tom in about how Tomquist had registered as R. Johann, and had subsequently befriended Edna Connor.

"Damn! I saw the name Tomquist, but never put two and two together," Tom exclaimed."

"You're not alone, Tom," Warn replied softly. Thus far, Warn had been doing a terrific job of keeping his feelings in check, for Tom's sake as well as mine.

I understood the magnitude of Tom's feelings. So, trying to get father and son focused, I said, "Let's proceed with a look at that jackass's activities the last two days, shall we gentlemen?" Tom smiled at me for saying this; and, out of the corner of my eye, Warn winked his approval. Looking at my notes, I informed them that Richard had arrived under the name R. Johan Tomquist, doubtlessly with the intention of deceiving any staff who might recognize the name, Richard Tomquist.

As I was about to continue, there was a knock on the screen door. Warn called out, "I'm sorry, we're in conference right now. Would it be possible for you to come back in a half an hour?"

I was incredulous. In my two days at the resort, I'd had four or five meetings with Warn. Every one of them had been interrupted, either by a department head, a staff person or a guest. It was no wonder Warn had seemed shell-shocked. But on this occasion, Warn was delighted when he recognized who his visitor was.

"Bill Norman, I haven't seen you for a few weeks. Come in for a minute. How is everything with your family?" And, before the man could answer, Warn said, "Tom, you know Bill, of course. Kary, this is Bill Norman; he has been a night watchman here for what, twenty years, Bill?"

Bill smiled, "Good of you to remember, Mr. Barson." This was just one more piece of evidence that Warn Barson was one CEO who did things right. He wasn't one of those myopic people who functions in a little cocoon sheltered from the lives of his employees. Warn probably encountered Bill Norman three times in a year, and usually in a cold, poorly lighted parking lot. Yet Warn cared enough to learn how long the night watchman had been working at the resort, and even knew the names of his family members. It was soon apparent that their relationship was more than superficial. "I'm doing fine, Mr. Barson, fine. My wife's back in Wisconsin visiting her family. So it's a bit lonely. But otherwise, no complaints."

"Nancy has just come back into town, too," Warn responded. "But she's attending a chamber of commerce function tonight in Colebrook. Say, I have an idea, why don't we have dinner together? We can eat in the dining room

. . .my treat."

"Thank you, Mr. Barson. That's too good of an offer to pass up."

"My pleasure, Bill. Why don't you meet me here at seven?"

"Before I go Mr. Barson, I have some information you ought to hear. I saw Reg early this morning when I came to get my paycheck. When I told him what I saw last night, he said that I should talk to all three of you gentlemen about it. That's why I came by. Sorry if I'm interrupting something."

I was the first to speak. "By all means, Mr. Norman . . ."

"Bill," he interrupted.

"Okay, Bill. If Reg thinks something you told him is important, we need to hear what you have to say."

"Well . . .it may be nothing," he replied.

Warn was encouraging. "Go ahead, Bill. Let us be the judge."

"Well, it's just that the other night, while I was doing my rounds . . ." He looked at his watch self-consciously. "It was right around 11:55PM. I saw a man parking his car and walking back and forth in all kinds of directions as though he were lost."

Tom said with a smile that looked pretty much like a sneer, "It must have been Billy."

Bill Norman looked at Tom and said, "If you mean that young punk, Billy Fenton; it wasn't. This man was older, and much bigger."

"Do you know who he was, Bill?" Warn asked.

"Of course I do, because I asked him. I stuck my flashlight in his face and asked for identification. At first I thought he was a guest who'd had too much to drink, because he seemed so disoriented. But, it turned out he'd just been driving for a long time and was just plain exhausted."

"I can't stand the suspense!" I finally said. "Who was he, Bill?"

"He said his name was Al Connor."

"Al Connor!" the Barsons and I said in unison. Tom followed that with a chorus of, "This is unbelievable!"

★　★　★

Bill left the office, while the three of us simply stared at one another without saying a word. I was the first to speak. "All right gentlemen; so now we have a third suspect. Although, there may not be a single soul who can place him in the Hampshire House."

"So now what, Kary?" Warn asked.

We had little choice but to keep examining the evidence. After all, Richard Tomquist still was our most viable candidate at that juncture. Then, I remembered about Reg Gill's errand. He certainly should have returned by that time. I turned to the younger Barson and said, "Tom, I've been expecting to hear from Reg. Has anyone contacted you on your two-way radio?"

"You'd have heard the squelch if they had, Kary. But that couldn't happen because I've had the radio off since just before our meeting started. I didn't want any interruptions."

To which Warn added, "And I've left instructions not to interrupt us."

"Then he wouldn't have been able to call, even if he wanted to?" I asked with noticeable relief in my voice. "Warn, can I use your phone to call the bellmen's desk?" He nodded his approval. I dialed the number.

"Professa, sorry I haven't had time to walk down there and talk to you," Reg said when I finally reached him.

"That's okay, Reg. But I've been concerned; is everything all right?"

"Well, not exactly. There's been a slight mishap in the Dixville House. So, I've been delayed. I should be able to head over to the theater in about ten minutes."

"Okay, Reg. No problem," I responded. But I couldn't completely mask my genuine sense of concern from Warn.

"Everything okay with Reg?" Warn asked.

"Oh sure," I replied. He's just been delayed working overtime for his ogre bosses."

Tom and Warn gave one another an amused glance. I decided not to say anything about the mishap in the Dixville House, for I knew that one or both of them would have wanted to find out what it was all about. With the sand running out of the hourglass, we didn't have time for that.

★   ★   ★

I continued to inform the Barsons about Tomquist's activities. I told them how Tomquist had been seated next to Edna Connor in the dining room, and how he had been assigned guest room number 168, right next to hers in the Hampshire House.

Warn looked at Tom and said, "I wonder what the odds against that happening are." To which Tom replied, "I'd say about twenty thousand to one."

I chimed in, "Well, unless the state police prove that this is somehow part of a conspiracy, I'd say the cliché about playing the lottery applies to at least one of them."

I continued with my description, which had been based upon input from the waitstaff, plus my own snooping. Richard Tomquist had honed in on the best built, and apparently most vulnerable person he could find. Once he had gained her confidence over the course of a couple of days, he began to follow his modus operandi of luring her into bed. I next told the Barsons what I had learned about the couple's red-hot night in the ballroom and then reconstructed, to the best of my ability, the walk back to their rooms. Next, using Billy Fenton's admittedly shaky testimony, I recounted the kiss at the door and Richard's temporary departure, estimating the latter to have occurred at approximately 11:15 PM. Finally, I told them how Billy had seen Richard leaving his room with the plastic bag over his shoulder at what I'd estimated to be about 12:30AM.

"Warn then looked at me and said, "Are you saying what I think you are?"

By this juncture I was beginning to think I could read minds . . . everyone's mind except Nya's, that is. "Yes." I replied, "Edna had three visitors that night."

Once again, we were interrupted by a knock at the door. Before Warn could answer, we heard Reg's voice, sounding somewhat strained, coming from the other side of the screen. "Is it okay if I bring this inside, Mr. Barson?"

Chapter 68

1 P.M. "Aftanoon, gentlemen." Not even the bulky bag he was carrying could dampen Reg's perpetual good mood. "This big plastic bag is a slippery bugger . . . 'specially with these rubber gloves on." As Reg entered Warn's office, the two Barsons stared at him, their jaws dropping in disbelief. Reg's shirt had been torn at the shoulder and he was covered with grime of various origins. The Barsons were not the only ones who were surprised to see what Reg had in tow. Our plan had been for him to leave Mrs. Connor's remains in a more remote part of the hotel, so as not to panic the guests or the staff.

"Reg, I thought you . . .'

"No sweat, Professa, I doubt there's anythin' here that will upset anyone," he offered before I could finish.

"You mean, that isn't Edna Connor's body, Reg?" Warn asked.

"No sir, Mr. Barson. It ain't heavy enough an' just don't feel like a body. Although it's damn near as clumsy as tryin' to carry one," he replied.

"Then what is it; and why did you lug that all the way up here, Reg?" Tom Barson asked.

I interceded. "I sent Reg down to the crawl space along the east wall of the movie theater to see if he could find anything."

"But why that particular space, Kary?" Warn asked me.

"Yeah," Tom interjected, "there are hundreds of places Tomquist could have hidden whatever that is. Why did you think to send him there?"

"I wish I could give you gentlemen a sound, scientific reason. Two things caused me to think about that particular space in the hotel. Number one, Billy said he last saw Richard walking toward the stairs in the Hampshire House."

"So?" Tom asked.

"So, if Tomquist were looking to hide something in the catacombs, he would have taken the service elevator down, not up, where there's nothing but guest rooms."

"That's true," Tom agreed. "Go on."

"And if he were going to take something directly outside, he could have either thrown it off the outside fire escape stairs along the east wall of the Hampshire House, or else used the balcony overlooking Lake Gloriette. Then he could have acted like he was going out for some late night air and simply walked out the front door, gone around the building and retrieved the plastic bag."

"Okay, Kary. I follow you so far," Warn said.

I continued. "But he didn't do either of those things. Which, in my mind, indicated that he'd found a nice, quiet, storage place right there in the Hampshire House."

"All of this makes sense. But there are plenty of places he could have stored that thing, whatever it is," Tom said. "I still don't understand why you thought of that particular crawl space."

163

"This is where intuition and luck come in," I smiled. "Remember, I'm not a complete amateur at this investigation stuff. Right, Warn?"

Warn looked at me with a broad smile on his face and nodded his agreement. I continued. "Knowing intuitively that Richard was carrying something he clearly didn't want anyone to find for a while, I ruled out any place in or around the children's recreation area immediately."

"But why?" both Barsons asked in unison.

"Because young children are fearless explorers. If the bag were anywhere near the rec room, it would be found . . . possibly within a matter of hours."

"Wouldn't that also be true of your crawl space," Tom asked.

At this point, Reg interrupted. He described to all of us how Tomquist had lain the bag horizontally between the base of the Hampshire House's outer wall and the base of the outer wall of the theater's backstage area. "I'll tell ya' what," he said, "if I didn't know that I was lookin' for something in a large plastic bag, I'd have overlooked it."

"Why, Reg?" Warn asked.

"Because the way it was settin', it looked just like floor insulation."

"Okay, I'm buying all this," Tom said. Then turning to me, he added, "But I still don't understand why you'd honed in on that particular space.

I smiled and looked Tom right in the eye. "Luck," I replied.

"Luck?!"

"Look, Tom. Investigative work of any kind . . . even the academic research I do . . . is really a matter of designing some workable hypothesis, then doing your research. Frequently our hypotheses fall way wide of the mark. Once in a while that educated guess we have taken is so right-on it's scary. The truth is, I had a strange feeling both times I walked by the door to that crawl space. I just sensed that something was in there."

"And it was," Tom added, with an expression of admiration and mild amusement on his face.

Chapter 69

Having thus discussed the location of Richard Tomquist's stash, Tom was all set to open the large plastic bag and find out what was inside. I noticed that Reg had been wearing a pair of rubber gloves. "Should we be tamperin' with this evidence?" he asked.

"Yeah, let's open it," Tom said.

"Not so fast, gentlemen," I interceded. "Does anyone besides me notice something familiar about the bag." The others looked at one another, then back at me, with blank expressions all around.

"Warn, will you please get me the envelope with the stories about your niece's murder." Warn seemed frozen at first; so I added, "You'll see what I'm up to in just a minute."

Warn retrieved the envelope and handed it to me, the ashen expression having returned to his face.

Looking at them for a minute, I said, "Yes, I was right . . . take a look at these pictures."

Tom was the first to speak. "I've seen these pictures before, Kary; there's nothing here that . . ."

But, Reg soon spotted what I had noticed. "It's the knots, ain't it, Professa?"

"Good for you, Reg."

Warn, then Tom, noticed what I had seen, too.

"The knot that was used to tie the bag shut is really unusual," Warn said.

"Sure ain't the kind of double knot I tie my garbage with," Reg chuckled.

Then, with an anguished cry, Tom added, "The bastard used a big plastic bag, too!" Warn placed his hand on Tom's shoulder. Both men were being tortured by this revelation.

"Do you have someone on staff who might be able to identify this knot and tell us something about it?" I asked.

"Yes, Chris Buckley, our nature guide; fortunately, he just returned from vacation this morning," Warn replied. Then, needing to feel that he was making a contribution, Tom added, "I'll call him in here." With that, he picked up the telephone and, after a brief conversation, told us that Chris was on his way.

Within five minutes, there was a knock on the screen door. Opening the door, a tall, lean rugged man of about forty strode into Warn's office.

Recognizing everyone except me, he stuck out his hand and said, "Hi, I'm Chris Buckley." Chris Buckley was ruggedly handsome, with a look of intelligence and self-assurance, just the kind of person I'd entrust my life to, should I ever decide to change my sedentary ways.

Warn introduced us. "Chris, this is Professor Turnell; he's a guest at the resort."

"Oh, so you're the novelist; I've heard a lot about you. But, I feel sort of left out. It seems you've interviewed everyone else around here."

Not wishing to arouse suspicion at that juncture, I replied, "Don't think you're off the hook, Chris."

"Well, that's good news. I'd be happy to talk with you anytime."

"Thanks, I'll take you up on that. But, what I'd like to know for the time being is the name of this knot." Still wearing the rubber gloves, Reg held up the bag so Chris could get a closer look.

Chris let out a whistle. "That's a beauty! It's a Yosemite bowline. You don't usually expect to see something like that in a resort hotel."

"What's it used for?" Warn asked.

"It's primarily used by climbers, spelunkers and serious campers," Chris informed us. "I've never used one. We learned to use a figure eight; although, we studied these in the boy scouts. Your weekend camper usually sticks with a half-hitch."

"I've never heard of the Yosemite bowline before; how does it differ from a half-hitch?"

"How much do you know about knots, Professor?"

"Almost nothing," I admitted.

"Well then, the simplest thing I can say is that the Yosemite bowline offers more security than the basic half-hitch." Then moving toward the plastic bag, he asked, "Is it all right if I touch this?"

When we all replied in unison, "No!" Chris arched his eyebrows suspiciously.

Warn interceded at this point. "Chris, you're going to have to trust us and keep this entire conversation quiet for the next couple of days."

"Sure, Mr. Barson," he said. But it took Chris a few seconds to recover enough of his composure to continue. Finally, taking a pencil from his pocket, he pointed out how the knot on the bag was secured by taking the end of the plastic tie . . . which had been cut for the purpose . . . and threading it back through the knot. Then, using his pencil and a pad of paper from Warn's desk, Chris showed us why the more familiar half-hitch didn't provide the same level of security. "Not as many knots," he offered with a wry smile.

We thanked Chris and allowed him to get back to work, but not before Warn reminded him of the importance of secrecy in this matter. Before he left, he looked back at me and said, "Nice meeting you Professor; I'm looking forward to that interview . . . more than ever."

After Chris left, we continued our discussion.

"That was very informative; but, now the question is, is Tomquist a climber or a spelunker?" I asked.

"Was." It was Reg who spoke first. "Richard used to do some hiking and such when he lived out west, 'long time ago."

"But, was he serious enough to have learned this?" Warn asked.

"I remember him talking about climbin' cliffs in one of the national parks out west," Reg replied. "I think he spent his summers out there."

"And we have every reason to believe this is the same bag he carried out of his room," I said. Then, thinking a minute, I added, "This is starting to be

166

a lot more serious situation than it was yesterday."

"It sure is," Warn said.

Tom started to say something, but I interceded. Looking at Warn, I said, "Unless I miss my guess, the bag that Reg found may prove to be evidence in your niece's murder."

The full weight of this seemed to hit Warn. He sat down and, rubbing his brow with his right hand, replied, "I'd give anything to be able to nail Tomquist. It's been killing my family knowing that he's been running around free all of these years."

"Look, Warn, let's not jump the gun here. Besides, we have more pressing matters."

"More pressing matters, what could be . . .?"

"Let's not forget Edna Connor," I said.

For once, Tom proved to be the Barson with the more level head. "Kary's right, Dad. Besides, we may be able to kill two birds with one stone."

"Precisely," I said.

"So, now what, Kary?" Warn asked.

"I'd like to hear about this bag from the horse's mouth," I replied.

"Okay, let's bring him in here."

I wanted Warn to be certain he understood the possible consequences of bringing a reluctant, and probably uncooperative Richard Tomquist into the office.

"Let's think about this for a minute, Warn. First, without taking fingerprints off of the bag, we have no real proof that Richard is the one who put this into the crawl space."

"But, we have Billy Fenton's eye witness testimony that he saw Tomquist removing the bag from his room," Tom said. Of course, we all knew that this would not be terribly useful evidence by itself, given Fenton's own history.

"We sure as hell better make certain he can't touch it and say he got his finger prints on it afta' the fact," Reg offered.

"That's good thinking, Reg," I said. Next, I told the three men how we should proceed with an interrogation of Tomquist. Before putting my plan into action, we needed to find a more private place to meet. Also, it would be helpful to recruit two more people to restrain Tomquist, in case it became necessary.

The potential for nailing Tomquist seemed to revive Warn.

"Reg, go find Bill Norman and get Rolf, too. "We can do this in one of the far corner rooms on this level in the Hampshire House. See what's available will you, Tom? Oh, and Reg, please tell Bill to bring his restraints with him."

"I'll call Javy Olds about an empty room," Tom replied.

"And I know just where Bill probably is; the practice puttin' green is usually deserted this time of the day," Reg said with his typical smile.

It was 1:45PM when Warn, Tom, Reg, and I met in room 15, situated in the southwest corner of the Hampshire House's ground level. Rolf and Bill Norman had accepted the task of locating Tomquist and bringing him to the room, hopefully before one o'clock. Then, at precisely 1:48, we heard the sound of a card key being slipped into, then triggering the lock. A voice that sounded like Rolf said, "Let's go in here and talk, Richard." Rolf and Bill had been very clever. They had positioned themselves behind Tomquist. In the event that he decided to bolt when he saw us, they would be blocking his egress.

Tomquist was the first to enter. "Say, what the hell is going on here? You guys said that this would . . ."

"Sit down, Mr. Tomquist," Warn said, while pointing toward the mint green wooden chair we had placed strategically between two rows of inquisitors. You could see in his eyes that Tomquist was thinking about trying to make a run for it. But, with Rolf and Bill Norman on one side of him and Reg on the other, he was outweighed by nearly triple. And the looks on the three men's faces showed that they would have no qualms about using force if it became necessary. I doubted he would cause any trouble; Tomquist was one of those guys who described himself as a lover, not a fighter. I figured him for a coward.

By prior agreement, I would serve as principal questioner. Warn, who was now remarkably composed, would serve as my back-up. The other men were to remain silent throughout the entire process. I could see the instant he recognized me for the first time since he'd entered the room.

"Hello Richard," I began.

"Wait a minute. What the hell is this about? I thought you were a professor. You interviewed me about your book." In the background, I could hear Rolf whisper to Bill Norman that he'd thought the same thing. I gave Rolf a quick, cold stare. He immediately understood its meaning.

"What you said is partially true, Richard. I am a professor; but I've also been known to do a little investigating." I nearly smiled in spite of myself. This had been a clever way to make me sound more official than I really was. At the same time I was being entirely truthful. Warn immediately read into my meaning and gave me a subtle nod. I continued.

"Richard, these men and I want to know where you were between midnight on the 13th and one AM on the 14th."

Warn chimed in, "That's Friday night to Saturday morning, Mr. Tomquist." I looked at Warn. It was a signal to let me do the talking.

"I don't remember . . . wait a minute, is this a trick question? I was sleeping by eleven that night."

"Really? We have an eyewitness who saw you wandering the halls at that time."

He was not being moved. "Yeah, well so what? Even if I was, there's no law against that, is there? Not that I'm saying I was doing any such thing, mind you."

Now it was Warn's turn. "Mr. Tomquist, you're in much deeper trouble than you may realize."

"Why should I believe you, Mr. Barson?"

Now it was time to play our trump card. Owing to Reg Gil's ingenuity, we had fashioned a little display for Tomquist. From behind the bed, Warn pulled out a large piece of poster board with four Polaroid shots attached to it.

"Take a careful look at these, Mr. Tomquist," Warn said.

Tomquist blanched noticeably when he looked closely at the photos, each depicting another angle of a large plastic garbage bag. "How did you . . . wait a minute . . . I'm not saying anything."

Warn started to speak again, but I waved him off.

"Richard," I began, "it looks to us like you're the leading suspect in the kidnapping and murder of Mrs. Edna Connor."

"Kidnapping? Murder? I didn't kill anyone, I just . . ." Again he stopped before he could incriminate himself. He sat there in silence. With terrific restraint, the six of us also were completely silent. It was like a game of chicken, each of us waiting for the other to speak. Finally, Tomquist broke the silence. "Look, I admit that I knew Edna. We were kind of sweet on one another. There's no way I'd . . ."

Warn stepped in at that point. "We know all about your relationship with Edna Connor. We know that you had meals together; we know about the nightclub and your attempt to get a bottle of champagne on the 13th, just before midnight. Why don't you save us all a lot of trouble and just tell us the rest?"

Again, Tomquist was silent for a long time. He seemed to be thinking hard about something, attempting to bring it to mind. When at last he spoke, he sounded more like a boy in his early teens than a man in his mid-thirties.

"Do you know how much I loved this job?" he cried. "Do you have any idea how proud I was to come to work here every day? Do you know what it meant for someone from my background to be able to tell his parents and his friends that he works at the nicest resort in all of New Hampshire?" He was fighting back tears as he said this.

"Most of the men in this room share that pride, Richard. Only, they play by the rules. Apparently, you didn't," I said. Several of the others nodded as I said this.

"I had sex with a few people. It was consensual, for Crissake. I have needs; the people who work here aren't children!"

Warn spoke next. "This is a resort, not a brothel. We can't have that kind of thing going on between the staff and guests."

"Why not? Every woman I did it with was as satisfied as I was," he blurted.

"Because," Warn replied, "those people came here to have a first class leisure experience. Reg and Rolf . . . and you, Mr. Tomquist . . . all were hired to make certain that happened, while being as unobtrusive as humanly possible. If we start allowing staff to fraternize with the guests, where will it end? The next thing you know, Reg will call Rolf on his two-way radio about an emergency and Rolf will say that he can't come because he's Mrs. Johnson's second for bridge. That situation would be untenable. The resort would get a terrible reputation. And, the rest of us shouldn't be brought down by one person's irresponsibility."

"But I was off duty," he whined. At that moment he sounded like a grade schooler. I couldn't help feeling a little bit sorry for him.

"No, you were not off duty all three of those times. Twice you were on duty and, the third time, you were in the process of coming on shift. Once again, there's a reason for not allowing any fraternization."

Now it was my turn. I finished summarizing what we knew about his whereabouts. I then placed the poster board and photos near enough that he could see them clearly.

"Now Richard, do you have something to tell us?" Realizing that he might ask to speak with a lawyer, I decided to take steps to preempt that. "Do you understand; if you don't answer my questions, you'll be interrogated by the state police? They aren't likely to be as gentle as we've been Richard. So if you cooperate, I'll ask Tom Barson over there to record your statement; then you sign it and we'll submit it to the police. It will save you a lot of trouble"

Of course, this was a bluff. The state police were more likely to boil me in oil than Richard for my role in this charade.

"I don't need a lawyer," he mumbled. His voice was so muffled that he was barely audible.

"Fine, Richard. Why don't you start at the beginning?" I said.

Tomquist told us how he had arrived at the resort several days before, with a chip on his shoulder. He had carried the shame and anger of his firing for ten years. Now, even though he had gone on to operate a successful business and had accumulated a healthy bank account, he was unable to put that embarrassing episode to rest. One day, upon seeing an advertisement for The Balsams in his local newspaper, he decided to return to the resort, but this time as a patron. He made his reservation and prepared for the visit. As the time drew closer, he found that the old mental wounds were festering more than ever. So he resolved to do something to get even. "A gesture, mind you, nothing major," he said.

At this moment, Tom Barson had unfortunately decided to break my gag rule. It was nearly a very costly mistake.

"A gesture. Murder's a gesture to you, Tomquist?"

"Why do you guys keep saying that? I didn't commit any murder."

Unfortunately, Tom wasn't finished. "No, not one murder . . . two!"

"That's it, I'm out of here." He stood up and turned to leave. "I'm leaving and don't try to stop me." But that is exactly what Reg, Rolf and Bill Norman did. Still, Tomquist was not ready to give in without a fight. He began to flail at his captors. Finally, Reg put an end to his thrashing. Grabbing

Tomquist firmly by the throat and looking him straight in the eyes, Reg said, "Don't make me hurt you, Richard. I don't want to do that."

Realizing that his flight plans had been futile, Tomquist slowly calmed down.

Several minutes had been wasted by Tom's outburst. When I was convinced that Tomquist was ready to listen again, I resumed my position near his chair and said, "Let's get back to the point where you said you were planning to get even, Richard."

"Okay, but I'm no murderer," he said.

"We'll talk about that soon. Let's finish hearing what you were saying earlier."

But Richard wanted a symbol of faith. Pointing at Tom, he said, "I'm not saying anything else until he's out of this room."

"Okay Richard," I said with a calm voice. "We'll send Tom out of here so you can talk to us some more."

Tom had started to protest, but Warn cut him off with a stern look. Tom knew he had been out of line. So he left the room, stopping only to let his father know that he had calmed down.

I was concerned at that moment. We had built up momentum with our questioning process. I feared Tom's outburst had undermined everything we'd accomplished, and wondered if we could still meet our deadline.

"Please continue, Richard," I said.

Tomquist proceeded to tell us how he had brought some devices with him that could be used to remove and carry items away without arousing much suspicion.

"My plan was to steal something from the Dixville House, something they really valued, like an old book, or maybe one of the portraits."

For an instant, I had visions of Tomquist stealing my photograph from the Wall of Fame.

He continued, "But, as time went on, I got to know Edna Connor better. At first, I was interested in her because she had a nice rack." Others in the room suppressed the temptation to smile. "That lady's body is pretty damned good, for someone close to forty." Something deep inside of me groaned; but I decided it wasn't the time to teach this jerk it wouldn't be long before forty would seem young to him, too.

"So, your plan was to seduce Mrs. Connor, but that was all; is that correct, Richard?" I asked.

"Yeah, but when she sent me on a wild goose chase to get champagne, I started to get really pissed off. When I got back to my room, I got into some more comfortable clothes and I knocked on her door. She wasn't going to let me into her room, but I threatened to make a ruckus unless she changed her mind. When she finally let me in, I tried to make a move on her; but she blacked out."

"Is that when you decided to take stronger measures?" Warn asked.

"Hey, what is it with you Barsons? I told you, I didn't kill Edna . . . I didn't even hurt her. Not really," Richard replied.

"What does not really mean, Richard?" I asked.

"It means I was pretty mad and I shook her up a little bit. But nothing more than that."

I looked at my watch. We needed to cut to the chase. "Then what happened, Richard?"

"Nothing . . . well . . . I had to beat it."

"Beat it? Why?" I asked.

It was then that Richard described how there had been a knock on the door. He then left Edna's room through the connecting doorway both he and Edna Connor had opened a few minutes before. He was able to close her door but could not lock it. So, he locked the door in his room, hoping it would be enough.

"That fits what I saw," I said. Then realizing my error in allowing this to slip, I gave Reg a look of panic. Warn had caught my expression. Fortunately, he was too shrewd to repeat his son's earlier outburst. He simply looked at me, and then at Reg, and said softly, "I'll deal with you two later." I looked across the room at Rolf who was absolutely gloating over my predicament.

Fortunately, Tomquist had missed my faux pas. He told us he had taken a quick shower. This had been his alibi in case someone burst into his room and accused him of accosting Edna Connor. When he'd finished showering, he listened at the door that connected his room with Edna's. Almost immediately, he had heard a man's voice, then he heard a woman who sounded like Edna-he couldn't be sure-and finally, the sound of Edna's room door closing.

What did you do next, Richard?" I asked.

"Oh, it was a freakin' nightmare," he replied." He proceeded to tell us how angry and disgusted he had been. Not only had he failed to upset the Barsons, he had missed out on having sex with Edna. Then it had suddenly dawned on him how he could embarrass the resort, while simultaneously getting back at Edna. "Two birds with one stone," he said. With Edna out of her room, his plan was to take some of her valuable clothes and jewelry-as it turned out, she didn't have any-then stash it some place where no one would find it . . . at least not for a long time. He used the connecting door to gain entry into Edna's room, then loaded the plastic bag he'd brought to the resort with as much as it, and he, could carry. "It didn't seem to weigh anything at first, but after a while . . . holy cow!"

Next, Tomquist described his ill-fated attempt to enter the theater through the front door. He described how he had thought about simply going through the catacombs, but figured it was too risky. He told us in laborious detail how he had resigned himself to taking the service elevator back upstairs, stopping briefly in his room, then carrying the bag down the side stairs to the recreation room. "That damned bag felt like it weighed a ton by then," he said.

I then interjected, "So you used a master key of some type to gain access to the back of the theater through the recreation room, didn't you?"

"Yeah. That's pretty smart of you, Professor," he replied.

Rolf couldn't resist making the comment, "So, that old legend about you having made a copy of the master key is true." It was more of a statement of realization than a question. Tomquist nodded; and as he did, four hands reached out, simultaneously. Reluctantly, Tomquist reached into his pocket and placed the infamous key in the hand of Warn Barson.

Looking at the gash on the left side of Tomquist's face, I said, "It looks like you had a bit of a problem negotiating the crawl space near the theater." He nodded, "Yeah, that was kind of the last straw." As he rubbed his face, I saw Reg fondling the tear in the sleeve of his own shirt. There had been two victims of the tight quarters in the crawl space.

Warn was to have the last word. "Then you took Edna Connor's belongings and hid them as a payback to her, and all of us as well. Is that correct, Mr. Tomquist?"

"That's right. So, you see, I'm no murderer. The bag in those photographs is filled with a bunch of Edna's junk. The most you have me on is a misdemeanor. So, why don't you just forget the whole thing, and I'll promise to stay the hell away from here," Richard said. Now that the truth was out, he was feeling more sure of himself.

"Not so fast, Richard," I said. "There's one more picture I'd like you to see."

I removed a photocopy from a folder I had borrowed from the business office. Looking at it, I remarked, "You know, it's amazing how clear these new copies look. I think you'll agree, Richard."

Tomquist took the picture from me and, recognizing the large plastic bag pictured in the article about the murder of Warn Barson's niece, he panicked. He knew that he needed to run; there was no time to waste. This time, with Rolf and Bill leaning over to see the photocopy, Tomquist saw his best opportunity to escape. Grabbing Rolf's arm, Tomquist used all of his strength to shove the maintenance chief into Bill. Bill, in turn, lost his balance and fell to the floor, knocking Reg down in the process. Warn and I were still on our feet, but had three large, prone men separating us from the fleeing Tomquist. In the thirty seconds it took the three men to get untangled and to regain their feet, Tomquist had opened the door of the guest room and exited.

★   ★   ★

Within two seconds, Tomquist was in the hallway. Then, despite hitting his left shoulder against the pillar situated outside the guest room where he had been interrogated, Tomquist ran with all of his might down the corridor of the Hampshire House. Richard was moving on adrenalin now. He had a quick decision to make. If he took the stairs toward the basement level, he would need a key to gain entry into the theater. But, he didn't have his master key anymore. He could run the full length of the corridor to the stairs leading to the lobby; but, then what? The chances were that someone had alerted other staff in the hotel. They'd already be heading this way. So, that left him with only one choice . . . the fire escape.

A few more strides . . . twenty-five in all . . . took him to the doorway leading to the fire escape. He pulled open the door. There was no time to heed the warning, "Emergency Use Only." Besides, this was an emergency. If Richard couldn't get away, they'd nail him for that girl's murder. Why had she resisted him . . . all those years ago? They had gotten along so well. All he'd wanted was a little sex. Why had she suddenly become so uptight? A few days later, when he'd learned she had been related to Mr. Barson . . . he didn't feel so bad . . . the bastard had fired him, hadn't he? All of that had happened so long ago . . . he'd refused to think about it for years . . . why did the damned professor have to find that old newspaper article?

Tomquist was in a blind fury. Having torn open the door to the fire escape, he failed to see the metal utilities box mounted along the right wall. Now the searing pain in his right shoulder matched the throbbing in his left. There was no time to worry about that now; he had to get to the parking lot. He ran along the concrete corridor, moving wildly toward the ladder that served as the fire escape for the Hampshire House. So blind with fear was he, that he failed to negotiate the steel link chain that separated the corridor from the ladder. Catching his heel on the chain, his momentum carried him outward, parallel to the building. Reaching in vain for the ladder, he hurdled forward, rotating so he was falling head first toward the ground. Had he fallen feet first, Tomquist might have survived the twenty-five foot fall with little more than a broken leg. But, by landing on his neck and head, he was killed instantly.

Chapter 71

It was now nearly 2:30. Because of Tom Barson's outburst, a meeting that should have taken thirty minutes had lasted an hour. With Richard Tomquist's body lying along the outside wall of the Hampshire House, Warn had placed an urgent call to the state police. Thankfully, his friend the captain had returned earlier than expected. Tom Barson did not join us; having helped Reg secure a tarp over Tomquist's body, he was taking the rest of the day off. This left Warn and me to tell the state police our version of what had transpired. For his part, Warn appeared one part relieved, and one part anguished. The knowledge that Richard Tomquist had finally received the justice he had long deserved was briefly satisfying to Warn. However, there would be no escaping the sensationalism surrounding Tomquist's death. Once people tied Tomquist to the decade-old murder of Warn's niece, both the authorities and the media would be coming around for quite a while. Besides Warn and Tom, some of the other loyal, long-term Balsams employees dobtlessly would be questioned about Tomquist's untimely tumble.

"Well, it's been an interesting weekend, Warn," I began. "One piece of good news . . . the stuff Tomquist told us about Edna Connor corroborates what we learned from Billy Fenton and our other witnesses," I said.

"Billy Fenton!" It was a tone of disgust as well as Warn's expression of annoyance that Billy had slipped between the cracks and into The Balsams employ.

"I have to say that I trust the information we have; which, unfortunately, exposes a serious shortcoming in my investigation."

"Namely?" Warn asked.

"Our missing third suspect; Al Connor."

Warn then informed me he had already instructed his secretary to try calling the Connor household while we were interrogating Tomquist. "There was no answer; and, there's no answering machine at the house either. We even tried his cell phone . . . nothing." Warn also had given instructions to try another telephone number that had been listed on Edna Connor's registration information. The latter had proven to be Al Connor's business telephone. "No one was there either. It's strange, Kary; the Connors vanished from different places, but on the same day."

"There is one clue. We do know that Al was in touch with Edna more than once that day."

"That's right; the telephone records. And of course, he was seen here last night by a very reliable source, Bill Norman."

"So what do you make of Tomquist's story about the knock on the door while he was in Edna's room?" Warn asked.

"And what about the voices and the room door closing that Tomquist heard?" I added.

Warn's attention was diverted momentarily as the telephone rang. It was Jay calling from the front office.

"Thanks, Jay; put the call through." Then, following a brief pause, he said, "Yes, I understand. I guess you guys aren't immune from that either. 4:00 will be fine; we're not going anywhere. Thank you for calling."

"What was that about if you don't mind my asking?"

"The captain can't get here until 4:00; it seems the cruiser had a blowout on Route 3 just north of Groveton."

"So the inevitable gets postponed a little longer," I added wryly.

"It does," Warn replied.

"Well, I know you have things to do; and I have a wife who I've been dying to spend some time with. So let's meet back here at 3:45. Is that okay with you?"

"I'll be here," Warn replied.

I took two steps toward the screen door. But before I could grasp the handle, it opened and Nya walked into the office.

"Nya!" I said with unrestrained enthusiasm. "I'm so glad you're here. I was just coming to find you."

"So I overheard. Well, I've saved you the trouble." If she'd overheard anything I'd just said, she didn't let on.

By the tone of her voice, I figured I was still in hot water. But Warn's office wasn't the place to explain myself. So I said, "Let's take a walk."

"Fine; where would you like to go?"

"Let's see . . ."

Then Warn interjected, "Why don't you walk up toward Lake Two Towns. It's a nice walk up the hill toward the golf course."

"Can we make it there and back in time for 4:00?"

"Sure; it's about three-quarters of a mile. And the lake is beautiful this time of year; Nya will enjoy the lily pads."

"It sounds lovely Warn. Thank you," Nya replied.

Nya and I walked up the road toward the small lake. She didn't take my hand . . . not a good sign. As we strolled, I gave her a short version of what we . . . or mainly I . . . had been doing for the last two days.

"Oh my God," Nya cried. Then looking at me, she added, "So this is why you've been the invisible man ever since we arrived."

"Yes; I hope you'll forgive me for keeping you in the dark. Warn and Tom made me promise to keep this thing under wraps."

Nya did not look pleased. I'm certain she was about to tell me how I didn't understand marriage is a partnership and that husbands and wives should share everything, when I saw something that froze me in my steps. About a hundred yards up the road was a middle age couple-a woman walking next to a very large man.

"What is it Kary? You look as though you've seen a ghost."

"I may well have, Nya. I may well have." I couldn't contain my excitement. "Quick, Nya come with me!"

"But why . . .?"

"We need to catch up to that couple walking near the lake."

Nya didn't question my sanity; and, although she probably thought about pushing me into the lake, she deferred. She matched me stride for stride as we closed the distance between ourselves and the other couple. As we strode along, I continued to assess the two people ahead of us. Having heard the two us coming, they had stopped walking and were now facing us. The woman was smiling and the man initially appeared unfazed by our approach. It was the man who had first caught my eye. He appeared to be at least six foot-five inches tall and more than 250 pounds . . . Al Connor's size, according to Bill Norman's description. The woman appeared to be about five foot-six and, dressed in a tight fitting t-shirt, certainly possessed the physical attributes that Tomquist had ascribed to Edna Connor.

I called to them. And as I did, I could feel Nya's eyes focused upon the side of my face. Doubtlessly she was wondering what outlandish odyssey her husband was embarking upon with these two strangers.

At the risk of all three people thinking I'm crazy, I called to them, "Hello."

The woman returned my greeting while the man stood transfixed.

"I know this may seem like an odd question; but are you, by any chance, the Connors?"

"Yes. But how'd you know that?"

"It's a long story. But, if you'll walk with my wife Nya and me back to the hotel, I'll explain."

As we walked, I turned to Edna Connor and began, "Mrs. Connor . . ."

"Please, call me Edna," she said. Her husband patted himself on the chest and added, "And you can call me Al."

"Edna, I have to tell you that the state police have been called to begin an investigation of your disappearance and rumored murder"

"Murder! Me? Oh, that's crazy."

I continued, "You checked into the Balsams on the 10th and then disappeared a few days later." I let this sink in for about five seconds before asking, "Will you please tell us what actually happened on the night of the 13th?"

Edna was understandably embarrassed and upset, but proved to be most helpful. Over the next several minutes, she described to Nya and me how she had arrived at The Balsams a very lonely woman. She felt that her husband was pushing her farther and farther away. Shortly after Edna's arrival at the resort, one of the maintenance men had flirted with her, which she had reported to Al on the telephone. However, Al didn't seem very concerned once Edna had described Billy Fenton. Richard Tomquist had been another matter entirely. He was built somewhat like Al and he had been so flirtatious. When she told Al about him the first time, he said he wasn't concerned, but his voice told her otherwise. So she decided to continue to spend time with Tomquist, even agreeing to a quasi date with him. At that juncture, having failed to get the kind of attention from Al that she craved, she had briefly considering having an affair with this new suitor. She had called her husband at work at 4:00 on the evening of the 13th, and told Al about her impending date. She knew that she'd struck gold because, for the first time in years, Al Connor had become furious with her. The last time that had happened was when she'd mistakenly told a client that Al wasn't interested in doing business with him. Al had been angry about losing new business. At eight o'clock on the evening of the 13th, Al had returned Edna's telephone call, catching her as she was going out the door. He didn't tell her where he was at the time, or that he was calling on his cell phone from the car. Nor did he mention her impending date.

Thinking things between Al and her were status quo, Edna met Tomquist for the date in the spirit with which it had been arranged. Tomquist sensed that this attractive woman was lonely, and he knew exactly what he needed to do to close the deal. Edna described him as a smooth operator. He had very cleverly mixed the types of drinks he served her, and had spread them out so she wasn't aware she'd had too much to drink until it had been too late. As the two walked back to their rooms, Edna had to admit that, in her physical and mental state, she was torn between having sex with Tomquist or not. She needed time to think; so she sent Tomquist on a little errand. In the interim, Edna had gone to her room and was waiting for him to return, when the telephone rang. When Al called, he had told her that he was in his car just south of Colebrook and would be there by midnight.

At this juncture, Edna stopped telling her story for a few moments. She took Al's hand in hers and kissed it reassuringly. Al responded with a meaningful kiss on the cheek. I couldn't get over the difference between what I was seeing and the dormant marriage reported to me by Katyana, Edna's waitress.

"Okay, I'm ready to continue now." Edna had the enthusiasm of a new bride. She told us that she was about to change into a comfortable pair of slacks and a short sleeve top, when Richard Tomquist returned. She had tried to convince him to call it a night, but he wouldn't leave her alone until he saw her face to face. Knowing that Al was on his way, and hoping to silence this man, whom she now regarded as a total nuisance, Edna reluctantly agreed to open the door. But, instead of just talking the way he had promised, Tomquist began trying to undress her. Edna knew it would not be possible to hold him off for long, so she did the next best thing; she pretended to faint. Then, while Tomquist was trying to decide what to do with his now limp date, Al Connor had knocked on the door of her room. Edna said she'd waited about twenty seconds before she opened her eyes. When she did, Tomquist had already closed her part of the interconnecting doorway and disappeared into his adjoining guest room.

"I opened the door and Al came into the room. He swept me into his arms and out into the night," she smiled.

I looked at Nya out of the corner of my eye. She was dabbing her eyes with a handkerchief. I realized there was a lot of work to do if I was going to live up to the standard Al Connor had just set.

"Where have you been for the last couple of days?" I asked.

"Al and Bill Head, the golf pro, are old high school chums," Edna responded with a smile.

"Yeah, Bill an' I have known each other for more than twenty years," Al added.

It took a few seconds for things to register. "It's all becoming clear now," I said. "Mr. Head is visiting relatives in South Carolina; and he allowed you to stay in his apartment. Am I right?" I wouldn't have wanted to be in Bill Head's shoes when Warn got wind of this.

"That's right," Al said. "I called in an old favor . . . I actually used the car phone to call him after I'd already left home. Lucky for me he was packing to leave when I called. He told me where to find the key. So, I drove up here, picked up Edna and headed up to the golf course."

Then Edna added while blushing, "We haven't left Bill's apartment since the other night. Of course, we'll need to restock his 'fridge before we head back to Massachusetts," she added with a smile. Al then put his left large arm around Edna's shoulders and nuzzled her affectionately. Clearly these two were very much in love.

★   ★   ★

3:45 P.M. Nya and I returned to Warn's office with about fifteen minutes to spare before the state police were scheduled to arrive.

"You're certainly prompt," he offered as we entered. Figuring that I had told Nya what had been transpiring since our arrival at the hotel, he added, "And Nya, there's something I need to say to you."

"And what is that, Warn?"

"The buck stops right here, Nya. This mess is not Kary's fault. I needed help sorting things out. And, it had to be someone I could trust . . . someone without strong emotional ties to my staff."

"I see." Nya was being non-committal.

"Warn," I said, "I've been doing some more snooping; and I have a surprise for you. There are two people outside I'd like you to meet," Then I called out into the foyer, "Would you folks step in here, please?"

At first, Warn appeared annoyed at this intrusion. "This hardly seems the time, Kary." Suddenly, the realization of who these people were struck him. Before he could say another word, I declared, "Warner Barson, I'd like to introduce Edna and Al Connor."

Chapter 72

3:48 P.M. Warn shook the Connors' hands warmly. Then the five of us sat facing one another. Warn spoke first.

"Mrs. Connor, I don't know whether I feel more like hugging you or throwing you into Lake Gloriette."

"I don't think I could let you do either of those things, Mr. Barson," Al Connor said. Next he took his wife's hand in his and placed a soft kiss on it. Edna beamed and put her head on her husband's shoulder.

"Of course, I'm being somewhat facetious," Warn replied. "But, do you have any idea how much trouble you have put people at this resort through because of your disappearance."

Edna was still feeling a bit defensive. "But all I did was leave for a couple of days. Surely, that couldn't have hurt anyone."

When Warn stifled a groan, I felt it best to intercede. "Edna, as I tried to explain on the way here, at a resort property like The Balsams, if you don't make yourself visible for more than twenty-four hours, the staff becomes alerted and reports your absence to management; in this case, to Mr. Barson or his son. The truth is that people who miss more than one meal around here are rare indeed." Then I continued, "Not only did you miss meals, but it was reported that you hadn't slept in your bed. And according to your housekeeper, it didn't appear that you had used the bathroom."

"That's not true," Edna smiled. "But I do understand why you may have thought that. You see, I'm a neatness freak. Since I checked in last week, I've made my own bed every morning, and even cleaned the bathroom. Frankly, I'm surprised my housekeeper hasn't told you."

I was feeling a little queasy at that moment, mostly due to my failure to interview Edna's maid. Nya, on the other hand, was beaming as she watched the way the Connors acted together.

After a moment, Al chimed in, "Yeah, she's super neat." As he said this, Al gave Edna's hand a squeeze and another kiss.

Warn was still bewildered. "That's a lovely story, Edna. But, why didn't you two just stay here in your room?"

"Please don't be offended, Mr. Barson. The Balsams is a lovely resort; but it was so romantic being whisked away like that. Al was being my knight in shining armor; and I wasn't about to do anything to dampen his spirit," Edna added with a giggle.

Al Connor interjected in his monotone, "It sure was nice of my friend Bill Head to loan me his apartment."

When Edna saw the look on Warn's face, she felt compelled to say, "I hope Bill won't be in too much trouble for this, Mr. Barson."

Warn smiled and replied, "Some, but not too much, Edna."

Just like that, the mystery of Edna Connor's disappearance had been solved. Edna asked Warn if it was okay for Al to join her at the resort during the next week or so. Warn said he would arrange everything with Jay Olds in reservations. Warn also told Al that he would have any necessary toiletries delivered to room 167. Finally, he told the two that the large plastic bag with Edna' valuables would be returned as soon as the police had finished dusting it for fingerprints. With that, the happy couple left Warn's office and walked hand-in-hand toward the Hampshire House.

I spent the next five minutes bringing Warn up to speed on how we had found the Connors during our walk to Lake Two Towns.

"What an unbelievable stroke of luck . . . for almost everyone concerned. I sure wish we didn't need to have the police in here conducting a full-scale investigation." Then he looked at me and said, "But, you know you're something of a genius detective, don't you, Kary?" And, with a wink he added, "I can't wait to tell Tom how you not only solved one mystery, but two." Then, his smile faded. "Now my niece can finally rest in peace."

Before the police arrived, Warn excused himself to make one of his frequent daily visits to the reservation desk. He did this with the full understanding that this action left Nya and me alone in his office.

"That was so beautiful, Kary" Nya said, while dabbing her eyes. "After years of living together, but really being alone in a sense, the Connors really have rediscovered one another."

"I have so much to say to you, Nya; and it's difficult to pick a place to begin. What do you say we take a walk down by Lake Gloriette?"

"But, don't you need to stay and talk with the police?"

"Something tells me they'll be busy with Warn for quite a while." I smiled.

Chapter 73

4:15 P.M. Nya and I walked along the grassy western shore of Lake Gloriette. For several minutes, neither of us said a word. Finally, I broke the silence. "This has been hard on you, Nya; and I want you to know I'm sorry."

"It wasn't what I had expected; that's for sure. I thought we were going to take walks, lounge around the pool . . ."

"I wasn't referring to our vacation; I was talking about our life together."

"Our life?"

"Don't deny it, Nya. I could see it on your face the whole time we were listening to Edna and Al Connor talk about how they had rediscovered one another. You may not believe me, Nya, but I was taking all of that in, too. In fact, during the last couple of days, I've sensed an emptiness between us I'd never taken the time to notice before. And now that I'm aware of it, I can't understand for the life of me why it's taken so long. You know, it's funny; it wasn't until I had a front row seat in Warn's office . . . watching how protective and caring he is about his staff . . ."

"And you're equating Warn's relationship to his staff with our marriage?" The look of disapproval on Nya's face told me I'd just lost some valuable points.

But I needed to make my point, so I continued, "Yes. Yes, I am. These are people who Warn has worked with for years. He's seen them every single day during that time; he's heard about their marriages, and about the loved ones they've lost. He's enjoyed their triumphs and shared their pain. Isn't that a big part of what marriage partners and their families do? The only thing missing is the sex," I said.

"Let's not go there just now, okay?" She said. "But, all kidding aside, I suppose there is something to what you're saying." The expression on Nya's face indicated she was not just patronizing me.

"I really believe that, Nya. I believe that Warn loves this old place enough that he was willing to give it up . . . to take the fall for The Balsams . . . in the event that the Connor business had turned out badly. Warn never thought about what he wanted, or what this mess might cost him. He wasn't thinking about himself at all . . . only the others who would be hurt by the scandal Edna's disappearance would have generated. Warn Barson is a giver, Nya. You, on the other hand, have spent the last thirty years wet-nursing a taker."

"You sound so different, Kary. I feel like I'm talking to a stranger . . . a nice stranger."

"In a way, I am a stranger, Nya. I'll tell you this . . . I'm a person who's learned its time for me to stop thinking solely about Kary Turnell." I took both of Nya's hands in mine. As I did, I said, "And I owe you nothing less than Warn was prepared to do for The Balsams. I've made a shambles of our marriage. All I've ever done is take your love and your kindness and repaid you by giving you loneliness and the chore of looking after an empty shell.

I've committed every transgression in the book, except for one."

"And that is?"

"I've never cheated on you, Nya."

Nya sighed. It looked and sounded like an expression of relief. "Yes, but you have no idea how many times I've wondered, especially late at night after you'd rejected me time and again. I'd lie there and wonder, 'Is it another woman? Is it the way I look?'"

"The way you look? You look . . . beautiful. I am so sorry, Nya." As I said this, I put my arms around her and continued to look directly into her eyes. "My part in this marriage has been a disaster. But now I'm prepared to offer you what you deserve."

"Are you saying what I think you are?" Tears welled up in her eyes.

"I'm offering to get out of your life, Nya . . . to leave like a gentleman. You're young enough. And, just look at yourself; you're still a beautiful woman. Trust me, if you decide to take this offer, I won't ask for a thing . . . the house, the car . . . you paid for virtually all of it anyway. This could be a second chance for you, sweetheart."

Nya stood there looking up at me, the tears now streaming down her face. "Is this really what you want, Kary?"

At that moment my voice began to crack. "It's the last thing I want, Nya. What I would like to do is start over, to live the rest of my life the way I should have lived my first fifty years. What I want is to go to sleep every night with you in my arms and wake up every morning with you by my side. But I can't blame you if you're no longer interested."

"Interested! These are the words I've been waiting to hear for so long, Kary Turnell." Then she took a step back and released my hand. "But, I can't stand the thought that things might return to the way they've been. I'm not willing to put up with that any more, Kary. However," she added with a slight smile, "you really do have a few redeeming qualities. So here's my offer. Let's take things one day at a time." Then, with an attempt at a wink, she said, "If you behave yourself, I'll keep you around for a while."

"Do I really have to behave myself all of the time?" I asked as I held her hands again.

"I certainly hope not!" Nya smiled. I kissed her gently on the lips. We walked back up the hill toward the Dixville House; and as we did, I couldn't help but revisit the Connor situation. "It's still amazing to me how Al Connor went from being an insensitive lug to being such a romantic. I guess the shock of nearly losing Edna really straightened him out."

Nya was facing me now. "And, are you straightened out, Kary?"

"Just try me, sweetheart; just try me."

★   ★   ★

4:40 P.M. As we walked through the foyer, we could see that the police were just finishing their first conversation with Warn. There were certain to be others. Looking up, Warn waved us toward his office. He introduced me to a young police officer, Wesley Dow.

After a few minutes of casual conversation, Officer Dow looked at me and said, "You folks are going to be staying here for a few weeks." It was more a statement than a question.

"That's right officer," I replied.

"That's good; because I'm going to need a statement from you, Professor Turnell. But, it will keep until tomorrow." Then, reaching for the hat he'd left on Warn's chair, he said, "Goodnight, folks."

After he left, Nya remarked that Warn seemed in remarkably good spirits, especially given the circumstances.

"I should be. That interview went better than I could have imagined. I think the state police completely understand that what happened was an accident. And, with Edna Connor safe, I'm beginning to think this place is actually going to survive the media scrutiny."

"Yeah, but something else is going on, isn't it, Warn?"

"How did you(?) . . . you know something, Kary, you really would make a heck of a detective."

"Over my dead body!" Nya interjected.

We laughed. "So what's going on, Warn?"

"I have some news to share!"

"What is it?" Nya and I said in unison.

"I've decided to stay on and keep running this old place . . . at least for a while." We could see from his demeanor that having made this decision had been a huge weight off of his shoulders. "You know, I was ready to walk out that door just a few hours ago. You're the one who tipped the scales in this direction, Kary."

"You're giving me too much credit," I said.

"You helped me to rediscover my sense of purpose. Thanks to you, and owing to all of this craziness, I realize that I can't abandon this old place and all of the people who depend on me. But, more than anything else, it was your willingness to risk your own happiness to help me that made the difference. You made me realize what a mistake I'd be making by quitting without a fight."

At this point, I couldn't resist saying that I was having difficulty getting used to my new reputation for putting others first. Warn's response came quickly. "You are a great friend, Kary; even if you are too hard on yourself."

"What I do know, old friend, is that Nya and I are thrilled about your decision. But let's get the record straight, shall we? You've done more for me in the last two days than I could ever possibly tell you. However," I added with a smile, "I'm willing to call it even, if you are."

"Done," Warn replied with a smile, a handshake and an embrace.

Then, to change the subject, I said, "You know, I wouldn't wish the last two days on my worst enemy. Not even Billy Fenton." We all had a good, long laugh at that last pronouncement.

Then Warn's tone turned serious for a moment. "You do realize, don't you Kary, that Tomquist came awfully close to ruining this place?" We all stood silently for a moment, contemplating what Warn had just said.

None of us wanted to hang around for any more small talk. Warn was anxious to leave the small office where he had been captive the past two days. Besides, with Nancy back in town, and the revelation that Sarah's murderer was dead, the extended Barson family would be gathering at his residence. Nya and I were looking forward to finally enjoying a quiet meal together, hopefully without any intrusions. But, as we opened the door to leave, Warn called out, "Hold it you guys. With all of the commotion, I nearly forgot." Holding his left palm up like a traffic cop to emphasize that we shouldn't leave, he bent down and removed a large, flat, rectangular object wrapped in brown paper from beneath his desk. He placed the package on top of his desk and tore back the paper revealing a black and white photograph in a black, wooden frame.

"I'm certain that you'll be happy to see this, Kary. I wanted to tell you about it earlier, but never got the chance until now. You see, when Nya called for your reservations, she asked to talk with me. She wanted me to know that you two were coming up here and had me make a special point to remove any dust from your Wall of Fame photograph. Of course, Nya was kidding; but, you know me . . . I took her remark literally and asked the housekeeping staff to be certain that the frame and glass were spotless. Well, wouldn't you know that Murphy's Law would rear its ugly head? It was a new housekeeper who was assigned to do the dusting. She was a little overzealous in her effort to please Lucy Laflamme, I guess. So, what did she do? She knocked the photograph right off the wall, breaking the glass and gouging the frame."

"Oh no!" Nya laughed.

"Oh yes," Warn replied with a wan smile. When I heard about it, I was really upset. So, when Reg headed down to Twin Mountain to pick up one of our guests who flies his private airplane wherever he goes, I told him to drop it off at the frame shop in Colebrook, and to ask for a quick repair." Nya and I smiled at one another, knowing how anguished Warn must have been. Warn continued, "I knew right away there was no way it was going to be ready in time for your arrival; so I sent you that note to see me on Friday night."

"Of course, you couldn't have known that Kary would want to make a visit to his personal shrine our first order of business," Nya added as she touched my hand.

"No, I hadn't planned on that scenario," Warn agreed. "Then with the Connor mess cropping up, I never had the opportunity to explain this to you until now. Let me assure you, my friend, this photograph will be joining the others on the Wall of Fame by the time you're ready for breakfast tomorrow morning."

"Don't bother, Warn," I replied. "In fact, you can put that old photo in the trash if you'd like." Warn and Nya looked at one another, a quizzical expression on each of their faces.

"But Kary, I thought you loved having your picture mounted along the Wall."

"Oh, I do; I do, Nya. But, I haven't looked like that picture in years. And besides, the guy in that photo was a one-hit wonder and a lousy husband to boot." As I took Nya in my arms, I smiled and said, "Besides sweetheart, thanks to Warn here I have an idea for a new book that's going to earn me a better place on the Wall anyway. And I can assure you the new and improved version of Kary Turnell is a husband you won't want to miss." With that I gave my wife a kiss that was as expressive as the hotel's decorum would permit.

Nya and I left Warn's office. As we walked hand in hand across the foyer, the normal quietude of the resort was shattered by the sound of a picture frame meeting the metal bottom of Warn's waste paper basket.

THE END

About the author:

Mark Okrant is a university professor and long time tourism researcher. He is the author of one other murder mystery, *Judson's Island* (Wayfarer Press 1995, 2002). Mark lives with his wife Marla in Plymouth, New Hampshire.